Occult Detective Quarterly

CONTENTS

FICTION

"Got My Mojo Working" — 4
    David T. Wilbanks and William Meikle

"When Soft Voices Die" — 12
    Amanda DeWees

"Don't Say I Didn't Warn You" — 20
    Adrian Cole

"Orbis Tertius" — 28
    Josh Reynolds

"MonoChrome" — 36
    T.E. Grau

"Baron of Bourbon Street" — 62
    Aaron Vlek

"The Adventure of the Black Dog" — 71
    Oscar Dowson

OCCULT LEGION: "The Nest" — 78
    William Meikle

ARTICLES

The Occult Files of Doctor Spektor — 54
    Charles R. Rutledge

The Man Behind Doctor Spektor:
    An Interview with Don F. Glut — 59
    Charles R. Rutledge

"How to be a Fictional Victorian Ghost Hunter (In Five Easy Steps)" — 86
    Tim Prasil

REVIEWS — 91

editorial

What's in a name? Well, in the case of Occult Detective Quarterly, a lot more than you might think. The stories and articles that await you in the next few issues will be the result of months of pondering over the meaning of such an apparently simple term as 'Occult Detective'. With this first issue, we have a chance to talk about what came out of our deliberations.

Were we hunting the classic period investigator, from the consulting detective to the enthusiastic amateur? Shades of Sherlock Holmes, and lashings of Carnacki, Dr John Silence, Flaxman Low and other characters. Did we want to evoke images of seedy offices in which a jaded Forties or Fifties PI drinks whisky from a cracked glass? There he slouches, waiting for the next haunted dame to walk in that door. Sam Spade and a ghost who won't stay dead.

Or were we treading contemporary ground? John Constantine, trudging through a modern-day wasteland and regretting almost everything; Harry Dresden with wizardry to hand, or Felix Castor, freelance exorcist with problems of his own. Even Sam and Dean could qualify.

The answer is all of the above, but much more. From a simple idea and a lot of questions, there arose a recognition that the occult detective has many faces. It's going to be a challenge to do those faces justice, but we're up for it. At heart, we're seeking out stories of those folk who investigate strange, occult and supernatural phenomena. That process might be out of curiosity, because they have no choice, because they're paid, or an accident of fate. We don't mind.

We'll always have room for a Carnacki or a Constantine, but we want to go much further than that. Our basic definition doesn't stipulate that the occult detective should be some white guy with troubles. We'll be looking for the best written and most interesting interpretations of the theme we can find. Investigators of every creed, colour and culture; wise women and foolish ones. Japanese Shinto priests, First Nation law enforcement officers and gay Edwardian psychologists. Not forgetting detectives who aren't even human. You get the idea.

For our debut issue we've unashamedly included some 'classic' interpretations. So you can burrow into Adrian Cole's world of Nick Nightmare, a hard man with a hard job, or step into the 1920s with Josh Reynolds' ever-suave Royal Occultist, Charles St Cyprian, and his somewhat blunter companion, Ebe Gallowglass. Sold on PI stories but want a different take? Share a banana or two with Gus, a rather different detective brought to you by Willie Meikle and Dave Wilbanks. And if you like Edwardian strangeness, then try Oscar Dowson's tale of Dr Henry Jerusalem Crow

We've also thrown in some great stories which don't follow in the footsteps of the usual suspects. Ted E Grau brings a quite different tilt to things, an original and nightmarish story of the fall of what we know and the rise of... let's just say that if you've come across the work of Robert W Chambers, you'll get there very quickly. Aaron Vlek shares her tale of Baron Samedi himself, stalking New Orleans with a puzzle on his mind, whilst Amanda DeWees takes us back to earlier times – her character Sybil Ingram needs somewhere to stay, but the room she gets may already have an occupant...

Finally, our exclusive extra is the first story in a great series by the Occult Legion, a collective of talented and experienced writers sharing a world of supernatural dread. Willie Meikle brings us Part One: The Nest, where it all begins, and more of the Occult Legion's tales will unfold in each issue of ODQ.

We hope that you enjoy our first selection of fiction, and that you check out the articles as well. There's something for the comics fans in Charles R Rutledge's pieces on Don Glut and Dr Occult, and something for the classicists in Tim Prasil's handy guide to being a Victorian ghost-hunter. Plus reviews, of course.

That's us for now. We're delighted to say that we already have some cracking tales to come in Issue Two, and we look forward to seeing you next time.

Sam Gafford and John Linwood Grant

Publisher:
Travis Neisler

Editors:
Sam Gafford
John Linwood Grant

Consulting Editor:
Dave Brzeski

Layout & Design:
Sam Gafford

Logos & Headers:
Bob Freeman

Cover by:
Terry Pavlet

"Monochrome" by Ted E. Grau first appeared in THE COURT OF THE YELLOW KING, edited by Glynn Owen Barrass (Celaeno Press, 2014)

OCCULT DETECTIVE QUARTERLY #1, WINTER 2016/2017 2nd printing published by Ulthar Press. All Rights Reserved. Not for copy or distribution. Subscriptions available.
Submissions guidelines available.
Contact us at:
Occultdetectivequarterly@yahoo.com

"A community of dark stories and verse."

RAVENWOOD QUARTERLY

Issues 1 and 2 now available from
electricpentaclepress.bigcartel.com

Got My Mojo Working

David T. Wilbanks & William Meikle

I hate shaving—always have, and I suspect I always will. But a gorilla's got to do what a gorilla's got to do to get by in the City of Angels, and mankind isn't yet ready for the real me.

But I'm working on it.

Eight-twenty on a Saturday morning and I was already up and trying to clear hair from the plughole Too much gray in it nowadays, too much fat around the gut, and too many thinks in my head—I miss the simple, no thinks required days of my youth when all I had to worry about was jungle. Booze helps—mostly—but when I drink, I remember some things, forget others, and when my thinks get really foggy I tend to hit people. Mostly bad people, but that still doesn't

Illustration by Wayne M. Miller

This particular Saturday I hadn't hit anybody yet, and I'd had a coffee, so I was pretty mellow when I heard the footsteps on the stairs. I looked up to see a thin, mousy man in a sharp suit and wearing a cologne I could taste even while he was in the doorway. I opened a window before showing him a seat, and even that didn't help, so I lit up a Lucky. He didn't like that—but I didn't like him, so we were even.

He stared at me, his mouth hanging open like a dope. I get that a lot, but then I'm not what you'd call attractive to most hairless monkeys, even after I've had a shave.

"Didn't your mother ever tell you it's rude to stare?" I said. His eyes widened as I spoke—I guess because other gorillas didn't have the capability.

He staggered to a wooden chair I kept in the room for customers and plopped himself down. "I-I was told about you, but—but..." He had a high voice, piercing to these ears. I didn't like that about him either. But I could smell fear on him so I let him gibber. I wanted to hear what the human had to say.

I went to my desk and sat in the leather chair behind it, swiveling to face the stammering buffoon. "What's the story, bub? I haven't got all day. Now's around the time I usually take my morning swing through the park." I didn't really take a morning swing through the park, but what can I say? I like to mess with the hairless apes.

"It's my sister. She saw something that frightened her terribly and now all she does is lie in her bedroom and stare nervously about—that's if she's not sleeping, which is half the time. She sleeps like she's trying to escape from something. I've tried to talk to her about it but when I do it's like I'm not even there."

I tapped my cigarette into the ashtray sitting on my desk, the one with "Big Lake Motel" printed at the bottom. "Sounds to me like you might need a doctor, not a private dick."

"I *did* talk to Lucille's doctor—that's her name by the way: Lucille Bennett. Mine is Jim Crawford. He said to let her rest and maybe she'd be better in a few days. But it's been two weeks now, and I can't afford many more house calls, especially since he has no real idea what's wrong with her."

"You know, Crawford, I don't exactly come cheap." I said.

"But I was told you specialize in...this sort of thing."

"What sort of thing is that?"

He wrung his mousy hands together. "The supernatural."

There it was. My reputation precedes me.

"I'm not sure how the supernatural comes into play here. How did you jump to that conclusion?"

A sheen of sweat covered Crawford's face as he continued. "For the past couple weeks, I hear Lucille's...shrieks in the night. I go to her room and turn on the light, but there's nothing there. Yet I find her in bed, the covers held up to her chin, staring at something that I can't see, a look of terror on her face. And the continued shrieking." He paused to wipe his forehead with a white handkerchief from his jacket pocket.

I lit another Lucky, my stomach rumbling because I hadn't had my morning yellows. "Forgive me for being so blunt, but your sister getting the heebie-jeebies and staring at nothing doesn't prove we're dealing with forces from beyond."

"B-but there was this one night when I felt something that made me momentarily doubt my sanity. I can't tell you exact details because it wasn't a noise or a touch precisely—just a sudden feeling of impending *doom*."

I knew that feeling—only too well—I'd had it myself just before I got the way I am now. I spoke quickly before the thinks could kick in.

"So, this Lucille dame, what's her line?"

"Line?" he said.

"Yeah—how does she get by—seamstress, librarian—escort?"

Now he wasn't scared—he was offended. That's when I started to smell the money.

"She is my sister," he said, as if that explained everything. "And she's an artist, if you must know."

"Oh, I must, I must."

I thought about getting the booze out from the drawer—the sap looked like he might need it nearly as much as I did—but it was too early yet and, besides, I was intrigued, despite myself.

"I think I'll come with you and see her—but it'll cost you a Benjamin a day plus expenses," I said, and his eyebrows went up his forehead.

"I don't think I like that," he replied.

"There's the door, bub," I replied. "See ya, wouldn't want to be ya."

He didn't get out of the chair, so I knew I had him. He took out his wad, I took out the bottle and we sealed the deal over a couple of shots of rye. On the way out I thought about taking the bottle in my jacket pocket, but it was kinda busy in there already, what with the gat, my smokes and the juju bags—and I thought I needed all of them more than I needed the booze—for the moment.

***

We took his Caddy—I just about fit in the back seat—and I had him get out and get a bunch of yellows for me at the corner shop—no sense in advertising I was on a job until I knew the lay of the land. I felt excited despite myself as he drove us along the Boulevard and up onto the canyon road. This was no penny-ante deal—I really could smell the money, nearly as strong as the bananas. I didn't throw the skins out the window—I stuck them, hard, into his ashtrays where the stink would remind him to clean them later. Then I just had time for another Lucky and we were there.

I'd been right about the money—it was an architect's dream of concrete and glass and sat on a rocky outcrop with a view out over the city. I could have sat on the roof and made like Kong on the Skull Island mountain ledge—if I felt like reinforcing the stereotype—and if the maid let me in. She looked me up and down and sniffed at me. I tried not to look offended, but it's kinda hard for me to look anything else—even when I wear my best thick striped Zoot suit, brothel creepers and Homburg, I still look like I'm ready for war.

But she was kinda cute, and she wasn't scared of me, and when she stepped aside to let me in she called me 'sir'. If I went for that kind of gal, I might even have thrown her a line, but by this time the client was already off and away across a hall bigger than my apartment. I settled for giving her a wink and waddled after him, trying to keep my back straight and wondering if she was still watching me.

But my thinks of inappropriate romantic entanglements were forgotten all too soon—I had only got as far as the foot of the long sweeping staircase when I knew this wasn't a case of a lonely gal with night terrors. I felt it in the air, at the hackles at the back of my neck, thumping in my gut like a jungle drum. Crawford and his sister weren't the only occupants of this house—there was something in here with them, something old, something hungry—and I didn't think bananas were going to satisfy it.

Whatever it was, it was up that staircase, somewhere on the floor above—but Crawford hadn't headed that way. Instead he led me into a huge living area dominated by leather chairs that even I could get lost in and a view over the city that stretched away into the wild blue yonder and, somehow, instantly made me nostalgic for home—real home—jungle home. A long thin dame sat on a long fat couch by the window and I tried to focus on her rather than the view—it was making me misty eyed just to look at it.

"Lucille?" Crawford said. "This is Gus—he's here to help you."

She turned, saw her brother, then looked at me—and screamed, fit to bring the roof down.

"Look," I said, "I know I'm no hunk, but that's uncalled for."

Uncalled for or not, she wouldn't stop. She went red in the face with the effort of it, and the sound went through me like a knife. I felt the jungle drums beat in my gut again and I knew this wasn't a reaction to my good looks—well, not just that anyway. I put a hand in my pocket, got out a juju bag, and squeezed it under her nose. I smelled the jungle, smelled death and ash and the potency of blood and old bone.

Her eyes rolled up in their sockets, she went as limp as a fish and fell into my arms. This time there were no thinks of romance in me, inappropriate or otherwise.

"We'd best get her to bed—she's going to sleep for a while."

I carried her while Crawford led us upstairs.

The hungry beast somewhere up there seemed to swell and grow, and the jungle drums in my gut beat louder than ever as we went into the lady's bedroom. I put her down on the bed and shoved the juju bag in her hand. She was breathing easily, and all the fierce redness had gone from her cheeks. She appeared to be fast asleep.

I had a look around the room. There were several easels, all with paintings in progress on them, all of the same thing—thick brush strokes, and dark, almost black spirals, winding away down into infinity. The black pulsed in time with the drums in my gut. This room too had a view over the city, but I had no thought of looking out over it—I was going to need all my wits, all the time.

There was something here—and it was ready for a fight.

I turned to Crawford. "What are these paintings?"

His mouth twisted in disgust. "She has always been a creative person but she had never painted anything like *these* before. I assume it has something to do with whatever's going on around here. If she's not sleeping or screaming, she's standing in front of one of her easels, painting madly. I tried to have our man remove these from her room, but it only made her worse, so here they stay, as repulsive as they are."

I cocked my Homburg back and scratched my forehead. "These look familiar. And I don't mean familiar in a good way. I've seen these patterns before, or maybe I dreamed about them."

I turned to the man, who was wringing his hands again. I figured him for around thirty years and her a few years younger. "Have you always lived with your sister? Forgive me for saying so but shouldn't she be mated? She's a fully grown adult female."

"She was married once, but it ended badly—about a year ago—and I let her come here and live with me. Really, I have plenty of room here and it's no problem as we tend to keep to ourselves—me with my writing and her with her paintings."

"Artistic types, eh?"

He simply nodded and continued mauling his hands.

I looked at the paintings again, moving from one to the other, wondering how I knew these images. Maybe I had never seen them before personally, but it was as if they were something I had been given an excellent description of. Or maybe I'd read of them in one of the occult books I kept around the office for research. Whatever they were, they were bad news.

"You said the screaming mostly happens at night?"

He nodded again, unconsciously edging towards the door as if in fear that some insanity from the paintings might leech into his brain. He did have a point. Having given them a good look-over, I wasn't feeling too swell myself. In fact I was beginning to understand that feeling and realizing what I was dealing with here.

"Maybe we should go outside and let her rest a while."

I followed Crawford out the door, closing it behind me, and took a Lucky out of the pack. The house's owner nodded, giving me permission to light up. I walked across the wide landing to one of two comfy chairs and sat down to make use of the giant glass ashtray there.

Crawford sat in the other chair. "Do you know what's going on yet? Can you help my dear sister?"

"I have a feeling I know what's going on, yes. But you're not going to like it." I tapped my cigarette in the ashtray and leaned back in the soft chair. "You might not even believe it."

"Well, what is it, man?" He was starting to get excited and losing his nerve, but I didn't take it personal.

"*Man*? I'll let that one slide." I winked at him and pursed my lips into a monkey kiss to lighten the mood, not that I was feeling particularly jocular. Old habits.

"I've had me a think about it and diagnosed that what you probably have here is a demon, or maybe even *demons*—plural."

"Demons? You're mad!" He rose from the chair and began pacing back and forth in front of me, gnawing on a knuckle. "Why, there's no such thing!"

"Hey, bub. I wasn't the one coming into my office, talking about the supernatural. Deep down, you know what you have here—and it's nothing good!"

"So, what do we do now? Don't you have some sort of voodoo magic you can perform to rid the house of this...thing?"

"I'm not going to do much of anything until I collect more information, and I have an idea about that: When it's time to hit the sack tonight, I'll perch out here in one of these swanky chairs and keep an ear open for anything strange happening in Lucille's bedroom. All you need to do is act natural, and I'll most likely have more information for you in the morning."

"Well, you have the run of the house until then. Please feel at home."

"That's awful nice of you, Crawford. And you can call me Gus, seeing as how I'm a house guest and all."

He nodded and turned to leave, but I wasn't quite done.

"One—okay—two more things. Could you get your gal to fetch me some bananas?"

"I'll see what I can do—what was the other thing?"

"I assume you have a library somewhere. You mind if I spend some time in there later? I'm a big reader."

"As you wish...Gus. It's downstairs, through the back where it's cooler."

I nodded and he trotted down the wide staircase.

I lit another Lucky and blew out the smoke in a nice stream, leaning back in the chair. After a while the maid brought me some bananas and a smile to go with them. Tonight, all hell might break loose but for now, I was goddamn comfortable. An ape could get used to this life.

***

My good mood lasted only as long as the daylight—and that went at the same time as the bananas did. I heard Lucille moving around, and I smelled cheap paint and rich perfume. I figured she was okay as long as she was up and around, so I took the time to seek out the library.

He was right about it being cooler—a ceiling fan moved the air about nicely and I had to fight off an urge to strip off and let it at me—he might be paying me, but I don't think he was quite ready to see me *au naturel*.

There was something about those damn paintings I couldn't place, and it was itching at me. I went through the library—lots of European white man fiction, a couple of encyclopedias, some nice pulp era Tarzan that made me smile, remembering—and finally, after I'd moved nearly every damn book he owned, I found the thing. I'd thought her art was African, and old—I'd been right on one, not the other. What I was after was in a book of rock art. It was well thumbed—I smelled paint and perfume again as I looked through it—and it had her name handwritten inside it—from Daddy, Nineteen Thirty Six. The pictures were Australian. Aboriginal Dreamland stuff—old stuff—not to be messed with lightly.

I was thinking, about caves and spirals and summonings, when the screams started from upstairs. I gave the staircase a miss and went up via a dresser and the chandelier, swinging onto the balcony and crashing through the bedroom door even as the echoes of the first scream were fading.

She stood in front of her latest painting, a hand to her mouth, her eyes wide. The smell of her fear was stronger than either paint or perfume, and I saw why when I looked at what was on the easel. The black lines spiraled away into an impossibly deep distance that hurt the eye to look at too closely. The woman screamed again—whether it was at me or the painting this time I'm not sure. The noise was distracting me from the job in hand so I got her outside—her brother was on the landing and took charge of her, giving me a chance to get back inside to see what had spooked her so bad.

Way down in there something seethed and roiled, coming up the spiral, looking to be born. I had half a mind to let it come—all that leaping about had got me ready for action—but with the gal so close by it was just too dangerous. The painting flowed and swelled—whatever it was it was coming up fast. I took a juju bag out my pocket and tossed it, hard. It hit the surface of the painting—and fell into the spiral, following the lines down and away. Somewhere, in the deep distance, something squealed in frustration and went still.

Then, as quickly as it had got loud, it got quiet.

***

The client was not amused—I'd pulled a chandelier half out of the ceiling and busted a door that cost him a bunch of dollars. I heaved the door back onto its hinges and straightened it up with a push and a shove, but he still wasn't happy. He yakked at me like an over excited chimpanzee.

"Next time, I'll let her scream," I said, and that calmed him down a bit. He got calmer still when we all went downstairs for a stiffener and I showed him the book.

"Here's where the trouble comes from," I said.

The man took the book in his hand.

"She was obsessed with this when she was ten," he said softly. "It was the last thing Father gave her before he died."

"It's maybe not the best thing to be obsessed about. Over where these pictures are made, they're used to give the menfolk access to their dreamlands, to see their future, their past, their present—everything at once, all singing, all dancing, all at the same time."

"That doesn't sound too bad," the client said.

His sister didn't add anything—she was back on the couch again, back staring listlessly out the window.

"That depends," I replied, sipping some of his fine scotch and lighting up a fresh Lucky. "What do you think she dreams about? Happy thinks? Or dark ones?"

He didn't have to say anything—I could smell the answer on him, see it in the dark in his eyes.

When it came time for another round of drinks, I went and made them. I slipped a Mickey Finn into the gal's—I had a plan of action now, one that didn't involve any screaming on her part. By the time I'd had another Lucky and finished my Scotch she was out for the count.

I carried her upstairs, laid her on the bed, and started to get ready.

***

First I had to send the man away—this definitely had to be done *au naturel*, and I don't think he'd want me around his sister if he saw me in that state. Once I'd shooed him out and closed the door, I got down to business. I stripped off, and left the man-clothes, shoes and hat at the door, taking only the juju bags, the Luckies and my gat with me when I went back to stand by the easels. I used up one of the two remaining bags to keep her protected, splitting it open and sprinkling the contents over the eiderdown—she wouldn't have liked the smell, but she was too far down and out to complain and at least I knew she wouldn't be harmed.

Then I was ready. I turned my attention to the easels, let my mind drift, and watched the spirals turn.

"Come to daddy," I whispered.

A black smudge appeared in the middle of her latest artwork. I knuckled some carpet and slammed the juju bag against the painting--the stuff inside puffing out in an obnoxious, brown cloud. Despite the force of the blow, the easel didn't tip over; not only that, but it felt as if I had slammed my fist against a brick wall. That told me my hunch was right—if any of these paintings were indeed the entrance to the dreamtime, it had to be this one—the other paintings just helping to charge it with mojo. I stepped back and watched the portal closely, squinting against the cloud of magic dust to see what was happening.

The black smudge grew and took on more solid form—a shapeless, amorphous, flowing blackness. I don't know if I could describe it to you even if I took a million years. There was no way to depict it in words except to say that it was dark, multi-limbed and my gaze slid off it as if preserving my sanity by keeping it on the periphery of my thoughts. If I had not worked my trance up beforehand to keep me in the zone, I'd have hightailed it out of there, dollars or no dollars.

But I was in the mystic now and there was just no backing down. My juju bag had done nothing to slow the demon's climb up out of the spiral. So I had to rely on my instincts, my experience, and the few small gods and entities who have my back in times of need—and sometimes don't. They're fickle, and bad travelers, and L.A. isn't among their favorite places, so they don't always answer my calls—sometimes they're real jerks.

The bulbs in the light fittings pulsed twice and then went black. Now the only light in the bedroom came leaking in from outside, from a yellow moon half hidden by clouds and distance streetlights. That suited me fine; the less I could see of this thing the better for my simian brain.

The demon came up out of the spiral and started to emerge into the room. I raised the gat and fired, emptying the cylinder. Something shrieked—could have been the demon, could have been me. Things were getting out of control fast, and the demon kept coming. I dropped the empy gat, made fists and beat them against my chest, sniffing deeply of the magic dust that still hung in the air between the easel and me. My head spun as I called up my mojo, feeling it rise and build. I swung my arm up and let fly a searing bolt of blue energy right into the very heart of the spiral.

The demon yelled as only a demon can, burst out of the painting and went swirling around above my head, flying along the high ceiling of the bedroom, bouncing off the walls. I launched myself toward the bed to protect the sleeping woman should the unholy thing decide to perform some mischief on her unconscious form. I was high on magic now and primitive urges to destroy arose like the first putrid belch of stench from the very first tar pit from prehistory.

The thing dived at me, flinging me across the room, sending me crashing through the big window and joining a shower of glistening shards on the way out. At the last moment, I managed to grab the window frame with my fingers and pulled myself in a rangy swing back into the room, and, shrieking—definitely me this time—went up, into the main body of the demon. I was too close to blast it again—but I had both my paws around its throat—at least I hoped it was a throat. Claws like daggers raked down my back, raising weals, and I felt blood flow. The beast screamed wordlessly into my face and I smelled its foul breath, the stench far worse than any juju bag I had ever created. It tickled my nose—too much—I sneezed back at it, snot and dust and magic—and lost my grip. The hell creature flung me hard to the floor, where singing canaries flew around my aching noggin even as the thing surged and flowed and came at me again.

I grunted and pushed myself to my feet, my head still splitting. Now I was royally pissed off. The jungle mojo welled up in me, and I let it come. It was time to get *primal.*

The demon roared. I roared back, stood up straight, and beat my tattoo before going in, hard. The rage was on me, the magic filled my lungs, my chest, my head with jungle juice. The demon came at me, but I was already on my way to meet it. I grabbed at it, pulled at it, tugged, tore and chewed. Bits of ecto went splattering around the room, hitting walls, floor, bed, some of it even heading out the busted window. The demon roared again, but not in anger this time—in pain. It tried to retreat away from me but I can hold on pretty damned tight when I want to, especially when the mojo rises.

I held on, and kept tearing. It was strong enough to drag me toward the easel, back to the black hole where it came from, but not strong enough to take me down with it. I pulled more bits off it, throwing a ball of shining slime aside that hit the wall and ran down it like a lump of fresh snot.

What was left of the demon started to break up in my hands. A chunk of it retreated back to the easel—there was something in that part, something that pulsed and glowed, something from the dreamtime—and it wanted to go back there.

I knew I couldn't let it, for it would just return the next time the lady had a brush in her hand. At first I didn't know how to stop it—then I had a thought, My brain might not be as good as a human's, but it usually gets there eventually. I waited until the demon had slid into the painting and, before it had time to start the long slide back down the spiral, tore the picture out of the frame and ate it, cramming it down like it was young fine bamboo.

It takes a lot of mojo to make something like me, and most of that mojo is always there, hungry, needy. I fed it the painting and the thing that screamed inside it. It tasted like bananas that had gone black and putrid, but I forced it down, and it was gone before it hit my stomach.

***

I had my clothes on by the time I let the client back into the room. He wasn't too happy about the mess—ecto is a bugger to get out of carpets and soft furnishings. But I'd done my job—the demon was gone and the dame was alive and just waking up, although I had to warn him not to let her near paint for a while. The cute maid gave me a kiss and her number on the way out too, so I call that a job well done.

As for the demon, I sometimes see it, spiraling away down in my dreams—it's kind of comforting actually—its screams remind me of the jungle.

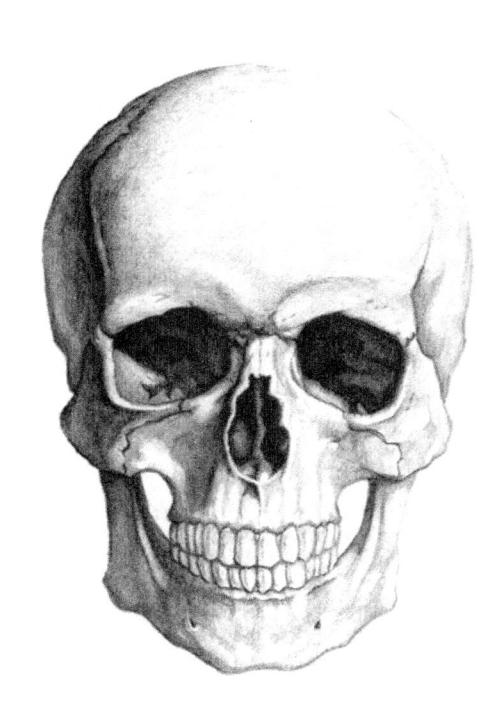

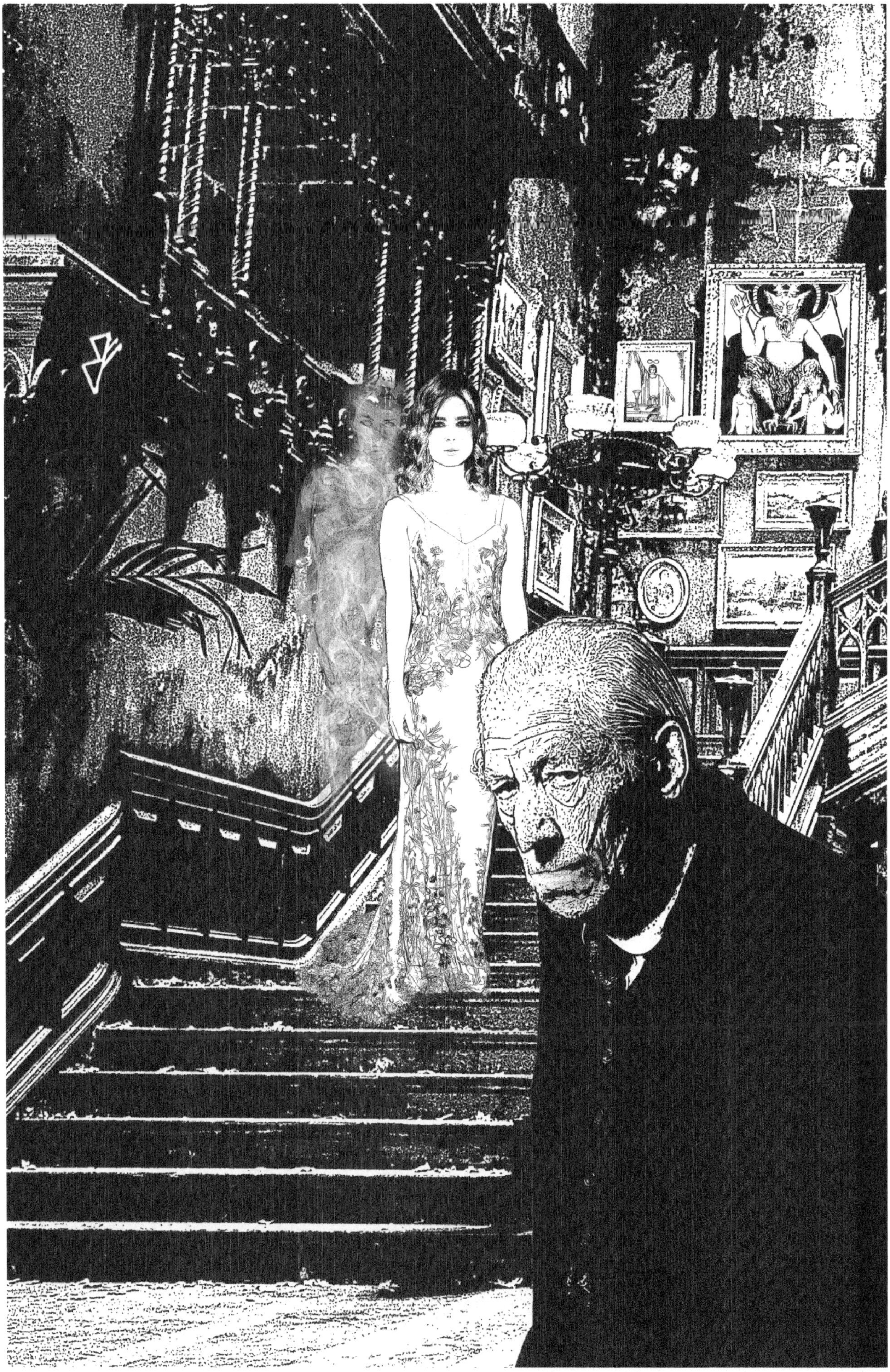

When Soft Voices Die

Amanda DeWees

A single woman can be a terrible inconvenience. This unhappy realization made itself known to me when fire destroyed my lodgings and I was forced to seek another place to stay.

"I'm so sorry, Sybil," said Arabel Keith, my closest friend. "But with my brother being a young bachelor as well as the village minister, it wouldn't be proper for you to stay with us. People would talk if we had a young widow as our houseguest, especially..."

Illustration by Robert Freeman

"Especially an actress." I repressed a sigh. Even in this enlightened year of 1873, it seemed that American sensibilities were too delicate to cope with me, and for a moment I was homesick for England. "The village inn refused me a room," I pointed out. "I can only suppose that they believe having an actress on the premises would transform it into a brothel."

Arabel blushed. She was still unmarried and had lived a sheltered life. "The neighbors are all quite sympathetic," she said hurriedly, "but they are afraid of being involved in a scandal."

If only my fiancé and I had been married already, we could have taken lodgings together. But the burning of Roderick's family home had thrown our lives into confusion, and it was not a propitious time for a wedding.

"There is one possibility," Arabel ventured. "It is far from ideal, and we may have to work hard to persuade her, but let us pay Deborah Sutton a call."

In the wilds of the Hudson River Valley, paying a neighborly call was more involved than I was accustomed to in London. When we reached our destination after half an hour's journey by sleigh over the snow-covered country roads, Mrs. Sutton received us in the high-ceilinged, airy parlor of a large Federal-style home. Unfortunately for me, she seemed just as reluctant as everyone else to take me in.

"We're very crowded at the moment," she objected after Arabel had explained my predicament. She looked to be close to fifty, with intelligent dark eyes and silver threads in her dark hair. "Our sons and their families are staying with us until spring, and of course my husband's father lives with us—"

"I would be grateful for any room, even a cupboard," I interrupted. "As far as I am concerned, the tiniest garret room would be as luxurious as a palace, no matter how many drafts, leaks, ghosts, and mice it may have."

Her gaze came to rest thoughtfully on mine. "Truly?" she asked, in a low voice that made me think of a mourning dove. "Ghosts would not bother you?"

"Not a whit," I said promptly.

"You don't believe in them, do you mean? Many scoff at the idea."

"I believe in them, but I don't fear them." Perhaps I was a bit too sure of myself, but I felt quite seasoned after my encounters with Brooke House's resident ghost. It (or rather *she*) had even borrowed me as a vessel to speak through, which seemed like a badge of acceptance from the spirit world. Arabel had witnessed this, which might be why she had deemed the Suttons' a suitable residence for me. But when I caught her eye and raised my eyebrow, she only smiled enigmatically.

"Perhaps it isn't a good idea." Doubt was drawing a furrow in Mrs. Sutton's brow. "I try never to put anyone in the haun—in that room."

"If you're troubled by a spook, perhaps I can persuade it to leave," I said recklessly. "I have some experience in these matters."

At this, my hostess brightened. "That is most reassuring! Very well, then, if you're certain you won't be afraid."

"What sort of haunt is it?" I inquired. Most likely it was not a ghost at all, merely a combination of folklore and overactive imaginations, but it was best to be forearmed.

She considered. "I don't want to predispose you to see something that isn't there," she said at length. "But you should not go in unprepared, either. Let us say that an unhappy spirit has sometimes made itself felt in that room, starting from about half a century ago. You won't come to harm, I feel certain—no one ever has—but it can be frightening."

"You've seen it yourself, then?"

She gave a self-conscious laugh. "Not exactly. But I've heard it."

This intriguing statement preoccupied me as my hostess introduced me to the remainder of the family. Her husband, Mr. Amos Sutton, was a hearty and unimaginative man who seemed to find nothing odd in the idea of inviting me to stay in the unused back bedroom that, he said, was the subject of a curious prejudice among his children and servants. The house seemed surprisingly new for a haunting to have taken root there, for the date painted over the parlor mantel was 1822. Moreover, the atmosphere of conviviality seemed ill suited to ghosts; I was warmly greeted by one cheerful family member after another.

The eldest member of the household was Mr. Sutton's father, a grizzled old sinner of seventy-five, who leered at me in a way that was all too familiar. My blonde hair tended to attract a great deal of masculine attention, not all of it welcome.

"Father Jonas, this is Mrs. Sybil Ingram Lammle," my hostess said. "She's the actress from England who was living in Brooke House until it burned down. She'll be staying with us for a while."

"An actress, hey?" he exclaimed, his close-set eyes brightening. "Come sit by me, missy. I could do with a few poetical speeches murmured into my ear."

"Have you an ear trumpet?" I inquired brightly. "If so, I shall be happy to oblige."

Suspecting that I was mocking him, he narrowed his eyes at me and chewed on the stem of his pipe while surveying my figure again. I resolved not to get within arm's length of the man.

Mrs. Sutton apologized for not having my room ready for me when it came time to retire, "but the servants simply refuse to enter it anymore." I helped her make the bed—a homely domestic task that I was unaccustomed to—while taking a good look at my surroundings. The room appeared to be furnished with odds and ends, as if Mrs. Sutton had made a gesture toward treating it as a normal bedroom but did not actually expect anyone to use it—at least, no one whose opinion mattered. It was the kind of room where one might stow an unimportant spinster great-aunt.

Because all of my belongings had been burnt along with Brooke House, Mrs. Sutton also provided me with a nightdress, sheepskin slippers, and nightcap. I could not suppress a smile as I regarded the last item. Roderick had once poked fun at me for wearing a serviceable flannel nightgown instead of something more alluring, and I could only imagine with what hilarity he would have greeted me had I worn a ruffled bonnet that tied under the chin. Still, I knew it would keep me warm, and even in this room well furnished with rugs and heavy draperies, warmth was elusive.

After the emotional strain of the last two days, I was more than ready for sleep when I climbed into the tester bed—so much so that thoughts of the ghost had actually receded from my mind. The feather mattress was soft, the quilt was warm, and my mind had drifted into a hazy place near sleep when a clatter sounded somewhere in the room.

Sitting bolt upright, I groped for the safety matches on the bureau and struck a light. From where I sat nothing looked amiss, but I lit a candle and rose from the bed to investigate.

The light of the candle glinted on a metallic surface on the floor just inside the threshold, where the floorboards were not covered by a rug. To my mystification, a silver dinner fork lay there, still vibrating slightly as if from having been dropped.

When I knelt to pick it up, I found that it seemed to be an ordinary piece of cutlery, though considerably tarnished. The simple pattern suggested that it dated from an earlier era, since the current fashion for such household objects was to be highly ornamented.

But that was all I learned from it. Though I examined the doorway and lintel, there was no place where the fork could have been hidden or where it could have fallen from.

The darting candlelight revealed nothing else out of the ordinary in the room, so I placed the fork on the bureau, blew out the candle, and returned to bed. All inclination toward sleep, however, had fled. I had seen objects materialize out of nothingness before, but it was still an unsettling thing to observe.

It was only a few minutes before the next occurrence. This time the sound was a muted *thwop*, and I felt something strike the bedclothes near my feet.

Instinctively I yanked my feet away. With my heart beating more quickly now that the intrusive presence was so close to home, I lit the candle again. A tarnished silver snuff box lay at the foot of the bed just inches from where my feet had been.

I swallowed. Even though I did not sense hostility, it was unnerving that some presence was summoning these objects out of thin air to rain down in my room. I picked up the small rectangular box with its old-fashioned scrollwork and opened it. Not even the scent of tobacco remained.

"Is anyone there?" I asked aloud, and was proud that my voice did not shake. "Are you trying to communicate with me? You may speak through me if you wish."

I saw nothing, heard nothing. My throat constricted, and for a moment I was certain I was about to speak with the spirit's voice, to articulate what it wanted and needed, as the Brooke House ghost had done.

But instead my throat closed, and a feeling of choking rose in me. In moments I was gasping for air, and a fear not entirely my own washed over me like a cold tide. My hands flew to my neck to protect it, but my fingers encountered nothing. I was strangling from within.

"*Stop*," I managed to croak, and the iron grip on my throat relaxed at once.

Panting for breath, I snatched up the candle again and shone the light into every nook and cranny where something might be concealed. Nothing was there. Or nothing that I could see. For when I had finally given up and stood still and helpless with defeat, I heard it.

A long, painful intake of breath. A choked rasp as if someone were desperately struggling to inhale... as if they were being strangled.

This time I did not extinguish the candle but wrapped myself in the quilt and sat wakeful in a chair through the rest of the night. The dying gasp did not come again, but the memory of that painful grip still lingered in my own throat and kept me from sleeping. Fear, pain, and the frustration of being unable to communicate—I felt them all, on my own behalf and on the visitant's.

Despite my boastful confidence, I was at a loss. The terrible futility of my situation mocked me. How could I hope to give voice to a ghost that could not draw breath to speak?

* * *

At length I did fall asleep, and I was almost surprised when I woke to find the fork and snuffbox still where I had placed them on the bureau. I had half believed them to be ghostly manifestations that would vanish in the light of day. When I showed them to my hosts at breakfast, however, the reaction startled me.

"Where did you get those?" old Mr. Jonas Sutton thundered.

"I merely found them in my room and wondered how they came to be there," I said, wondering at his show of temper.

"You lying baggage." His hand shot out to seize my wrist across the width of the dining table. "What are you playing at, girl?"

A surge of revulsion rose in me, and I flung off his hand with a violence that surprised me as much as his accusation. Collecting myself, I said more calmly, "I've no reason to lie. It's as I told you—they were in my room." Which was true as far as it went. With so many others present, including the children, I chose not to elaborate on just how the objects had come to be there.

Young Mr. Sutton prodded the fork. "That looks like something of my grandmother's. Eh, father? We don't use the old silver, though. Do we, Deborah?"

Mrs. Sutton shook her head. "There aren't enough place settings for everyone, so I keep it locked up. It looks as though this was somehow separated from the rest." Picking up the snuffbox, she regarded it thoughtfully. "Didn't your father collect snuffboxes, Father Jonas?" she asked old Mr. Sutton.

"I don't recall," he said gruffly. Without warning he turned on the two chattering great-granddaughters next to him and barked, "Can't a man have a bit of peace?" and the subject was dropped.

Later I was able to draw Mrs. Sutton aside for a few minutes to ask her for more details about the haunting.

"It's believed to be a servant who ran off," she said in a low voice, checking to be certain no little pitchers had brought their big ears to the linen closet where we stood. "The silver you found makes that seem quite likely. Eliza Southgate was a young maidservant who stole some of the family silver and ran away. She was never heard from again—at least, not in the flesh."

"People have heard her struggling to breathe, you mean."

"Yes, and once in a while she will return one of the silver objects she stole. That is why I believe she means no harm. Clearly it is her remorse that makes her haunt the house."

"Why do you think she is gasping for breath?"

She straightened a stack of table linens. "I've had a good many years to mull that over, and I think it may be the force of her guilty conscience. By all accounts she was a loyal and sweet-natured girl, just a young thing, so whatever caprice impelled her to rob the family must have weighed heavily on her breast—perhaps to the point that the guilt became an almost physical weight."

Guilt had not been among the emotions I had felt last night, however. It seemed to me that something more desperate was preventing Eliza's spirit, if indeed it was hers, from leaving the place that had been her home in life.

"What does your husband say about his family spook?" I asked.

She grimaced. "He doesn't believe in such 'foolishness,' and my father-in-law refuses to listen to any discussion of the topic. In truth, it's rather a relief to me to know that you have also experienced it and believe me."

Eager for another chance to communicate with the spirit, I was restless and impatient for night to fall. The day did bring one happy interval, when Roderick stopped by on his way to oversee further salvage operations at the wreckage of Brooke House.

"So you've already found a new ghost to lay," he said after greeting me with a kiss.

"Oh, you've heard about the Suttons' haunting?"

"The innkeeper filled me in." He flashed his devilish grin. Not for the first time I reflected that although Roderick's crown of dark curls was rather like a halo, his demeanor tended to mitigate any angelic qualities. "You can never resist a challenge, can you?" he teased.

"You should know," I said demurely, "being quite the biggest challenge I've ever taken on."

Conversation after that became more intimate and less verbal, and has little bearing on this account.

* * *

That night I did not bother undressing or going to bed. Instead I sat fully dressed in a chair in the darkened room, illuminated only faintly by the fire banked behind the pierced metal screen, waiting for Eliza. There was little noise from the rest of the house; for such a large family, they seemed to settle down upon retiring with little fuss or delay. Only occasionally did the night cry of some wild creature penetrate the closed windows.

I first knew I was not alone when I felt a tightening at the back of my neck. So quickly I could not prepare myself, it moved to my throat. The familiar drawn-out rasp sounded as I dragged my next breath into my lungs, and I coughed with the effort.

"Eliza?" I whispered, relieved that I could still speak on my own behalf. "I want to help you. What is it you wish to tell me?"

My throat convulsed but no words came forth, only a hoarse gasp. Frustration rose in me. I was here to serve a purpose, but how? Surely it only needed a bit of imagination to determine how I could help.

"You can breathe through me," I mused. "You move my lungs. Does that mean you can control the rest of my body? Can you lead me to something that will make clear what you want?" I had heard of automatic writing, though I had not attempted it. If the hapless spirit could guide my hand and put pencil to paper, we might be able to break through this barrier.

I felt a tentative hope brush across my mind. The idea was promising to her.

It seemed we had a plan. Taking a deep breath for courage, I stood, resisting the urge to reach for a candle. Eliza might be stronger in darkness. "Guide me, then," I whispered. "I am your instrument in any honorable enterprise."

How can I describe that bizarre nighttime journey? I could scarcely see, so I had to trust the spirit to know how and where to guide me. The sensation of my limbs being moved by another will would have awakened panic in me had I not experienced it before. Even so, it was a strange, off-balance sensation as first one foot, then the other, progressed toward the door, and in the dimness I saw my own hand reach out for the latch.

We traveled slowly through the dark and silent house. She made no sound any longer; perhaps moving my limbs took all of her strength. My booted feet noiselessly conducted us downstairs and then, to my astonishment, to the front door. My hands worked at the bolt, and then I drew open the door to a shockingly cold gust of night air.

The first real fear touched me then. How far was the ghost going to take me? What if our journey lasted for miles? I would risk dying of exposure or being set upon by whatever dangers lurked in the wilderness. Too late I wished that I had asked Mrs. Sutton to sit up with me to be a witness.

The spirit must have sensed my alarm, for in a peculiar gesture of reassurance she lifted my left hand from the door latch and clumsily patted my right hand.

Very well, I thought, *I'll trust you a bit further.* But I was more confused than ever when after guiding my steps down the porch she took me around the side of the house.

The moonlight glowed eerily on the snow, and the rustle of wind in the treetops served only to remind me of how very isolated I was. Then I found myself approaching a low, arched structure of brick, and even as I recognized it as the entrance to a root cellar my hands were drawing the bolt and opening the door. Without even a moment to prepare myself I was propelled down a staircase that was invisible in the darkness. My footfalls struck hollow echoes from the wooden treads, but soon I stepped onto soundless packed earth.

The only illumination was the faint glow of moonlight through the open door. My spine prickled uneasily as I realized that I could be surrounded by anything—anything at all—without knowing it. Surely Eliza's restless spirit was leading me toward something that would expiate her crime, but what was good for her might not be good for me, a corporeal human, and I heartily disliked being unable to see my surroundings.

Five paces she took me, curling the fingers of my right hand toward my palm, one by one, to count them. Then she raised my hand to place it against what my fingers told me was a brick wall.

At the first touch of my fingertips against the rough surface, my mind was suddenly flooded with memories and images so horrible that I snatched my hand away with a cry. I backed toward the stairs, appalled. I knew now what had made Eliza restless all these years... and it was not a guilty conscience.

Gathering up my skirts, I stumbled up the stairs, not even pausing to close the cellar door behind me. I was already through the front door of the house before I realized that my body was my own again, no longer under Eliza's guidance. But she had communicated what she needed me to know. The rest was up to me.

I hammered on the door of Mr. and Mrs. Sutton's bedchamber until the man of the house opened the door a crack. When he saw me in the moonlight that fell through the window on the landing, he blinked drowsily. "Mrs. Lammle? Are you unwell?"

"This house is unwell," I said recklessly. "Bring lights. Come at once."

"What the devil? At this hour?"

"Do listen to her, Amos." Mrs. Sutton joined him in the doorway, drawing on a dressing gown. "Mrs. Lammle would not disturb us were it not vital."

Grumbling but compliant, her husband put on a dressing gown and lit a spirit lamp. In my agitated state he seemed to move with agonizing slowness. Sleepy faces appeared at other doors as we passed, and Mrs. Sutton spoke placatingly to send them back to bed, but even so our procession had gained a few more curious family members when we made our way to the root cellar.

Mr. Sutton glanced at me quizzically when he realized this was our destination, and I grabbed at his sleeve to hurry him. "We'll need a pickaxe," I said. "Or something of that nature, perhaps a mattock. Have you such a thing?"

To his credit, he did not dismiss my disjointed words as babbling, although when he replied "I'm certain we do," his voice was the soothing tone one would use to placate someone out of her wits.

"I'll fetch something," said his elder son, to my relief, and departed on this errand. I was fortunate that curiosity was strong enough to overcome the natural human desire to dismiss me and return to bed.

Not until we stood at the place Eliza had led me, with the lamplight casting eerie shadows on the brick walls and arched ceiling, did I realize that old Mr. Jonas Sutton had joined us. "What in blazes is that actress woman up to?" he snapped. "This is pure nonsense, dragging us out of our beds in this fashion!"

"No one forced you to accompany us," I said, "so I find it all the more significant that you did. But then, you are the only one besides me who knows the secret hidden in this cellar."

"What secret is that?" asked his daughter-in-law, since the old man just glared at me without replying.

"Eliza Southgate's final resting place," I said. "She didn't run off with the family silver after all. The burglary was just to lend her disappearance plausibility. Isn't that right, Mr. Sutton?"

In the lamplight the old man's features looked distorted, twisted by evil. But my new knowledge of him was coloring my perception; it was actually his inner being that was ugly and warped. His eyes narrowed at me, and a chill raced over my skin as I realized that had we been alone, he might have tried to kill me to keep me silent.

We were not alone, though—and evidently he felt it was not too late to protect himself from the truth. "Poppycock," he said roughly. "I don't have any special knowledge of the matter, Mrs. Lammle. I was a lad of scarcely eighteen when she ran off. I had nothing to do with it."

"You had everything to do with it." Emotion made my voice shake. "She was carrying your child, and you wanted to be rid of her. So you told her to meet you in secret with whatever silver she could carry to finance your new life together, saying you would take her away and marry her someplace where scandal wouldn't follow. And that innocent girl believed you. Her heart was full of love for you right up to the moment when you wrapped your hands around her throat and strangled her."

All eyes were on old Mr. Sutton now, and he licked his lips and glanced toward the stair as if gauging his chances of running. But his son stood between him and freedom. "Father, is that true?" he asked in astonishment.

"It's rubbish, I tell you! The woman is mad. She's simply trying to stir up trouble." His face was venomous when he turned back to me. "I'm no murderer, you lying baggage."

"You're certainly not a very good one," I said coldly. "You crushed her windpipe but did not kill her right away. So while you were walling her up here, where the cellar was still not quite finished, the poor girl was struggling to draw breath. You could hear her fighting to breathe, fighting to live, almost until you put the last brick in place."

An appalled silence was broken when the old man burst into a storm of curses and imprecations. I let him rail at me as much as he wished, but when he made as if to strike me, his daughter-in-law placed herself in his path.

"You can't believe this madwoman's tales," the old man expostulated. "She made this up out of the whole cloth."

"So if we were to tear down this wall," Mrs. Sutton said quietly, "we'd find nothing to support her story?"

The old man's face went sickly white. "I don't see why that should be necessary," he stammered. "Why should you credit something so farfetched?"

"It's easy enough to settle," said the elder of his grandsons, producing a sledgehammer. "Give me a little space, and we shall soon see if this is nothing but a wicked slander."

On that long-ago night when a young man walled up the body of his sweetheart, he had known precious little about bricklaying. So it was perhaps not greatly surprising that after just a few blows of the mighty hammer several bricks gave way, revealing a dark space... and a glimpse of bone and hair.

Mrs. Sutton's hand flew to her mouth, and her husband and son fell back with exclamations of disgust. Then a choking gasp made us all look toward the old man.

Laboring to draw breath, he clutched at his throat as if to dislodge the grip of merciless hands. His eyes stared wildly as his face slowly turned purple. Then, with a last gasping rattle, he collapsed to the earth floor of the cellar.

* * *

"Heart failure, Dr. Carfax said," I told Roderick the next day. "Evidently his heart gave out when he was faced with the evidence of his old crime."

"I'm not surprised," Roderick said, his hazel eyes grave. "Will Eliza get a proper burial now?"

"Yes, but they're keeping old Mr. Sutton's part in the matter secret." Shuddering, I remembered how the girl's body had gradually been revealed as the wall was taken apart, the skeletal hands still holding a moldy leather satchel containing the remainder of the missing silver. "As far as the world is concerned, he lived a righteous life and died in his bed. No one outside the family will ever know that he was a murderer." I shook my head in disgust. "It scarcely seems like justice to me."

Roderick laced his fingers through mine. We had the small back parlor to ourselves while the rest of the household busied itself with funeral preparations, so we could sit as close together on the settee as we wished, and that was very close indeed.

"But the family knows the truth, which they didn't before," he pointed out. "That poor girl's spirit will be at peace now because of you. Just think if another fifty years had passed and no one came to help her—or no one with your empathy and courage." Then a thought occurred to him that made him draw back and look searchingly into my face. "If the ghost had been male," he said, "would you still have allowed it—allowed *him*—to take command of your body?"

"I don't know," I admitted. "Being a medium is still new to me. I imagine I shall be making many decisions on the spur of the moment, depending on the circumstances." I could see that this answer did not satisfy him, however. "Does it disturb you to think of my being under another man's control?" I asked.

His piratical grin flashed. "I'm sure it would... if I thought there might somewhere be a man capable of controlling you."

That made me laugh. "You don't think you will be equal to the task?" I challenged.

Hearing the trap in my words, he leaned closer and wound a strand of my hair around his finger.

"I know better than to try," he said.

Don't Say I Didn't Warn You

Adrian Cole

In my business a guy makes more than a few enemies. Most of them I don't worry about. If I did I wouldn't sleep at night. I'd be a zombie and let's face it, there are enough of them cluttering up the world, one way or another. When you've as many enemies as I have, it doesn't pay to waste time fretting. But sometimes you got to make the first move. You need to have a clear out, before someone gets ideas about maybe clearing you out.

Let's go back a year, to the first time I met Isiah Constantine Massamboula. He was reckoned to be one of the richest men in the world, the heart of his financial empire based in Africa and built on diamonds, although my guess was he dealt in a whole lot of other stuff, as much under the counter as over it. He had an outpost here in the US, a combination of fortress and palace, and his parties were said to be something else, rivalling anything Bacchus ever put together. So when yours truly got an invite – a personal invite – I already started to feel those cold fingers down the back of my neck. Why should Massamboula want anything to do with a two bit private dick like me?

I packed my twin Berettas and set off to find out. I don't drive, so I took a taxi beyond the city limits to the private retreat of the magnate. Expensive, but as Citizen Kane was paying the bill I figured - what the hell. At the gates two armed guards, who looked like they'd just stepped out of an African war zone, checked my invite and the taxi with military precision. My driver, Fritzy Caraldo drove on through the endless forest like he expected to be fired on at any moment.

"Jeeze, Nick, this guy you're visiting has a private army?"

"Sure. Don't sweat it, buddy. You and me, we're just two flies on the wall. When we get to Castle Dracula, stick around. I don't want to spend the next week walking home. You'll be okay for dough."

Massamboula's place was set high upon a ridge, overlooking the ocean of trees. Half the limos in the State were parked outside it. This would be some do. I left Fritzy to his cigarettes and jerking nerves and was met by more of my host's goons, only these didn't wear military uniform, just slick suits and terrifyingly shiny shoes. They studied my invite, nodded and led me up wide steps into the reception area. I could have been in Fontainebleau - opulence screamed at me from every direction as I was left to mingle. So I mingled, but I won't dwell on it.

I'd been there an hour or so, twiddling my thumbs, although the food was pretty damn good and the booze, too, but I didn't indulge. Whatever I was here for would need a clear head. Eventually one of the suits took me up a small staircase and I knew that I was about to be ushered into the presence of the master, like I was visiting the Pope.

I was asked, very politely, if I'd mind leaving my guns with the guards, and I couldn't argue with that, although I hated to feel naked.

We entered a room the size of a cavern, and it was every bit as lavishly decorated as the rest of the place, with antique furniture, paintings and chandeliers that would have embarrassed the Rockefellers. The man who approached me dominated the room, about the size of a grizzly bear and maybe twice as wide. Matter of fact, if he'd wrestled a grizzly, my money would have been on him.

Massamboula was a gleaming monster of a man, his smile as wide as the Congo, his teeth flashing. One of his huge hands reached out to engulf, and almost pulverise, my fingers. He was dressed immaculately, ludicrously expensively, and I noted several rings on both hands that would have bought him a small island – say, Madagascar. He waved his stooges away and we were alone.

"Mr Stone," he said in a deep, rolling voice. "It is such a pleasure to meet you." His English was perfect. I knew that he was from West Africa originally, and had been educated at Oxford University. He retained a very cultured accent which didn't strike me as affected. He waved us to a couple of chairs that looked like the last person to sit in them would have been a King Louis.

"You're undoubtedly wondering why I invited you to my little gathering." I let him do the talking. "Well, you are a man of many talents, Mr Stone. Or Mr Nightmare, I believe some people call you. I like that. Well, it's very simple. I want to employ your services. I'll pay you *a lot* of money, and in return I would ask for your exclusive attention. I'm sure the type of work I want you to undertake for me is well within your capability, but beyond that of most other men."

"I'm flattered."

He laughed and it was a surprisingly warm sound that rolled around the room like a big wave. Easy to be sucked up into its embrace. I was waiting for the catch.

"I'm a collector, Mr Stone. I collect very unique objects. In a moment I will show you some of them. I'll be blunt. I want you to help me increase my collection. You have access to certain places, one might almost say, other *dimensions*. Oh yes, I know of these places. I have long ears, so to speak. I gather, however, that it is only given to a select few to slip in and out of these realms. Men like you are necessarily very secretive about such matters. That doesn't concern me and I'm not about to subject you to some barbarous ordeal in order to extract your secrets from you. It will be enough to know that you'd work for me, and carry out errands on the other side."

I said nothing, waiting while he studied me, his smile fixed, but no warmer than that of a Great White. I didn't think the shark would have fared any better with Massamboula than the grizzly.

"The Pulpworld, someone called it," he said. It was no surprise to me that he'd heard of it. A lot of guys in powerful places had, but it didn't necessarily give them access. "You are more than familiar with it."

"Sure." There was no point bluffing. "I've been there. Though crossing's not like opening and closing a door."

"No, of course. It's no matter. How you get there and back is not my concern, although I'm sure I would find a visit there highly gratifying. Well – let me show you something." He rose, looming over me for a moment. We went to the far end of the room to a door that looked as if a craftsman had spent his life whittling away perfecting it. My host took out a small bunch of keys, using one to unlock the door.

Beyond was a long hall. Its walls were lined with statues and artefacts of all sizes, and from as wide a variety of cultures as you could shake a cutlass at. My guess was Massamboula's contacts had raided more tombs and maybe museums, to get hold of this collection, than I'd eaten hamburgers. And that's a lot of hamburgers. As an investment, the statues alone would have been priceless, an emperor's ransom, and as my host walked me down the hall, it was obvious he revelled in his gathered hoard, like a dragon with its gold.

Some of the statues were amazingly life-like,

whether marble or dark wood, or whatever. The detail was startling and Massamboula grinned hugely at my fascination.

"You are a man who appreciates fine art," he said. "Are they not beautiful? As you can see, they are from all periods and parts of the world. And – beyond."

One of the statues caught my eye and I had to mask my sudden shock. It was a thinly clad twenty-something girl, cast in what looked like bronze, her face looking upward in surprise. If I hadn't known it was a statue, I'd have said it was alive, someone frozen for a second in time. I half expected the eyes to swivel toward me.

"There are things in the Pulpworld that I desire for my collection. I'd like you to negotiate on my behalf. I am a patient man, Mr Stone. And a very busy one. I will give you one year to decide. You can contact me at any time within that year. Go away and think about it."

Thankfully he didn't appear to have seen my reaction. My guts were crawling. I nodded, feigning general interest.

"My people will give you a private telephone number where you can reach me personally. Give it to no one. *No one.*" No two words ever conveyed a greater image of extreme pain and unpleasantness.

And that was it. I was given back my guns and ushered out. I went back to where Fritzy Caraldo was dozing in his cab, listening to late night jazz. He jerked upright when I tapped the window and we were quickly on our way back into the forest. I didn't say a lot on the journey home. My mind was too occupied with thoughts of the life-like statue I'd seen of the girl. A girl I'd once known and who'd disappeared completely without trace a few years previously.

***

That had been almost a year ago. I hadn't got back to Massamboula. From time to time I mulled it over. It was another unexpected meeting that had me thinking about him again.

I was in one of the seedy bars downtown, curled up in a corner with a cold beer and a battered pulp magazine I'd haggled for at *Kikbak Komix*. I'd still paid more for the book than it was worth, but it was my little luxury of the week.

The guy who stood in front of me, emerging from the shadows, was no regular. He looked like a runaway from Men in Black, but I had a shrewd idea who he worked for. I'd had dealings with the Feds before.

"Mr Stone?" He flashed his ID. I'd been right, FBI. "I'm Agent Collins. Spare me a moment?"

I waved him to a seat. He was rangy, with neatly cropped hair and chiselled features. Aged about thirty and a tough guy, I guessed, but I didn't think he'd come here to rough me up.

He declined a beer, which, in this joint, was sensible. "I know you've helped out the local police with some difficult cases," he said. "And my people too."

"All in a good cause. What's eating you guys this time?"

He looked at me as if I was the last resort. "I'm on a murder case. It's connected to trafficking. Women being brought in from Eastern Europe."

My face would have clouded – I'd had some nasty experiences dealing with that kind of racket. Experiences I didn't want reminding about.

"A colleague of mine was on to a ring, five men. Somehow getting the women into the States, and then – nothing. A whole string of girls vanished into thin air. But the five men ended up dead." He pulled an envelope out of his breast pocket and slipped it over the table. "We think maybe it was a revenge killing on behalf of the women."

I got the photos out and studied them. Five separate killings. Nasty. Each of the men had had their back opened up – I mean, ripped open – and whatever had done this had made a real mess. Looked like a small bomb had gone off under their spines and scattered meat every which way.

"We drew a blank," said Collins. "Ordinarily we'd have shut the case. The trafficking ring was smashed, the dealers eliminated. Suited us. But there was a problem. A sixth corpse, just like those."

"Your colleague," I said.

"You got it in one." He stopped looking at me like I was the last resort. "No one does that without we take action. Mike – my colleague – left a few clues. He'd tracked the ring to a place he called the Pulpworld. I've drawn a blank. Brick wall. Except for one thing, Mr Stone. I was told you know something about this Pulpworld."

"Maybe. So what do you want from me?"

"Find my colleague's killer, Mr Stone. We'll pay whatever you want. And we won't get in your way."

"Mind if I keep these?" I tapped the photographs.

He nodded.

"I'll see what I can do. Give me a contact number. If you don't hear from me, meet me here in a week."

After he'd gone, I sat back, my head spinning. There was a jigsaw puzzle waiting to be put together here, but I didn't reckon on having all the pieces yet. I knew who – or more precisely what – had done the six killings. Those creatures kill in a certain, distinctive way. And I knew where the killer was based. No wonder the Feds hadn't been able to find it.

I knew someone who would have the information I needed. Someone I hadn't seen for a long time. Someone who'd threatened to cut off certain tender parts of my anatomy the next time she saw me. And it hadn't been an empty threat.

I finished my beer and put the paperback away. I needed to visit a certain woman.

***

It was a cold and foggy night in the Pulpworld. Seemed like it always was whenever I'd visited this insalubrious area of the city, which hadn't been for a long time. I stood in an alley mouth across the street from the *Exquisite Red House*, whose bright pink neon sign flashed on and off like a winking eye. For a while I re-ran some of those events, good times and bad, centred on the woman I was here to see, now calling herself Lady Arabella. She ran the place I was watching. Rod of iron in a velvet glove, if you want to mix a couple of metaphors.

I gave one of the guys on the door my details and asked to see her. In return he gave me a look that suggested I must have escaped from the local funny farm, but he sent someone inside to inquire. His ugly expression rearranged itself into an even uglier one when word came back for me to go in. I stepped into the semi-lit darkness of the club and steeled my senses against the perfumed smell, the dim light and discordant noise that passed for music. I was taken upstairs by a young guy in the most crumpled suit in the world. The kid looked like he'd slept in it – since birth.

Arabella had better accommodation on the top floor. A tough stood either side of the door, probably carrying more hardware than a SWAT team, but I ignored them and went into the lair. It was tastefully decorated, not too expensive or avant-garde. Low lighting, velvet drapes, nice antique furniture. Arabella had come from humble beginnings but I'd always known she had potential class.

She sat in a high backed chair, wearing a one piece full length dress of deep purple that clung to her figure, tight as a second skin. There were no spare inches, no lines, nothing to suggest she'd reached the threshold of middle age. Except for her eyes. They were very cold, almost icy, like they'd seen more things in life than most. She tried to smile, but it was obvious her mouth wasn't used to that particular arrangement of muscles and it came out wrong, like she was about to do something very unpleasant. I'd been expecting it.

"It's been a long time, Nick," she said, voice as cold as her eyes. "A very long time."

I nodded.

"This must be very important. I told you what I'd do to you if I ever set eyes on you again. You're not dumb enough to think I still won't."

"Hear me out before you get your claws out." I didn't sit down. We were alone, but if the two meat grinders outside came in, I wanted to have half a chance of nailing them.

"It better be good."

I took an envelope from my pocket and slid out the photographs agent Collins had given me. "Take a look at these." I handed them to her.

She spent a moment or two shuffling them, her expression indifferent. "Nasty. Do I know them?"

"Traffickers. Five of them. The sort of scum who trade off human misery for a quick buck. Some of those girls could have ended up here in the *Red House*."

"My girls are well looked after, you know that. Nothing's changed. They're protected. Anyone gets funny and they pay, big time."

"Then these guys must have been hilarious. They've practically been shredded."

I got that smile again. "Too bad," she said. "Who's the sixth guy?"

"He's the bad news. He was after them. FBI. And the Feds are not happy."

Her eyes narrowed and the temperature dropped another degree or two. "You work for the Feds?"

"I know what killed these guys, Arabella," I said. "You've got a firedrake. Tell me I'm wrong."

She watched me for another long, cold minute or two, lifting a glass beside her and sipping at the liquid. She didn't offer me a drink. "That's a cynical assumption."

"You have to deliver it to me."

She lifted her head and laughed, a short bark and just for a moment I caught a glimpse of her as I'd known her, all those lost years ago. We'd been young, not exactly hell-raisers, but wild enough to treat our lives none too seriously. For a year we'd enjoyed each other to the full and we'd shared everything, not just our bed. It had got to the point where I'd been thinking this was the love thing and we were going to build something special.

Then I met her kid sister, Maria. It changed everything. Mostly it made me realise I wasn't in love with Arabella. I tried to be. She knew something was wrong. And being a smart woman, she figured it out pretty quick. I wasn't two-timing her with her sister, other than in my head, but Arabella could read my mind. I'm no saint, but I didn't cheat, even though I knew Maria would have welcomed it.

Things got heated, stretched, hellish. None of us said what was on our minds, but we all knew. In the end, Maria settled the problem, or thought she did. She took off, without saying anything. Walked out of our lives. In some ways it was a big relief to me. I thought I'd just pick up where I'd left off with Arabella and everything would go back to being hunky-dory. I got that wrong.

Arabella and Maria were very close, like twins I guess. Now there was no contact, almost as if Maria had died. I got the blame, maybe rightly so. Arabella and me were finished. It didn't take long for the rot to set in and she kicked me out, along with that promise of retribution. As for Maria, no one found out where she'd gone. Arabella had feared the worst. The world we knew was a pretty sleazy place, with few compromises, and Maria would have been hard put to make a go of life on her own.

I'd tried to find out where she'd gone, but drew a blank.

"What makes you think I have a firedrake?" Arabella said.

I tore my thoughts away from the past. "I may have kept my distance from this place, Arabella, but in my job I need good ears. Word is, the *Red House* is very well protected. This isn't the first time you've used the firedrake to eliminate troublesome patrons."

"You always were a smart cookie, Nick. But I went through some tough times, *very* tough times, to establish myself here in the Pulpworld. If you think I'd give up the firedrake, you're losing it. Why should I? The guys in the photo were scum, like you said. The Fed was unlucky, but that's the price you sometimes pay. Go back to your world, Nick. Let the Pulpworld take care of its own."

"There are others who prey on the Pulpworld. These traffickers were small fry. What if I told you there's something much bigger and nastier nosing about? Something from my world."

"I'd say it's bugging you and you want to settle its hash. Oh – I get it – you want the firedrake to do your dirty work. You're a fool."

"I have something in exchange."

"Your head on a plate would barely cover it," she said, with some feeling and I would have been genuinely terrified if I hadn't been holding the one card that would trump her.

"I know where your sister is."

If she'd been stark naked and I'd hosed her down with icy water, she couldn't have reacted more shocked. She stood up, taller than I remembered, and for a moment she seemed to *glow*, fury personified. If she'd been holding a gun, my guess is she would have emptied it into me. When she spoke, her voice was glacial.

"She's not with you. Don't tell me she's with you."

I shook my head. There was nothing for it but to give her the bad news.

***

I rang the number on the card Massamboula's goon had given me. Like he'd said, it was a direct line.

"This is Nick Stone."

"Ah, I was wondering if you'd forgotten me. Glad you rang, Mr Stone. Have you thought about my offer?"

"I have."

"You'll work exclusively for me. All expenses paid. No contract, no records, but you'll be a rich man."

"Sounds pretty good."

"Come and see me in two days. I'll have a car sent for you. It will collect you at six pm. Name your pick up point."

I gave him a convenient place downtown. "I have a little something for you," I said. "A token of my appreciation for your offer."

"Really? How intriguing." If he was apprehensive, his voice didn't show it.

"From the Pulpworld. For your collection."

I could just picture that widescreen smile. "It's the least I can do," I said.

"I look forward to seeing you."

***

Massamboula's palace was a lot quieter on my second visit. Without all those people it seemed twice as big, twice as glittery. I was shown into another state room, this one with a sweeping view of the lawns outside the window, dropping away into the darkness of the forest like it was another world. The goons still took my guns.

My host offered me a brandy and I'll give him this much, it must have been the kind of nectar the gods liked to sip. Massamboula sat opposite me, a monarch sprawled comfortably among his riches. My guess was, when a man had as much as he did there was nothing left to collect except for the exotic and the bizarre. Which sort of explained his obsession with the Pulpworld and what he could get out of it.

"That gift I mentioned," I said, and at once he was all teeth.

"Yes, it still intrigues me. You have it with you?"

"She," I said, flashing a grin of my own.

He leaned forward. "Now you are really whetting my appetite, Mr Stone. She?"

"I saw from my first visit you're a man who admires beauty. The ladies who attended that gathering were as beautiful as any in the world. And your statues. Real classy. Especially those in the private collection you showed me."

He gave a low laugh, deep down in that huge chest. It sounded like distant thunder and just as ominous. "Of course. There is nothing more wonderful in life."

"How is it done?" I was sticking my neck out, but if we were going to play this through, I had no choice.

"I don't understand," he said, but his wry grin told me the opposite.

"The statues. Some of them are very life-like. Almost too life-like to be true. My guess is, they didn't start life as statues. Matter of fact, that's why you're employing me. You want me to bring the objects of your desire here, from the Pulpworld."

"Go on, Mr Stone." He sat forward, his eyes gleaming. He was enjoying this.

"Beautiful women. You have them brought here, and you transform them. They wind up in your private collection." I kept my eyes fixed on his.

A shadow crossed his face, but it was momentary. He was smiling again. "Ah, you are an astute man, Mr Stone. I like that. You'll make a good employee. Yes, you are correct. That is what I do."

"So – how is it done?"

"It's a very ancient process, the secret handed down over generations. Call it black magic, voodoo, whatever you like, but in truth, it's far more than that. I am from a very old family line. My people were in Africa before Rome was built. Can you believe that?"

"Sure. We know a whole lot less about man's past than we like to think."

"I'm glad you have an open mind. I could show you how the process works, but alas, I have no subjects available at the moment."

"You will have, soon."

He sat back and studied me as if he would prize whatever he wanted to know out of me. "Go on."

"My gift." I looked at my watch. "Pretty soon, she'll be at the outer gates, in a taxi. Tell your guards to let her in. You won't be disappointed."

"I see! Yes, of course. A girl – and is she from the Pulpworld?"

"Oh yeah. She won't be followed. Once she's here, she'll be all alone in the world."

He grinned like a kid and I thought he was going to rub his hands with glee. We were interrupted by a knock on the door. One of the guards entered and walked over to Massamboula, bending down and speaking so I couldn't hear. I knew what he was saying.

"Yes, yes," said my host. "Let them in. I will

meet them at the main entrance." He rose and turned to me. "Perfect timing, Mr Stone. We have a visitor."

A short while later Massamboula and I stood at the top of the main steps into the house, watching Fritzy Caraldo's cab pulling to a halt on the gravel. Fritzy got out, looking more than ever like a frightened chimp and opened one of the back doors. Slowly the girl emerged. She wore a sleek coat that swept down to her ankles, and some kind of mantilla that hid her face.

Massamboula could hardly contain himself, his own Achilles heel exposed. He took the girl's gloved hand and bent to it like some regal nobleman, and then led her up the steps, like she was Cinderella in all her finery, come to grace the ball. At the top of the steps, she regarded me through her veil, but my own expression was bland, like I had no real interest in this affair. She was about to lift the veil but Massamboula gently restrained her.

"No, no, please. Not yet, I implore you. Come into the house. There will be time enough to get to know each other."

I heard the cab drive off. No doubt Fritzy would be back in the city in record time, and I knew he'd keep his mouth shut. I followed Massamboula and the girl, back upstairs to his private chambers. She moved languorously, and if I hadn't known better, I'd have thought she was drugged. Maybe Massamboula thought so. It suited me.

When we were alone in yet another of his rooms, he directed the girl to a central area, its thick carpets woven with exotic patterns that hinted at the loops and spirals of some kind of pentacles. The whole room was like a miniature temple to whatever strange gods and powers Massamboula worshipped. The lighting was subtle, the incense sharp, the air humid, as if we were in a tropic zone. The man knew how to create an atmosphere, I'll give him that.

The girl stood quietly in the centre of the room, which was on a lower level than its perimeters. She still wore her coat and the veil, but waited for instructions.

"Is this where you work your magic?" I asked Massamboula.

"Yes. We won't be disturbed. We are locked in, Mr Stone. What I am about to show you has only been witnessed by very few. It will bind you to me, you understand? You are a fortunate man. Your ability to enter the Pulpworld singled you out for me." He went to a very ornate stand, carved out of dark wood and embellished with the usual twisted carvings — snakes, demon faces, claws, all wound together effectively. The stand held a fat book, a grimoire I guess you'd call it, that looked like something one of those early printing presses in Europe would have churned out, and it was probably just as old.

"There are rituals for all these things," said my host. "Once it is set in motion, the words have power. When spoken, the sounds become currents in the air, forces that interact with us and our servants. I have opened the book at the appointed place for the ritual of transmogrification. Everything is in readiness."

"Do you need me to do anything?"

"Not yet. Watch and learn. Oh — before I perform the ritual, I sometimes like to indulge myself." He looked keenly at the girl.

I knew what he had in mind. It hadn't come as a surprise. I just nodded. We were getting to the interesting bit.

Massamboula walked slowly down the low steps to the girl. "My dear," he said, "you may remove your coat."

She did so at once, pulling it off and dropping it carelessly. She was wearing a skin-tight dress that left nothing to the imagination. She took off her headgear, including the veil, and revealed her face for the first time.

I barely managed to mask my shock. When I'd told Arabella that I'd wanted her firedrake, I'd guessed that the creature was embedded in one of her girls at the *Exquisite Red House*. I'd gambled that she would give the girl up to me in exchange for knowing about her sister and how she'd wound up in Massamboula's kinky collection. I'd gambled — and lost. Instead of sending me the girl and the firedrake, she'd come herself, obviously hell-bent on revenge.

Except that I'd only got half the picture.

Arabella saw my horror but something in her eyes warned me not to speak or move. She turned to reveal that her dress was backless, her bare skin gleaming in the lurid half-light of the room. From the nape of her neck down to the base of her exposed spine, the embossed tattoo of the firedrake stood out, its fabulous intricate details etched in vivid splendour, so that Massamboula gasped, instantly captivated by the sight. Which is how the damn thing works. It had just not occurred to me, the dumb-ass, that Arabella carried the firedrake herself.

I should have done something, but the air was crackling, alive with the firedrake's magic and whatever strange powers Massamboula had already set in motion through his preliminary rituals. I watched, hypnotised, as he reached out and ran his fingers down Arabella's spine. She shuddered, but it was all the firedrake needed to begin its deadly business. Massamboula was no match for it. Mechanically he took off his jacket and tossed it aside and unbuttoned his shirt. No doubt he thought he was in charge here, but nothing could have been further from the reality.

He couldn't take his eyes from the firedrake and watched as it shifted and then began the slick process of becoming three dimensional, its shape writhing, the skin rippling until the wings slowly unfolded and the body rose up from Arabella's back, half her size, as if she was carrying a child. I'd never seen this process before, but I knew how it ended.

"You wanna pleasure yourself, Mr Massamboula?" Arabella said to him, her lips drawing back over teeth that looked suddenly sharp as needles. "Go ahead."

If he realised the firedrake was unfurling long arms and claws that would have shamed a sabre-toothed tiger, Massamboula didn't show it. The thick, cloying magic had him totally snared and he seemed to be enjoying his own personal kind of ecstasy. Arabella abruptly swung round and gripped him with both arms, pressing her mouth on his in a kiss and embrace that no amount of struggle would break.

I wanted to stop it. Sure, I'd brought the firedrake here, knowing it would destroy him and exact the revenge that both Arabella and I wanted – but not her!

All I could do now was stand, mesmerised, as the firedrake rose up over its host and dropped like a cloud on Massamboula as she held him. Now it swung round and dug its talons into his shoulders, its legs interlinking with his lower legs in a horrifying parody of a clinch. Arabella drew back her face and Massamboula's was a bloody ruin. He screamed, a combination of horror and agony, but for all his huge strength, he was no match for the thing on his back, which began to tear and rend, reaching inside his opened flesh as though it would drag out his spine.

Arabella stood back, blood soaking the front of her dress. For a moment there was nothing human about her. Nothing I could have said to her would have got through.

As Massamboula fell to his knees, still screaming, the firedrake roared its fury. Arabella pointed to the stand and the huge book. "The ritual," she said in a voice of pure icy. "Read the words of the ritual."

I got exactly what she meant, because it was the thing I'd planned. I went to the grimoire and, as Massamboula had said, the pages had been opened conveniently at the ritual he'd used so many times to create his statues. I read, intoning the words carefully. I was too freaked out to care whether I sounded like an idiot.

Through his agony, Massamboula must have realised what was happening. He shrieked a warning. I knew as I continued that the thing was working. He and the firedrake were slowly *turning*.

I'd almost finished, when Arabella leapt forward, to give Massamboula what I thought would be a last kick, a final venting of her anger. I was wrong again. She grabbed him and locked her arms around him: the terrible metamorphosis extended to her. She looked at me and I saw her face as I'd once known it, and in her eyes there was no hatred, no fury. Something softer, something only I had known.

I slammed the book shut, but it was far too late to prevent the climax. It was over very quickly. I leaned on the stand, my legs threatening to collapse.

There was a new statue, a trio of mingled bodies, cast in dark wood, the details alarmingly life-like. The huge Massamboula, his body almost torn in half from neck to lower spine, the rearing, fanged firedrake, eyes glittering scarlet jewels, and Arabella, bent backwards, one hand on Massamboula's throat, the other raised as if fending off the daylight. Her eyes, though, looked at me.

I'd see that look for a long, long time.

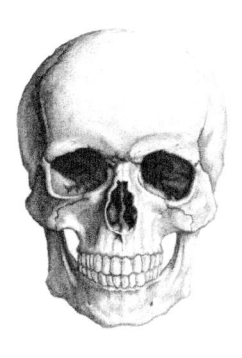

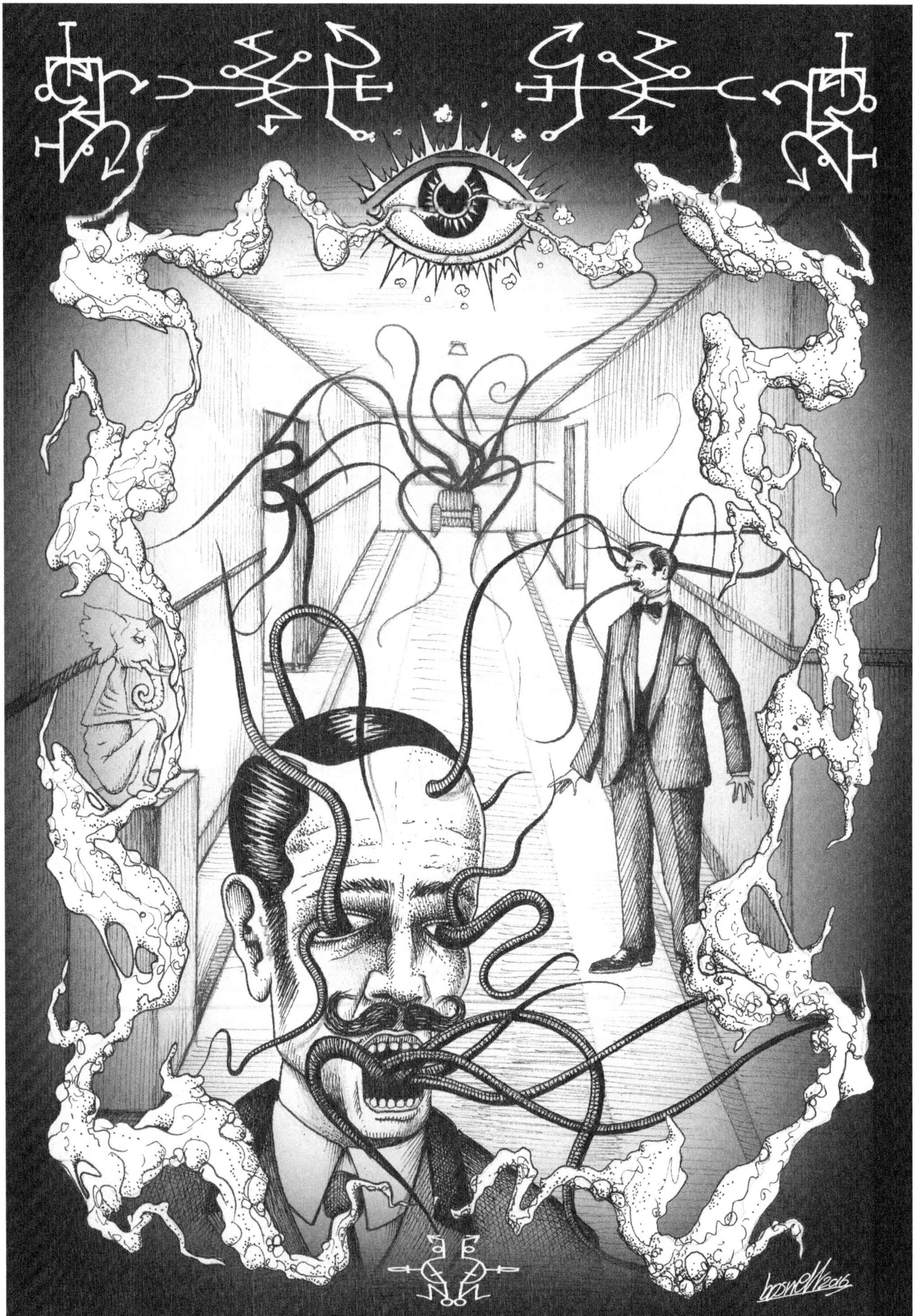

ORBIS TERTIUS

Josh Reynolds

'I now held in my hands a vast and systematic fragment of the entire history of an unknown planet, with its architectures and playing cards, the horror of its mythologies and the murmur of its tongues...'

-Jorge Luis Borges

"Tlon, Uqbar, Orbis Tertius"

"So, this would be one of those things that I should be paying attention to, innit?" Ebe Gallowglass said as the black Crossley pulled up alongside the pavement. Rain thudded against the windshield and the roof of the car as she peered up at the front of the Voyager's Club. "Place looks like it's going to smell like cigar smoke and musty clothes." She was a lean young woman, all sharp angles. With her battered flat cap and baggy coat, she wouldn't have looked out of place in a Soho dive or a smoke-filled betting shop.

"In this weather, quite possibly, and, yes, you should be paying attention," the driver of the Crossley said in exasperation. "Paying attention is what you're here for. Why else would I be remunerating you?" In contrast to his companion, Charles St. Cyprian was tall, dark and slim, and dressed in one of Savile Row's finest sartorial creations.

"You don't," Gallowglass said. "I don't get paid."

Illustration by Mutartis Boswell

"And you never will, with that attitude. You're here to learn."

"Are we going in?" Gallowglass said. She shifted and her coat fell open, revealing the shoulder holster and the butt of the heavy Webley-Fosbery revolver secured within it. A Seal of Solomon was engraved on the butt of the revolver, picked out in ivory.

"*Après vous*," St. Cyprian said as he got out. The rain pounded down, instantly soaking his clothes despite the heavy officer's greatcoat he wore. "I don't recall asking you to come armed, by the by."

"You never have to ask," Gallowglass hunched her shoulders against the downpour as they made for the steps of the club.

"I mean, there was no reason."

"I like to be prepared. Why are we here, anyway?"

"Tradition, mostly," St. Cyprian said. "Responsibilities of the office, what?"

As Gallowglass knew, said responsibilities included the investigation, organization and occasional suppression of That Which Man Was Not Meant to Know—including ghosts, werewolves, ogres, fairies, boggarts and the occasional worm of unusual size.

All such oddities fell under the purview of the offices of the Royal Occultist, by order of the King (or Queen), for the good of the British Empire and those who dwelt within it. Beginning with the diligent amateur Dr. John Dee, the office had passed through a succession of mostly steady hands, culminating with one Charles St. Cyprian and his erstwhile assistant, Ebe Gallowglass. "Someone went somewhere unpleasant, found something odd and now, after carting it from God alone knows where, across trackless deserts and vast mountain ranges, they'd like to know what it is, please."

"And that's where we come in?"

"Well, me at any rate," St. Cyprian said. "You, eventually." St. Cyprian had inherited the offices from its previous occupant, as Gallowglass would eventually inherit them from him, if she survived. Neither of them cared to discuss it.

He looked at the door, with its ornate knocker, shaped like a stylized compass. From the outside, the club didn't look much different now than it had the last time he'd visited. St. Cyprian didn't normally go to the clubs, though he was a member of several, from before the War. He'd had a whole life, before the War, before...everything.

The clubs reminded him of that earlier, emptier, happier time, and he had enough sour memories without inviting more. Absently, he rubbed the spot on his leg where a Hun bullet had left him something to remember Kaiser Wilhelm by. It ached in the rain. He knocked on the door. "I used to come here regularly with Carnacki, looking at one artefact or another in the Club's possession." He coughed and knocked again. He wondered where the hall porter was. "They collect what could be politely termed 'unique' antiquities. They've got cabinets filled with old manuscripts, shrunken heads and idols nicked from a thousand different temples, a whole ruddy museum."

"Lovely," Gallowglass said.

"Quite." It was usually a bad idea to bring home chunks of the local occult landscape as souvenirs; the locals frowned on it, but so too did the items themselves, on rare occasions. Whether it was dacoits coming down the chimney or ghosts slithering out of teapots, it rarely ended well. The Voyagers Club was a citadel of bad decisions, occupied by men with more bravery than sense. On the rare occasions when the members had called on Carnacki to help identify an object, he had always tried to convince them to send the item back to where it had come from. 'Let old gods rest in familiar climes,' was Carnacki's motto. The honourable members rarely listened, however.

"It never hurts to stay on good relations with men on the sharp edge, however," St. Cyprian said. "While I don't have Carnacki's eye for the outré, I can muddle through, make them feel as if they've got the Grail in their hands."

"What if they do?"

"Grab it and run." St. Cyprian knocked again. "Where is that dashed porter? I was told they'd be expecting us..." He knocked once more and the door jerked open. As he stumbled back, surprised, hands reached for him. Desperate claws fastened into his lapels and a blistering stream of gibberish assaulted his ears.

St. Cyprian didn't resist as he was pulled inside the Voyagers, though Gallowglass let loose a steady stream of curses. Men huddled in the corridors, hands clapped to mouths and ears alike as others grappled with one another, howling nonsense into each other's bewildered faces. He and Gallowglass were passed from hand to hand like gin bottles at a pyjama party. The words that assaulted their ears were in no language he recognized, nor, it seemed, in any language recognized by the speakers themselves, judging by the expressions of confused horror that surrounded him.

He'd seen worse in his time. Nonetheless, the hairs on the back of his neck bristled, as if he were at the eye of a building storm. He shoved free of his captors easily and they fluttered away, gazes vacant. Gallowglass had kicked and bit her way free, and her hand was on the butt of the Webley-Fosbery. "What sort of greeting do you call that then?" she snarled, eyes darting about.

"Not the one I was expecting, that's for sure." For a moment, he was tempted to leave, to let whatever was happening within these walls happen without him. Lord knew, they'd likely brought it on themselves. Unfortunately, he had certain responsibilities. He looked at Gallowglass, who grinned crookedly.

"Glad I brought the pistol now?" she said.

"I commend your foresight."

"How many you say were in this club then?" she said as they made their way through the club, shoving through the crowded corridor, relying on St. Cyprian's dim memories of the layout. His mind ran down a list of possibilities. Curses, possessions, poisons...given the proclivities of the Club members, it could be anything causing the members to curl up into sobbing balls, spouting gibberish.

"Forty or so members," he said, "I—hsst!" He held up a hand and they stepped back, into an alcove as stumbling men, armed with a variety of weapons, lurched from room to room as if looking for something. "Well, that's a rum do, what?"

"Is that a cricket bat?" Gallowglass whispered.

"The Club's armaments aren't what you'd call vast," St. Cyprian said as the mob lurched away, around a corner. "Even so, I'd suggest we stay as inconspicuous as possible."

Gallowglass grunted and shook her head. "What?"

He glanced at her. "I said—we should play it inconspicuous."

"I thought you said—never mind. What are we looking for?"

"Anything out of place," he said. He turned around, examining the alcove. It was occupied by a statue crafted from jade in the likeness of a crippled man with an elephant's head. It sat cross-legged and weary in its alcove, and he felt a strange sense of pity sweep over him as he reached out idle fingers to stroke it. There was a temple somewhere missing its deity, he thought. "A god in his own land and a curiosity in ours," he murmured.

"Sticky-fingered sods,"

"Yes, well, conquest goes hand in hand with pillage, doesn't it?" St. Cyprian said. "You can tell how successful an empire is by how much stolen culture is in its museums." He frowned. "And then something like this happens, or a mummy wakes up or chaps start sprouting rosette birthmarks and asking for raw meat and for a moment, just a moment, everyone can clearly see how bad an idea it was to filch the Blessed Eye of Kushiel-Ra and bring it back to Blighty to show off to the Oxford Old Fellows."

"Doesn't take them too long to forget," Gallowglass said. There was a scream from somewhere in the club, and the sound of breaking furniture.

"No, it doesn't." He shook himself. "When in doubt, follow the screams, eh?"

"Because that plan has never gotten us into trouble."

"Pish, walk in the park this," St. Cyprian said. He realized what the mob had been searching for a moment later, when they turned a corner and saw two Clubmen pulling a third out of a lavatory. One spat gibberish into the struggling captive's face with machine-gun like precision. The man bucked and squealed and began to babble as his captors released him and let him flop bonelessly to the floor. It was while St. Cyprian was considering this that a piscine idol nearly caved in his skull.

"Bugger," Gallowglass yelped as St. Cyprian jerked to the side. His attacker stabbed the soapstone statue into the wall, gouging the panelling with frenzied strength. He babbled nonsense syllables and slung the statue at St. Cyprian. As he stumbled back, he saw Gallowglass levelling her pistol. He batted the barrel aside. "Don't shoot him."

He thought he recognized the madman frothing unintelligibly at him. Sir Augustus something-or-other from somewhere, whose steely gaze and bluff, archaic manner had dissolved into rabid fury. It was as if whatever had taken his mastery of the King's English had also stripped away his humanity. Hooked fingers swiped at St. Cyprian, who drove a fist into his attacker's belly. Sir Augustus bent double, wheezing. St. Cyprian, never one for school-boy ethics, struck him again, dropping him flat to the floorboards.

A revolver barked, spattering his cheek with splinters from the wall. He turned and lunged for the gunman, who screeched simian curses at him as they collided. St. Cyprian twisted the man's wrist and forced him to release the pistol. Even as he dove to snatch it up, Gallowglass crept around the slobbering gunman. She brought the butt of her Webley down on the top of his skull, knocking him senseless. "Figured you wouldn't want me to shoot him either," she said.

"Not cricket, topping the doo-lally." St. Cyprian cracked the revolver open and checked its ammunition. Satisfied, he snapped it back into place and stood, happy to be armed. Boards creaked and shapes filled the other end of the corridor. A croquet mallet, decorated with blood and scalp, was extended towards them, and mad eyes blazed as orders in a strange language were barked.

"Yeah?" Gallowglass said, extending her revolver.

St. Cyprian grabbed her arm. "Yes. Not unless we have to. Run."

Feet trod the boards and they fled before them. His eardrums itched with the growing, growling cacophony that was filling up the air in the Club. He wondered if Gallowglass were feeling it as well. Her face was drawn and pale as they ran.

"Looks like inconspicuous has gone out the window," Gallowglass said, but for a moment, St. Cyprian thought she had said something else. The vowels had floated and stretched strangely, and then he was shaking his head and her words were normal.

"Yes," he said, as they ducked into a room and booted the door shut. He pressed his back to the door and closed his eyes. The ache was omnipresent and he massaged his temples. "Something's out there," he muttered.

"Several somethings," Gallowglass said, as feet stomped past the door.

"Not what I meant," he said harshly. She looked at him in confusion for a moment, as if she hadn't understood him. Then, abruptly, she shook her head.

"You're not going to do what I think you're going to do, are you?" she said.

"I don't think we have much choice," He traced the sacred shape of the Voorish Sign in the air with a finger, so that what was unseen might be seen, and let his inner eye flicker open. The spirit-eye, he'd heard it called, though acquaintances in the Society for Psychical Research insisted that it was merely a very focused form of extrasensory perception. Whatever it was called, it had taken him several years to learn how to utilize it safely. It was still a chancy thing at the best of times, but useful, in these sorts of situations. A bit of the old psychic howsits could reveal all sorts of interesting things that one might otherwise miss.

The world became soft at the edges and more vibrant as his senses expanded to fill the void left by his thoughts and physical sight. The walls became porous and gossamer and he could see the dim shapes of the afflicted members moving around and behind them, the lights of each man's *ka* flickering like a candle in a kaleidoscopic fog. Gallowglass' *ka* burned almost painfully bright. And something else, something dark and far too solid for his liking. It was reminiscent of oil spreading across water, or hundreds of thousands of words, spilling across a page. Tendrils of boiling black matter, stretching and twisting through the corridors and doorways, ignoring mundane barriers as they sought—what?

He saw a tendril slide past their hiding place, its tip planted in the back of a man's neck and as he watched, it drove its mount towards another man with gruesome undulations. The second man was without a ghoulish passenger and appeared to be trying to escape the Club through a window. The first man burst into the room and the tendril darted from his mouth, quick as an adder, to bury itself into the hazy shape of the second man's skull. St. Cyprian's eyes popped open and he jerked away from the door, revulsion creeping through him.

"What? What did you see?" Gallowglass said, reaching for him.

He shuddered and twisted out of her grip. He swept out his hand, inscribing the Third Ritual-Sign of Hloh on the surface of the door, even as tendrils began to cluster about it. St. Cyprian winced as the sound of muttering voices, in no language he recognized, built slowly, growing louder and louder before being abruptly silenced when his third eye snapped shut.

"It's..." he struggled to find the right word, "An infestation. Or perhaps an invasion..."

The first Clubmen began to attack the door even as he spoke, obviously alerted to his presence. Fists thumped against the wood and he looked at the revolver in his hand. He didn't want to kill anyone, if he could help it. Nonetheless, he aimed the pistol at the door and waited. Gallowglass followed suit. "If they get in, fire and attempt to barrel through them," he said. "Don't kill anyone you don't have to."

The deranged club-members were a threat to life and limb. The issue of the tendrils was another matter entirely. They weren't really there, he knew, not physically, but *psychically*. No way to barrel through those. He racked his brain, trying to think, cursing himself for being stupid enough to walk into the situation without proper preparation. He glanced at Gallowglass, and felt a stab of guilt.

Then, a larger worry: What would happen when the—infected, for lack of a better term—spilled out into the city streets? Would they carry this ailment with them, into London? He thought of the scene from earlier, when the afflicted had bellowed into the face of their prey. Was that how it was spread, through sound?

The door bucked and shuddered in its frame. Then, abruptly, it fell quiet. St. Cyprian took a breath and seized the moment, jerking open the door. The corridor was empty. From the shouts, they had found new prey.

"What's the plan?" Gallowglass asked. "Scarper or burn this place to the ground?"

"We're not burning anything,"

"You never want to burn anything."

"Because I have some sense of civic duty," St. Cyprian said. "I—what was that?" He heard a groan and they peered around the edge of an open door. He spotted the man he'd seen taken earlier. The fellow twitched and moaned, unintelligible words dripped from his lips as he tried to rise and failed. Like the chaps in the foyer, he seemed harmless. But how long would that be the case?

"Gone spare, innit," Gallowglass said. She sounded nervous, which was rare enough an occurrence to be unsettling.

Carefully, they entered the room. Gallowglass shut the door behind them. "This disease, this entity, whatever it is, it's spreading slowly," he said. There were maybe thirty or forty men in the Club at any one time, not counting staff. How many had already fallen under its sway? How long before the first gibbering berserker stumbled into the street and infected a random passerby? How long before someone noticed the noise and sent for the police?

"Which means?"

"It means that we need to find the epicentre. And quickly." He sank to his haunches before the groaning man and closed his eyes. He heard Gallowglass protest, but he ignored her and let his spirit-eye snap open. Something black and worm-like wriggled in the man's sinuses, spreading up into his brain and down into his mouth. Already, tendril like feelers were emerging from the back of the victim's neck and writhing searchingly in the air.

He steeled his nerve and opened his mouth. He felt a peculiar, yet familiar, chill as the first dollops of gelid ectoplasm were extruded from his mouth. His spirit-eye wasn't the only trick in his psychic tool-bag; there were many, some more useful than others, and all learned at great expense.

Hesitantly, he reached up, thrusting his hand into the mass as it gently tore free of his throat and floated in front of his face like some ghostly jelly-fish. It bubbled as it shrouded his hand, covering it in a foggy glove. He felt weak, as if he hadn't had a drink in days.

The black thing began to squirm as it sensed his intentions. Quickly, he plunged his ectoplasm-wrapped fingers into the man's throat and grabbed the writhing mass. It was like dipping his hand into soft lard. He gritted his teeth as the thing began to thrash in his grip. It was stronger than it looked and as he tried to pull it from its nest, its victim's hands suddenly fastened on his throat. Gallowglass shouted in alarm and grabbed his attacker's wrists. She cracked the man in the skull with her Webley, but he refused to let go.

St. Cyprian ignored the growing pressure on his larynx and dragged the thing from its hidey-hole. As it popped free, the man abruptly released him and flopped backwards like a marionette with its strings cut, his head bruised and bloody from Gallowglass' blows.

He glared at the thing in his hand with his spirit-eye, taking in its *wrongness* close-up. It struck at him and he tightened his grip. Even as he held it, part of it trailed away through the air, like smoke expelled from a pipe, exactly as he'd hoped.

"What now?" Gallowglass said. Her voice was dull and muted, as if he were listening to her from under water.

"Follow close," he said. He rose carefully to his feet, eyes still closed, spirit-eye wide. It was difficult to move in such a fashion, and dangerous, given the situation. But there was nothing for it. He had to risk it. Clutching his prisoner, he followed the trail out of the room and into the corridor, where more tendrils writhed and clutched at the air. He tensed, fear pulsing down his spine, both for himself as well as Gallowglass. It was like walking into the maw of some vast anemone. His body grew weaker the longer the ectoplasm was separated from him. There were men who could clothe themselves in the stuff, but he wasn't one; at best, he could protect himself and Gallowglass long enough to get to where they were going. He heard wood crunching, as if from far away. He hoped it wasn't a door.

He stepped into the heart of the thrashing tendrils and his mind cringed as they brushed up against him. Gallowglass made a sound, but he ignored it. This close, they took no notice, or perhaps they thought they were already mounted by one, thanks to his prisoner. Either way, he breathed a sigh of relief as he found the source of the things, pulling Gallowglass behind him.

It was in the study, of course. All new additions to the Club collection were brought to the study for examination by the Club president. It sat on the desk, as if waiting for him, innocuous and innocent amidst the paraphernalia of study, including papers and candles and magnifying glasses and other such odds and ends. It was a book. He circled the desk, examining it as best he could without touching it. Its cover had been scoured by hot winds and harsh sands, he thought, leaving scratches, scoring and tears. Gallowglass again said something, and tried to jerk loose from his grip, but he held on.

A title was stamped on the cover, in faded foil, illegible save for the volume number: VII. Strange words slithered into his head, and echoed like the clangour of church bells, deep in his mind. The book was large, and quite old, by the binding. Innumerable tendrils extended from its rough surface and filled the study with their writhing.

The thing in his hand began to struggle and he found his grip weakening. The mutterings he'd heard before were back, and louder, almost thunderous. They were voices, not just sounds. There was structure there, but it was incomprehensible to him. The sheer force of it threatened to drive him to his knees and he wondered what he was going to do now that he was here. What could he do? He could hear the flap of thin pages rustling and innumerable voices, reciting passages from a book in a language that was at once alien and impossibly familiar. He shook his head, trying to clear it.

He looked at Gallowglass. Black things writhed about inside her head like a midnight halo. For the first time, he realized that they were words—hundreds of strange words, composed of letters from an alien alphabet. The Webley rose, her thumb on the trigger. He dove aside as a bullet bit into the plaster behind his head. She tracked him with feline swiftness, firing. As he scrambled around the desk, he was showered with splinters and the crumbled shards of burst antiquities.

Desperate, he snatched up a Nemedian icon from where it had fallen. Gallowglass leapt easily onto the desk, the revolver barrel glinting hungrily as it swung towards him. Rolling aside, he hurled the icon. It struck Gallowglass on the head, knocking her backwards. She tumbled off of the desk and hit the floor in a heap. Even as he rose to his feet, however, one danger replaced another. A crawling wave of tendrils coruscated about him and he wracked his brain for a solution.

The tendrils drew close, as if sensing his hesitation. It was growing harder to think. He felt as if he were under water and struggling towards the surface, but too slowly. Everything was muffled, save the droning voices that clawed at his fraying attentions. They began to caress him gently, curling and coiling around him. He sensed its hunger through the squirming thing he held. How long had it been trapped in the book? Or was it trapped at all—he had a vision of something mammoth and monstrous, squatting in the pages and codices of many volumes, its vile seed in every page and paragraph, just waiting to be taken somewhere where it could—what?

What was it hungry for? What did it want?

More to the point, how could he stop it? He stared at the desk through bleary eyes, and couldn't find the word for 'desk' or 'stone' in his mind. They were gone, as if they'd been snapped out of the air and devoured. He looked up, eyes narrowed. The tendrils had risen over him, like hundreds of thin cobras. He could almost see their tongues flickering in eagerness, though he suddenly could not recall the word 'tongue' or even 'cobra'. Other words took their place, strange words like *hlor, u, mlo*...it was as if something were driving his own thoughts and words from his head and replacing them with something else.

The world twitched and grew sharp. Ectoplasm dripped from his hands as the tendril writhed and struck blindly. The other tendrils were gathering. They were preparing to strike and he would be gone, the 'him' that was Charles St. Cyprian washed away in the madness of thing. The desk blurred, becoming indistinct. Somewhere, a window shattered. He barely registered the sound. What was he missing, what had they—

He saw the slips of paper in the book and even though the word that was in his head was *scul*, he knew what it was. They had read it. Of course they had! They had opened it and read it and those who had first done so had recited the passages at their fellows, forcing them to listen, when they would have fled, and all he had to do was *assasaxsa u ult e-scul*. He shook his head, trying to dislodge the foreign words.

He tossed aside the writhing tendril and the revolver even as his spirit-eye snapped shut. He shivered as the last of the ectoplasm dripped away and he scooped up the book. He looked around frantically, searching for a solution. He gasped in relief as he saw the study fireplace. He felt a sudden sharp pain and strange noises burst from his lips as he blundered across the desk, sending everything on it tumbling to the floor. Gallowglass moaned and began to clamber to her feet, her hand groping blindly for her revolver. It--the book, no, the thing in the book--knew what he was planning, and it intended to stop him.

His hand snapped out, snagging hold of the carpet and he pulled himself bodily towards the fireplace. It wasn't lit, but he floundered around and found a box of matches on the floor. His head felt full to bursting and his back arched as the pain grew worse. He sat heavily on the floor and muttered gibberish as he tried to get the fire going with shaking hands. He tore pages from the book, ignoring the cuts that opened in his flesh as the book attempted to defend itself. The voices in his head were howling, now trying to cram the contents of the volume into his skull, to empty him out and fill him back up. Hard won knowledge slid from his mind as he watched the paper yellow and blacken after he tossed in the match. He forgot why he was doing it, as new desires flooded him.

Doors were not all one size and neither were worlds. Things could creep in, even through the tiniest crack and whole universes might spin within a grain of sand. New-made memories crashed through his head, displacing his old ones. Books brought knowledge; that was what an old tutor had told him, and this book brought knowledge both monstrous and magnificent. The magnificence of the other world buried the mud of Ypres, driving it down deep in his memories. In his mind's eye, invisible tigers stalked blind monks through a forest of stone mirrors. He felt the weight of a world unborn, a predatory world, and hungry for inhabitants, hungry for minds and thoughts and language.

But even predators could be beautiful, and kind. It was magnificent, wondrous and glorious and *sscha* and *hlel* and a hundred more adjectives that he had never before heard or seen but nonetheless knew, thanks to the pages lying crumpled and forgotten in his nerveless hands. It wanted all men to dwell within it in wonder and glory forever. Was not its language a beautiful one? Was it not a better place, where men did not wage war, for they all spoke and thought the same, and where there was no difference, there was no war, something hissed insistently—he had been wrong; the honourable members weren't mad, they were simply the first of many, and he longed to join them, to see the jade towers replace Westminster and the red reeds sweep aside Dartmoor andandAND—

And then, it was done. He fell back against the desk and felt as if he had been doused in icy water. Swallowing thickly, trying to work spit into his dry mouth, he looked at Gallowglass, who looked at him blearily. "Cor, what happened?" she groaned.

"Desk," he said experimentally. "Stone, cobra, hole, the quick brown fox jumped over the lazy dog." He felt obscurely sad as he said the words. He looked at the crackling flame in the fireplace. Carefully, with shaking fingers, he began feeding in the remaining pages, those that had sought escape in those last moments before he'd unconsciously shoved the bulk of the book into the flames. As he did so, he tried not to think about the numbers stamped on the cover, or those he'd seen on the pages he'd just fed into the flames. Volume seven of forty, which meant there were more doors out there in the world somewhere, waiting to be opened.

"What—what was that?" Gallowglass said. "I saw..." She shook her head.

"A better world," he said. He sat back and waited for the remnants of the book to burn to ashes. After that, he would seal the ashes in something more durable and drop it into the Thames.

He hoped that would be enough.

If the others hadn't been opened already.

8 Tales from the Master of Horror...
H.P. LOVECRAFT

Writer Brandon Barrows and Artist Hugo Petrus explore some of the lesser known corners of the Lovecraft mythos including a tale of humor from the master.

DIAMOND ORDER CODE
#SEP161503
PAGE 317

CALIBER COMICS

MYTHOS
LOVECRAFT'S WORLDS

Barrows
Cover by Dan Brereton
Petrus
Leto

MONOCHROME

T. E. GRAU

1. Wheelhouse

The phone rang on the nightstand, sounding like an alarm bell signaling the end of the world. End of a poor night's sleep, at the very least.

It was a rotary phone, robin's-egg blue with proper metal innards and a nest of copper wiring twisted up inside. A solid American-made piece of equipment, 25 years past its prime. The sound it made was horrible, and it kept coming with that relentless 2/4 beat.

A groan escaped from somewhere under a twist of quilt and sofa bed. The only thing visible of Henry Ganz was the lower half of a whiskered face peaking through the mass of patchwork fabric. He'd forgotten to pull the phone cord from the wall last night, and the anger at this sloppy oversight fired blood back into his limbs, forcing him to crawl back to the waking world. Worse yet, the phone wouldn't stop ringing on its own. Shards of plastic that had once been a nearly antique answering machine littered the corner of the room, broken under a boot heel three nights ago. So this hellish racket wouldn't stop until the caller decided to hang up, or we finally arrived at the heat death of the universe.

Ganz could have ended his suffering and just answered the goddamn thing, but he didn't particularly like phone calls, as they more than likely meant bad news. That or a conversation, which usually proved to be worse. But in his line of work, whatever that exactly was these days, Ganz needed a phone, good news or bad. He'd find an angle for either. That's what he was good at, which made him the cop he once was, the reporter he became, and the high functioning degenerate that he'd always been. Always with the angle. Finding degrees even when everything was bent into a pretzel.

After what was probably its fortieth ring, Ganz snatched the receiver from its cradle and mashed it against the blanket over his ear. The voice on the other end didn't wait for a greeting, as he knew it wouldn't come.

"Secretary quit?" Victor Baumgartner's barrel voice had a sarcastic chuckle to it.

Illustration by Dave Felton

"Ran off and joined the circus," Ganz rasped, unsuccessfully clearing last night from this throat.

"You hear the news?"

"I write the news, motherfucker."

"No, on TV."

"What time is it?" Ganz refused to open his eyes, not that it would have helped. The room was lit by a fat glass lamp with a stained shade, which rested on the floor next to his pull-out bed. The living room was mostly empty, as were the rooms beyond, aside from the stacks of books and newspapers that rose like dusty columns throughout the house. No natural light filtered through windows sealed shut with aluminum foil. Like a Vegas casino, never letting in the outside world to remind the poor bastards bleeding their baby's college fund at the craps table that it was time to get the hell out of town.

"2:30."

"AM?"

"What do you think?"

"Then no, I haven't heard the fucking news. Why are you calling me so early?"

"Turn on the TV. KTLA."

"You're an asshole, Bum," Ganz said. He'd long ago broken down "Baumgartner" into simply "Bum", which was far easier to say after a few cocktails. It had predictably stuck. "Goddamn Kraut bastard..." Ganz's head hurt, just like it always did when it was time to get up and sleepwalk through another day, counting his steps to the grave.

"You're just as German as I am," Bum said, feigning insult.

"I'm *Prussian*, you cocksucker," Ganz said. "I got more in common with the Polacks than you lousy fascists. How many times do I have to tell you this?"

"As many times as it takes to make it true."

"I'm going back to sleep."

"Turn on this news first. You still have a TV, right?"

"I'm going to shoot you, Bum. I'm going to find you and I'm going to—"

"Then turn it on. This is a neighborhood matter, and right in your wheelhouse."

"So?"

"*So*... the Park Plaza Hotel just ate four people."

…. "What?"

"KTLA."

Click.

2. The Hush of Pavement

Ganz stepped out from the porch shade and hit the first cracked step of his compact Queen Anne Victorian, built just a few years on from the turn of the 20th century. Its sash windows, gambrel roof, and offset turret were par for the course for Pico Union at the time, but now stuck out like a gaudy sore thumb, looking as out of place as Ganz. With the passing of years, the erosion of architectural variety led the parade for the general decline of the area, becoming just another one of the many gang-infested urban frontwaters taken over by cheap apartment housing, cheapo strip malls, and cheapjack drug dealers. Pico Union was left to rot by inches through the gutting of post-war factory jobs that drove out the blue collars, filling the gaps with style-blind investors and immigrants from Guatemala and El Salvador, on the run from brutal civil wars and therefore unconcerned with such bourgeois notions as curb appeal. Los Angeles was full of neighborhoods like this, mixed-race middle class bastions gone to shit, with a preponderance of them circling downtown like a rusted halo. Westlake, Crown Hill, Temple Beaudry, and all the Heights. South LA, which dropped the "Central" after too many black people made money off of it, and too many white people who wouldn't lower themselves to set foot in the neighborhood thought that rap music gave the place a bad name.

And Pico Union, where a broken-down white guy named Henry Ganz manned the turret in his kitsch relic in a tagged-up barrio hemmed in by streets and freeways that sounded better on paper, defined as they always were in the hearts and minds of Good America by the ritzier parts of town they bisected. No one wrote rap songs about Pico Union, as it was a ghost town in the middle of a teeming city. Not much to rhyme about. People just died here, shot drugs and each other here. Sold themselves in alleyways and marked the walls with machoglyphs of indecipherable rage. Very few people lived in Pico Union, and that included Ganz. Just ask Bum. That prick thought Ganz sold his TV for Ripple. Bullshit. He'd only sold his televisions for the good stuff.

Ganz squinted up and down the block as he walked to the gate centering his eight-foot-tall iron security fence, topped by anti-climb spikes the shape and warmth of shark's teeth. The neighborhood was quiet, which seemed odd for three o'clock on a Friday. Or was it Thursday? Whatever day it was, the block never sounded like this aside from that sweet, brief window of time between the downtown bars closing and the dope fiends making their final rounds before dawn. Those were the times when he could really think, and turn those jumbled memories into clay-like images so real he could almost reach out and throttle them.

He unlocked the gate, secured it behind him, and headed north up South Union Ave. He made good time, as the sidewalks were mostly clear. So were the alleyway fences and shop facades, which were normally decorated with colorful murals rendered in various levels of skill, accented by graffiti wars from the overlapping gang sets that crisscrossed the neighborhood, copyediting rival claims with deadly lines of spray paint. But most of the walls were now completely painted over with a color that seemed to be a treacle white from a distance, but upon closer inspection was a pale, industrial yellow. The color of the evaporated milk his mother used to pour out when he was a kid, for everything from biscuit frosting to a cure for stomach flu. The city council had been promising to clean up the graffiti problem around the city center since the invention of aerosol cans. Maybe the wrong business finally got tagged by knuckleheads, because the paint-over was extensive, stretching up and down the block in every direction, getting into every nook and defaced cranny. The windowless front of the Diamante Mercado, which only days before featured a vibrant Aztec mural depicting brick-skinned Mesoamericans, bundles of maize, and staircase pyramids was now yellowwashed from top to bottom, removing all trace of the cultural tribute. The city council wouldn't fucking dare mess with the Mayans. Too many potential voters were children of Chichen Itza.

Ganz strode on between the sour-milk walls, feeling now slightly detached from the neighborhood that he had loved and hated for the better part of half a century. The street level restoration seemed to drain the life from the block. Not much sound coming from apartment windows and the futbol cantinas that would normally be doing brisk and rowdy business at this hour. Even the impossibly shiny Tacos Tamix truck that normally posted up on 9th - specializing in such castoff delicacies as *lengua, cabeza, tripa,* and something similarly wretched sounding called *bucha* - was nowhere to be found, taking its reassuring silver gleam with it. The street children who made the pavement their everyday meadowland would have to go hungry today. He couldn't find them, either. Must have chased the truck to more lucrative parts of the city for their fill of grilled organ meat, as everyone loved a food truck in LA. The humble had become hip. Peasants to princelings. God bless us all.

Ganz scratched at the back of his neck, feeling the first uncoiling of The Thirst low in his stomach as he passed the Stuart Hotel and several other shooting galleries where he had rousted skagheads in a different life, then turned down 12th and up Alvarado and on toward MacArthur Park in Westlake, where a classic Neo-Gothic landmark built by the Elks had apparently decided to eat several members of the local population. Ganz walked where he needed to go these days, and caught a bus when necessary, flagging a jitney after hours. He wasn't allowed to drive anymore, which made him even more of an anomaly, not in his own neighborhood, but in Southern California itself. *Nobody walked in LA*, the song said. That bullshit singer never lived where he did. Everyone walked down here, because cars didn't grow on trees. Avocadoes and limes certainly did, but cars sure as fuck didn't. Nor did drivers' licenses for third-strike DUI dopes. But very few people were out walking today, and the ones that were kept their eyes down and hurried, ducking out of sight as soon as they could. The streets were different. Edgy as Ganz's stomach and twice as empty.

He stopped into the Araya Bodega on the corner of 8th and Alvarado for cigarettes and a walking beer, and found it deserted aside from the clerk and his boom box providing ranchero music to all customers at a shockingly high volume. Outside, Ganz popped his Tecate tallboy on the sidewalk, lit a Winston, and pulled out his notepad, an act he had performed a million times before as a homicide cop with the LAPD, then as a street reporter with the LA Times. Now he was neither, but very much both, as those two jobs never completely leave a person. Protector and documentarian come up from the bones of you, and either you have the DNA or you don't. Ganz had both in spades, and pink slips wouldn't change that essential makeup. After two unspectacular falls from grace, he now worked on commission as a freelance writer, sometime PI, and neighborhood fixer for anyone Bum – plugged in as he was to the aristocratic cream -- sent his way, which usually meant Hollywood location scouts looking for that "authentic gangsta vibe," or a greenhorn vice cop working a new lead about MS 13 or 18th Street. Ganz couldn't hold down regular work. His nerves wouldn't allow it, courtesy of the Mix Tape Murders case he worked 25 years ago that cost him his job, and then his marriage, and then everything else that mattered. This was followed by a brief stint at the Times, where he worked for City Desk Editor Victor Baumgartner, who kept his Pulitzer hidden in his desk where a bottle should have been. Bum was a grinder like Ganz but without all the toxins, and Ganz liked him instantly. The feeling turned out to be mutual, but after blowing too many deadlines while holed up in his home with a bottle collection and an array of loaded firearms, Ganz was let go. Now he wrote when he could, selling local interest stories to the Times, LA Weekly, various pay blogs and any other outlet on whatever platform that had the guts to publish unvarnished tales from the seamier side of diamond town. Ganz interviewed hookers, dope fiends, grieving mothers – anyone who fit the story or had a story to tell. Today, he'd be covering a carnivorous boys' club turned hotel overlooking the city's first leisure park. Ganz thought he smelled horseshit, as marketing mad men were clever these days, but he also knew that Bum wouldn't yank him from the safety of his reinforced domicile for an unsubstantiated lark. This was one of those Weird Stories, and Bum knew that Ganz was the guy to write it, as much for Ganz's talent as for the fact that the poor schlub needed to eat -- or drink -- and Bum wanted someone at the scene before the story got stale. Ganz was the obvious choice. Hence, the phone call. And now the walk.

He arrived on the northwestern side of MacArthur Park, the walking beer finished, crushed flat, and stowed inside his jacket like a hidden badge. Police cruisers and fire trucks and news vans and the gathered crowd all stood and looked up as a chorus at the front of the Park Plaza Hotel on the corner of 6th and Park View, facing MacArthur Park. The Tacos Tamix truck was parked nearby, just outside the media circus. No one waited in line.

3. Flesh and Stone

The massive carved head stared down from its perch overlooking the bronze front door of the Park Plaza. Above it was block lettering chiseled into the sandstone by the original builders back in the 20's as a calling card for their Lodge:

All things whatsoever ye would that men should do
to you
do ye even so to them

This clumsily constructed proverb was flanked on each side by a pair of war angels spaced twenty feet apart and thirty feet up, hands resting on sword hilts, blades pointed down, ostensibly at the ready for days such as this. Between the angels and the grim singular head, two drop cloths were slung across the wide matching expanses that made up the outer frame of the front entrance jutting out from the Park Plaza proper. The tarps mostly covered what was underneath, as the LAFD attempted to spare the locals from the latest indignity unleashed upon the populace. Their attempts were mostly in vain, as four heavy trails of blood had dripped from whatever was hidden beneath the draping, daring the mind to fill in the gruesome details. Far above this, a phrase was painted across the top floor walls and windows, the blackening blood contrasting sharply with the light yellow stone.

THE PLAY'S THE THING

How did someone reach down that low from the roof? Or how did someone reach up that high from the ground? Firemen's ladders weren't available for loan-out to the local punk ass graff crews. *THE PLAY'S THE THING*... Shakespeare. Taggers must be getting real uppity these days, or maybe spending more time in JUCO between lowering property values across the city.

The perimeter on Park View in front of the building was cordoned off by yellow police tape, holding back a growing crowd of concerned locals and rubbernecking commuters, cell phones taking it all in for safe keeping. Behind the plastic barrier, gray tarps covered four mounds on the asphalt, two on each side of the front door, shadowed by the building behind them. The size and shape of the shrouded remains seemed too small to be complete bodies, each one measuring what was probably three feet across.

The coroner's van pulled up and parked in the middle of Park View. Forensics was already on scene, snapping pictures and bagging up splatter, of which there seemed to be an abundance. A bouquet of lemon yellow roses lay in the gutter next to the van's front tire. Water from a burst pipe up the street streamed down the pavement, stripping off the petals and dragging them into the storm drain at the end of the block.

Ganz sidled up to a beat cop, blond crew-cut topping a sunburned cinderblock head that continued unimpeded into the navy blue uniform stretched tight over his juiced up shoulders and arms. He was eyeing the crowd through wraparound Oakleys, the white tan lines on the side of his face wider than the black plastic frames. New shades, purchased from a bygone era ruled by Jeep Renegades and Bon Jovi and wraparound Oakleys.

"How did someone get up that high?" Ganz muttered just loud enough.

The cop didn't take his eyes off the crowd.

Ganz pulled out his pad and jotted down a few notes. "I mean, they'd need some pretty heavy-duty equipment to get all the way up there, with their paints and whatnot... You think this is some new kind of guerrilla marketing?"

The cop noticed his notepad. "Who are you?"

Ganz shoved a Winston between his teeth and squinted a humorless smile. "You don't know?"

The cop stared at him, his hidden eyes – most likely the empty blue of February sleet -- most likely glaring. This wasn't a new thing, his anonymity amongst the LAPD uniforms, but it always surprised him nonetheless. He was all over the news back in '87. This thick-necked fullback in the 80's shades was probably still playing with his Transformers when Ganz was getting interviewed as the hero on the steps of the justice building downtown, when a routine investigation turned sideways and everything around him went to shit. Elijah liked Transformers. Ganz hadn't seen Elijah for 25 years. How old would he be now? As old as Ganz was back when... Jeep Renegades and Bon Jovi. The smashed can in his jacket itched at his chest.

"Local press," Ganz said, wishing he'd picked up another Tecate at Araya. He took a drag and pointed his cigarette at the building. "Do you know who did this? Some new tagger crew?"

"Who're you with? You gotta pass?"

"LA Times. Vic Baumgartner sent me."

The cop puffed out his cheeks and exhaled. "Fucking great... Talk to the Lieutenant."

"I have," Ganz said. "He told me to come to you. That you'd have the story."

The cop snorted. "I don't have shit. I'm just crowd control... and keeping my eye on those guys."

Ganz followed the hidden sightline of the uniformed fireplug out over all of the black haired heads and baseball caps and Pompano cowboy hats, toward the back of the crowd. There was space between the group of mothers and fathers and grandmothers and children looking up at the building and a half circle of figures standing behind them. All of them wore black canvas shoes, pants and hoodies, topped with featureless white masks covering their faces. Perfectly round black eye holes seemed to suck in everything that stood in front of them, including the middle-aged man with the itchy veins and notebook.

"Who are they?" Ganz asked, this time totally to himself.

"I have no fucking idea," the cop said, clenching his belt with thick hands. Walnut crushers. The leather creaked, and the .45 in his holster rode up higher on his waist. "They look like one of them dance crews my niece watches on TV, but no one is dancing around here today."

"And too early for Halloween," Ganz said, figuring that it was August or thereabouts, based on the heat and the thickness of the smog rimming the San Gabriels to the northeast. September would be worse. The worst month of the year, when the wind stopped and the foothills burned.

"Those ain't Halloween masks." The cop crossed his arms, stress testing the polyester fibers of his shirt.

Ganz left the cop and pushed through the crowd. It wasn't easy going, and as he approached the semi circle of masked figures, he couldn't tell if they were looking at him, as they hadn't changed the angle of their necks, nor their posture. And he couldn't see their eyes inside those weird, contoured masks. Viewing them more closely, it was difficult to tell if they were male or female, as their identical, baggy outfits rendered them thin and sexless underneath. They weren't physically imposing or outwardly dangerous, but somehow seemed threatening by their uniformity, and their stillness. Things on the streets were loud and obvious. Visibly aggro. This group was a mystery. And they didn't move a muscle, even as Ganz approached them with a white man's purpose, stopping only a few feet away from the group. Just like with the neighborhood walls, what Ganz thought were white masks were actually the same pale yellow as the new coats of paint all over Pico Union, as the stone hotel behind him. The last, tragic shade of yellow before the color fell into an eternal expanse of dead white. And at this close distance, he saw their eyes underneath. They were large and staring, each set of irises populating every shade of the rainbow save red and purple. And none of them blinked. Just stared, with an almost quivering intensity.

Ganz stepped back, and as he did, the spell seemed to break. The figures turned and walked slowly away from the crowd with hands shoved deep into pockets, scattering a flock of pigeons and stepping over nodded-out junkies curled up on the beatdown grass. The birds rose silently into the air, and instead of circling back, took off for another part of the city rather than settling back down on their home base. Ganz had never seen pigeons move with such determined direction, and with such speed. The masked figures continued walking toward the lake at the center of the park, their silhouettes fusing with the palm trees surrounding the alkaline lake that hadn't naturally hatched a live fish since the natives sold the swamp to the broken promise of the 18th century.

4. Of King and Kingpins

Ganz made his way home as the sun set, putting on a private show for him and him alone. He liked this time of day, when the sun gave up and packed it in, giving the night over to the darkness. The dying rays glinted off of the skyscrapers to his left, which lorded over downtown like protective pimps minding their stable. He blinked away the flash of dying daylight, rubbing his eyes with the back of his hand gripped around a fairly fresh beer.

The California sun always hit his eyes strangely, something he first discovered sitting in the back seat of his family's Studebaker all those decades ago, creeping along slowly with Friday afternoon traffic on the 10 Freeway on the outskirts of the city. While his father chain-smoked his curses at big city traffic, his mother had made a comment about finally being in Hollywood, and Little Henry Ganz sat up straight and pulled himself up to the window, expecting to see movie stars and limousines strobed by machine gun flash bulbs. Silver screen glamour girls like Marilyn Monroe and Jane Russell and Elizabeth Taylor, lounging in deck chairs on the shoulder, winking to all the new arrivals behind giant sunglasses. Frank Sinatra backed by a curtain of diamond palm trees, singing us home. But all he saw was a cloudless pale above him, and the blinding gleam of silver white chrome all around. So little color, and so much bright... He never knew he had sensitive eyes until that day, exposed by the endless snake of freeway, scaled with burnished steel that branded itself into Ganz's brain. The pallid gleam of those tentacles writhing from the heart of Los Angeles into the ashen desert overwhelmed his sight, accustomed as they were to mud and gray clouds, and his eyes had never gotten used to it, turning one shade of brown lighter that day.

Ganz stopped at an empty bus bench to jot down a few thoughts, leaning back into the jumble of magic marker graffiti scrawled across the backrest. Before he left the park, he'd overheard two detectives talking about the covered remains. What had hit the ground was only half of them. The rest of the four bodies were sunken into the building itself, integrated into the stone of the structure. ID found on the lower half of one of the corpses revealed that he was Hector "Little Death" Alameida, a heavyweight in the Mexican Mafia, presumed murdered eight years ago even though street rumors and *narco corridos* told otherwise. Not only had Little Death been discovered alive, but alive enough to be verifiably murdered in a bizarre and very public way. The other three half bodies didn't have identification, but the extensive Salvadorian prison tattoos on the legs of one of them made it seem real likely that Ernesto Dimas, the head honcho of MS 13 in Los Angeles, had met his end right next to his rival. The third vic was obviously a member of Aryan Nation, based on his own ink of fascist bon mots and Nordic runes, accented by bullet scars and the single shamrock on his backside, which told the cops everything they needed to know. The fourth was a black guy, wearing vintage blue BK "Blood Killer" tennies, and therefore most likely someone associated with the Crips. Probably Eight Tray or Rollin' 60's, as they both made runs at this side of downtown on occasion. If his identified cohort was any indication, he and the other unnamed were probably higher up in the ranks than your average drive-by foot soldier, and certainly specifically targeted.

Two, and possibly four, gangland kingpins shoved face-first and torso-deep into the side of a building, everything below the waist severed and left on the ground. Aside from the assault on known physics, this was a seriously fucked-up geopolitical situation, and could unleash spectacular waves of retaliatory violence and brutal repositioning that this city hadn't seen since the height of the gang wars in the late 80's, before Rodney King and Chief Gates and the riots that let most of the fizz out of the bottle, paving the way to the color truces and the Big Police Purge of 1993.

It could get ugly around here, Ganz thought, and began a mental checklist of items he'd need to secure for his home, should shit go south in a hurry. At the same time, he thought of the people in the game that he knew -- snitches, mostly, but also street-level dealers, couriers, and stick men -- who worked in the local gang scene. He smelled a big story brewing, and wanted to be close as it developed, and hopefully be the one to break it. He had so few joys left in life, but uncovering a truth that would eventually fold itself into history was one thing that kept him going. He wasn't paid to take down the bad guys anymore, so he might as well tell their stories, especially when "bad guy" and "good guy" were often only separated by differences in membership cards. Country clubs catered to more killers than any neighborhood gangbanger bar or backyard Inglewood barbeque.

Ganz paused to gather himself, feeling that familiar prickling sensation spidering up his spine that always meant he was on the cusp of a worthwhile new project, when he saw the smoke. It was rising hot and fast in black billowing waves, gathering over downtown like a shroud. Ganz left his beer on the bench and ran across the street, running toward the source of the smoke as the sirens took up their song in hidden fortresses all around the city.

5. Words to Smoke

He knew what was burning before he even got close. The layout of the downtown map was branded inside his brain from his time at the LAPD Headquarters on 1st and Spring and then the Times Building just across the street on Broadway. He came of age down here, and then slowly began to die, all within the same cement Skinner box.

By the time he got to Figueroa and dashed up to 5th, Flower Street a block over was closed off by the fire department, as the Los Angeles Central Library disintegrated from the inside out and spilled up its dead magic into the darkening sky. A million books and a trillion hard-won thoughts lost to the angry flames. The burn area was so vast that it must have been set in a dozen locations inside by a tanker truck of gasoline sprayed onto the moldering stacks.

Onlookers crowded the sidewalk, traffic froze, and still the library burned. Firemen fanned out and jacked their hoses into rarely used hydrants. It was clear by their positioning that they weren't going to attempt to save the building or its precious contents. They were just going to cut off any spread. Containment.

All around Ganz, amid the jostling mass of bodies both on the sidewalk and in their cars, a single arm of every person was held up in salute, cell phone in hand and pointed at the destruction, to capture a moment for social media and maybe the 11 o'clock news instead of experiencing with their eyes, feeling it inside that part of their being that wasn't connected to the goddamn Internet. These fools saw nothing and felt nothing but recorded everything for some later date that would never come.

Ganz became nauseous. His knees buckled and he collapsed to the curb, covering his face with his hands. He could feel the heat from the flames a hundred feet away and fifty feet up. They started from the top, eating away the roof and announcing themselves to the sky, then chewed their way down.

This was the place that had grown Henry Ganz, drawing him from the dirt and giving fiber and vein to the lost seed blown west, girding in tough bark the man in full who put down roots – thin, thirsty roots, but roots nonetheless. He'd spent rainy days and winter nights wandering the shelves, pulling books at random and forcing himself to read the first ten pages. More often than not, he read the entire book, immersing himself in worlds and subjects he'd never seek out on his own. For a boy who never found anything more substantial than Redbook around his childhood home, this was a revelation. An unlocking of a kennel door, with an unexplored wilderness waiting beyond. Everything Ganz knew – everything he *was* on a cellular level after he evolved from the muck – came from this place that was dying in front of him. The library was more of a father and mother than he'd ever had at home, or ever cared to wish for.

He rubbed his eyes, not sure if the brightness of the flames was making them water or actual tears were leaking out. He'd become a stranger to real feelings two hundred cases of Dickel ago, and they reemerged from the blur at unexpected times like acid flashbacks.

Ganz staggered to his feet and pushed through the gawkers. Their hunger for the train wreck was palpable, sickening. He had to get away from these goddamn vultures, and get his head around what was happening. He broke from the crowd and made a wide circle around the pyre, ending up on 3rd and Broadway. He stopped, realizing that he was heading for his former places of employment as if on autopilot, as that was exactly how he had arrived on so many occasions toward the end. Intoxicated to the point of blackout, legs moving stiffly, directional compass dug out of his lizard brain and hardwired into the robot.

Today was different. He wasn't drunk. He was in mourning. Ganz felt a presence behind him, high up and looking down. He turned, and while his internal map of the area expected to show him the vibrant Anthony Quinn mural painted on the old Victor building, what greeted him was an upturned rectangle of pale yellow. The mural was gone. The "Victor Clothing Co" lettering was gone. What replaced it was pure theatre:

TO UNCOVER THE CONSCIENCE OF A KING

Now it was time to get drunk.

6. Emperor's New Clothes

It wasn't until his third whiskey and water that his brain finally returned to the matter at hand. The work. The story. Had to get back to the story, and kick everything else back down deep into the bucket.

They didn't have Dickel, and even if they did, Ganz couldn't afford it. His disability had been cut in half thanks to the generous nature of the new California taxpayer taking marching order from Orange County, Utah, and a string of megachurches. The writing gigs had slowed, as print media transitioned to digital, and no one wanted to pay for anything they found online. So, he'd suck down whatever they had in the well while he fueled up for the dark walk home. It had been one hell of a day.

Ganz was drinking in the King Eddy Saloon on East Fifth, another one of his autopilot destinations programmed into his circuitry back in the Clinton Administration. He didn't venture out much these days, and when he did, he never made it this far east, so taking down cheap drinks in dirty glassware felt like a bankers' holiday. The place was mostly empty. The usual cast of vagrants and penny ante hustlers was cut down to a few choice stragglers, flavored by a stereotypical sampling of Silver Lake dropouts and choice West Siders who had dared cross the La Cienega Divide. A Latino woman with shock wig hair dyed orange and eyebrows painted up over the center of her forehead stared at the wall covered in old boxing paintings and a framed photograph of FDR. A toothless man with mechanics' hands mumbled over his nearly empty pilsner glass of beer. Two hipsters with newly minted 70's togs, strategically messy hair, and Amish beards strolled through the place, clutching cans of Pabst like they were holy water and looking at the pictures and faded out signage on the walls, peppering their discussion of a screenplay they were working on with cooed exclamations of "gritty ambience" and something called "gutterpunk."

The bartender walked over and asked if he wanted another. Ganz nodded and looked around the place one more time for the sake of the coming small talk, scratching behind his armpit.

"Kind of dead around here, huh?"

The bartender sighed, pouring another double with a heavy hand. "Everyone's checking out the library fire." Sully used to work the sticks back when Ganz haunted this place. Sully wouldn't be caught dead sighing in front of a customer, or even by himself. Sully killed two dozen Koreans back in the forgotten 50's.

"You notice the city painting over the murals around town?"

"Nope," the bartender said. "I live in Santa Monica. Don't really see many down there."

Good Christ. A 310 tending bar in an honest to goodness 213 joint. Ganz was appalled, and looked at him more closely. The tailored jeans, the factory-aged t-shirt, the ridiculously expensive shoes made from repurposed leather stitched with Humboldt County hemp. Who hired this fucking guy? Where the hell *was* he right now, anyway? Ganz glanced around, noticing that the barroom looked like the King Eddy Saloon, but something was definitely different. New ownership. Goddamnit. Some enterprising Gen X-er had bought the wormy old place, taking everything down, cleaned off the filth and grime and crime and motherfucking *character*, and rebuilt King Eddy to look like the potentate he once was. But these cash maggoting culture pimps never understood that they couldn't put the soul back into the revived body, as it had already fled this mortal coil at the registered time of death. History withers in the face of bleach and Behr paint, even in a place built basement deep by dead bootleggers.

"It ain't the city."

The directed voice shook Ganz, who looked down the bar. A man he hadn't seen come in was sitting on the corner stool and holding a pilsner glass in front of him like he was waiting to make a toast. He was a Hispanic guy, deeply tanned and even more deeply wrinkled, wearing his slate gray hair long and slicked back, curling up at the nape of his collared white dress shirt. He wore thick tinted glasses, like BB King. There was a distinguished air about him, from the way he held his glass to the golden pinkie ring on his left hand. In another version of Hollywood, he'd be a leading man on the decline, or a producer who owned half of the Hills. The fact that he was down here meant he was neither of those things. Old guys didn't go in for irony. "It's the street painting over them murals," he said. "The new street."

Ganz swiveled in his chair, every cell erect. "How do you know?"

"Because I got eyes under these things, and ears next to 'em."

"Then you've seen it, too."

The man drained his glass of dark beer, foam still rimming the top, and pushed it back away from him.

Ganz finished his own glass and motioned to the bartender for another round for the both of them. "What do you mean by 'street'?"

The man laughed, deep and wet. Smoker. "Come on, man. You know what I mean, right? The *street*. You know the street. You know it just like the rest of us."

Ganz squinted through the low light at the man's face. He looked familiar, but he couldn't place him. Maybe he saw him on TV.

"You're trying to remember, ain't you? You will. I ain't wearing no mask. I ain't seeing that shit."

Ganz's eyebrows shot up. "Seeing what shit?"

The man said nothing, flipping a Zippo between his fingers. A long thin cigarette was stowed behind his ear, poking through the drape of his hair.

"So the masks figure in somehow?"

The round arrived, and the man pulled out a twenty from a large roll of green, pushing it toward the bartender. "For mine." The bartender shrugged, took the bill and rang him up. The man poured the Modelo slowly into his glass.

"Yeah, they figure in." The man didn't elaborate, instead sipped his beer.

"Is this a gang thing? Some bullshit theatrical twist on colors?"

"I guess you could say that."

"Look, friend—" Ganz said, getting up from his stool and moving toward him.

"— I ain't your friend," the man said without turning, stopping Ganz in his tracks by the flat tone of his voice. "And you ain't mine, so why don't you stay where you're at."

Ganz slid back into his chair. He knew this drill and wasn't fazed. No matter how many years he had lived here, he was still the tourist. The interloper. White man on the bus.

"So what's with the masks?"

"You working a case, gringo?"

"No, I—"

The man laughed, cutting him off. "I know. You can't, right? Maybe writing a story for the paper?"

"Wait a minute—"

"Nah, that can't be it either. Maybe you just scared. Scared gringo. Gringos down here always been scared, ever since Avila Adobe. Maybe you got The Fear."

Ganz wanted to say something, but couldn't. The words stuck in his throat. Instead, he watched the man take a luxurious drink of his beer, then dab at his handlebar moustache with a white hankie.

"They don't talk on the street. None of them. They do what they do, quiet, then they put on the play again. Started around Olvera Street, under the church. Lots of things happen under churches. Lots of *things* under churches... Our Lady Queen of the Angels." The man chuckled to himself, finished his beer. "Angels." He slowly drained the bottle into his glass, the sediments dropping to the bottom as the foam built carefully on top, rising to the rim and stopping just short of spillage. "More people come, talking about Cassilda. Cassandra... One of them white girl names..." He sniffed, sitting up straight in his chair, freeing up the war in his lower back. "Everyone gathers round, goes down into the basement. Catacombs where the lizards hide out. See what the play says. Then they go out again. Marching orders. They snatch up the books, anything that ain't the play, and have themselves a barbeque. Fires all around town. Up in them hills around the stadium, north up the Arroyo Seco. Cops blamed the homeless, bored kids, but they know better. Maybe you seen one today, huh? Heard they had a big one."

Ganz wished he had his notepad in his hand, but knew if he reached for it, the story would be over.

"Then all the old *vatos* disappear. All the big boys. OGs. Then the little ones. Then..." He blinked under those thick lenses, long eyelashes fluttering. "Then they do another play. Then another. Same show, different showing, see? All over the *barrio*. Boyle Heights. El Sereno. Lincoln Heights. They grow, moving out from the underneath, from the back yards. Bell Gardens, Southgate, up to Highland Park, Eagle Rock. All along the Arroyo. The river walls, that cement, that's their theatre now..." The man snapped his fingers in front of his left ear, then laughed. "After every show, it just gets more quiet. This city wasn't meant to be quiet."

Ganz mulled this over. "Play... You mean theatre?"

"A week ago or so, a group of kids was standing on the corner, just down the block from here, over by skid row, all wearing them masks. They weren't just hangin' out, they were *standing* on the street corner, like at attention. Like military. Just standing there, not doing nothing. Not even moving. Four in the morning. Kids don't hang out down there. Not without baggies in their pockets, and that's a no-no with them guys."

Ganz's mind raced, looking for connections, angles... and found none. He'd need more fuel, so he shook his glass. "Weird."

"Fuckin'-a, weird. This shit happens every night, on different corners. Next day, them corners are all clean. Dope dealers gone. Graffiti, colors... gone."

He laughed again and motioned for another beer. Ganz tried to intercept the order, but the man shook his head.

"Your buddies roll up on them one night. Two cops, a black guy and some Italian dude. They grab a kid from the group and slam him on the hood of their car, cussing him. Scream at him to 'cooperate'. Kid don't move. They keep screaming, then the Italian pulls off the mask."

"What did the kid do?"

"Nothing."

"What do you mean 'nothing'?"

The man turned to face Ganz for the first time. "I mean nothing, motherfucker. The kid didn't do shit. Didn't do shit or say shit. He just stared at that fucking WOP who cuffed him."

"And then?"

"And then the ambulance comes."

"Why?"

"Cuz someone died."

A new beer arrived and was set in front of the man, who filled his glass, the statement lingering like a serial cliffhanger.

"Who died?"

The man turned to Ganz and held up his full glass in salute. "*Salud*, Detective Ganz, for my 25 years in Pelican Bay."

Ganz nearly choked on one of the slushy ice cubes in his glass. "I-I..."

The man drained half his beer, and set it down very slowly onto the bar napkin in front of him. "You put me away for what my brother did." The man dabbed his moustache. "You didn't have shit, but you had enough. You had the spic who did it, even when he didn't. Didn't matter which spic it was, as long as you got one, to throw to the wolves riding on the back of a white girl's honor."

Ganz sat back, replaying his three previous lives as if it was a 70's living room slide show, trying to find the right cell with all of the smiling and waving family members. But he couldn't. After a moment or two, he gave up. His brain was tired, and he knew he wouldn't make the connection, recall the damning collar, so he just lowered his head. "I'm sorry," Ganz said, hearing how trivial that sounded, considering. "I don't remember."

The man just nodded very slowly, taking another long drink that finished his beer, still not looking at Ganz. "Yeah, I suppose you're sorry for all of it, ain't you?"

"Yeah, I really am," Ganz said with a long exhale of breath, before draining his new glass in one gulp. He grimaced, sat up straight in his chair, and attempted to commiserate by pulling out a tiny shard from his personal litany. "Police work is a gymnastics routine between heaven and hell. Sometimes we stick the landing, and sometimes we don't."

The man turned in his stool and looked straight at Ganz, his dark eyes large and inscrutable behind those thick tinted lenses. After a few moments, he nodded. "Yeah, that landing is a bitch." He got up, headed toward the door. "The play's the thing, Holmes."

Ganz shrugged off the specific guilt and overall white man's burden that had poisoned his time at the LAPD long enough to process what he just heard. "What do you mean?"

The man stopped and turned his head slightly. "You done asking questions of me, Detective Ganz." He headed for the door. "See you on the other side. We'll all be waiting."

The door opened, briefly letting in the murmur of the night, and then closed again.

7. A Taste of Flame

Ganz left King Eddy's a few minutes later, his whole body shaking, and dove headlong into those murmuring streets. He could have hopped the last bus, but decided to walk. His legs needed to move under him while his mind worked, processing what he had just heard.

The spider crouching on his spine was now dancing. There was something growing inside the city, moving out from the core to infect the rest of the whole like a cancer. The play. The burning of the library. Olvera Street, the birthplace of Los Angeles. The spread. The rivers. The play. What fucking play? Shakespeare? *The play's the thing, to uncover the consciousness of the king*. Hamlet. College drama class. A poisoned king, a melancholy son. An immoral mother. Patriarchal bullshit. Still, those masks, those slogans... What did it all mean?

Following his legs while his head jagged elsewhere, Ganz caught Main and headed straight south until it found Olympic, the one major street cutting downtown that would allow him the best chance of getting home without getting rolled for his shoes. The fire at the library was out, but the smoke from all that smoldering parchment still filled the sky, white and fluffy and lighter than night above it. Ashes of dead books fell like a mockery of snow on a city that would never know it. Didn't deserve it after selling its soul for blue skies and room temp and a citizenry that burned down libraries. Ganz held out his hand and caught a falling bit of ash on his fingertip, raising it on his tongue, like he used to do as a child in Nebraska when the earth froze and turned brown and white and quiet. It tasted like fire. Motherfuckers.

8. Bugs

Downtown seemed to be in mourning with Ganz, or more likely annoyed by the heavy police presence, as it was nearly deserted, the major venues - Staples, LA Live, Nokia Theater, various spike heel clubs - shuttered for the night. The parking lot valets still manned their posts, waving their flags in the dark and ignoring Ganz as he walked past.

Ganz moved quickly away from the electronic circus at Olympic and Fig that advertised everything to no-one in the wake of the big downtown revitalization launched a few years back that didn't quite catch on. It was just like Hollywood and Highland to the west, with less TV coverage. Stripping off the grime and crime that made this city the chaotic pheromone that it once was and sterilizing it for minivan tourists and "Vegas baby!" cheeseballs. Ganz passed under the freeway and the cardboard campground that went up there every night, stepping around a few nodded-out sidewalk sleepers, and dove deeper into Pico Union. A fire was burning in a barrel behind an auto shop, like you see in those old movies about New York before Giuliani. Ganz wondered whose books were in that barrel. After several blocks, he noticed how quiet it was. And deserted. Street corners were free of shaved head Latinos, socks pulled up to meet their long blue shorts, waiting for west side party people to drive up and hand them money for a homegrown export shipped north.

Instead of loitering men, Ganz found mattresses. Up and down the block, every fenced-in yard and apartment building driveway featured rectangular slabs of fabric and stuffing propped up on the curb, on light poles, even on parked cars. On each mattress the word *BUGS* was scrawled in black spray paint. Ganz unconsciously itched under his armpit.

Minutes later at his house, Ganz dragged his mattress outside, pushed it through his gate and left it blocking the sidewalk, then headed back inside for a can of spray paint. Before he got to his door, he stopped and cocked his ear to the sky, listening. No revving engines, no shouts, no gunshots. He heard absolutely nothing. Nothing weighs on city ears more than an unexpected silence. Ganz headed back inside, flipping on his TV on his way to his tool closet.

Through his open door behind him, on the street corner opposite his yard, a figure wearing a featureless mask looked on. An identical companion joined him, then another, and another still.

9. New Numbers

Victor Baumgartner rolled up Union Ave at 6:00 pm sharp three days later. Ganz was waiting at the curb, peering through pitch black gas station shades up and down the empty streets as if waiting for something. He looked like hell, like he had spent the last 72 hours draining his house of anything remotely fermented and mostly liquid, before finally returning one of Bum's numerous concerned calls about an hour ago.

Bum's Mercedes sedan pulled to a stop. Ganz lurched to his feet and poured himself into the passenger seat, slamming the door behind him.

"Drive."

"Someone after you?"

"They told you?"

Bum laughed. "I was joking. The neighborhood's dead."

"Not dead, sleeping."

Bum chuckled, assuming a joke. "It feels like driving on Christmas morning. Like everyone down here split town. Maybe went back home. Hell, the mayor's already crowing about the new numbers, and they're only a few weeks old."

"What numbers?"

"Hasn't been a shooting or an assault in all the favorite places since that... *thing* at the Park Plaza. All the gun boys must be on vacation. Or maybe they all found Jesus at the same time. East L.A. is like a friggin' sewing circle right now. South Central is just as quiet. Highland Park, Bell, Venice. Ghost towns."

"They're still here, most of them, anyway. They're waiting for something." Ganz pulled down his glasses with a shaky hand and checked to see if they were being followed. DTs, Bum thought, as he could smell three days of whiskey worming its way out of his friend.

"The dealers went with them. The junkies down in tent city are ready to riot, I hear. Climbing the walls, and each other."

"There's a cleansing going on, from the top down."

"A *cleansing*? What the hell's that supposed to mean?"

"Everyone with a rap sheet longer than my pinky has gone missing."

"How do you know?"

"Can't get a hold of any of my snitches, or any of my 'select group of friends'. All MIA. I checked around online, and no one who knows is saying anything, and those wannabes who *are* keep talking about the masks, about there being a new king in town. Big time OG. Outlawing every gang color other than yellow." Ganz spotted something -- or someone -- out the window, and ducked down in his seat. "They know that I know and now they're watching me. Unblinking eyes burned inside the black..."

Bum glanced over at Ganz. He was talking fast, paranoid, like he hadn't seen for years. Getting poetic in that weird way of his when he had burrowed down too deep. This wasn't good. Ganz was slipping backwards in the tunnel, tumbling toward the bottom of the piss bucket where Bum found him. "You haven't been sleeping."

"Of course not. I got rid of my mattress."

"Why the hell'd you do that?"

Ganz rifled through the glove compartment. "Bugs."

"How long've you been up?"

"A couple days, give or take. Hard to tell, inside the compound... But it's good, because I got things to do, people to contact, the ones I can find, anyway. They'll come if I close my eyes. They'll come for my books. I've got thousands of them, Bum. Fucking *thousands*."

"Hank, I don't think anyone—"

"— And you can hear things at night that don't happen while the world's awake. The barks, the whis-

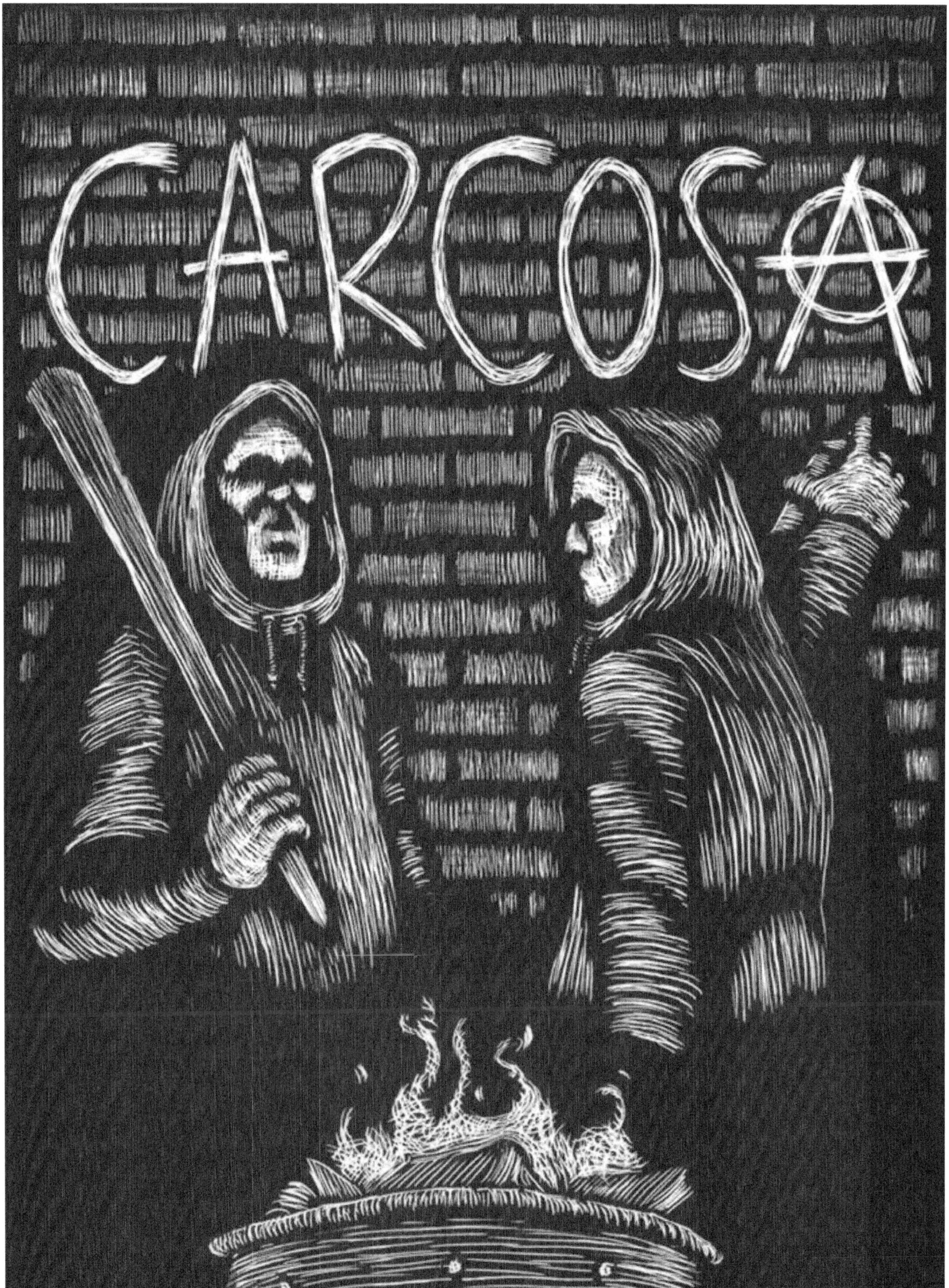
CARCOSA

pers. But mostly it's just quiet, which is scaring the proper fuck out of me."

Bum looked closely at him, with that smile he only created for Ganz that was a mixture of genuine affection and a measure of concern bordering on pity.

"How are you, Hank?" Bum handed him a half full Coffee Bean cup. Ganz took it, popped the top and sniffed the contents, scowling.

"Fucking parched. Pull over at the corner so I can heat this bitch up."

"First meatloaf," Bum said, driving past the liquor store, ignoring Ganz's gestures of protest. "Then refreshments. We gotta get some food in you, get you right."

"Fuck food. I'm right right now."

"I know you are, Hank. You're always right. At least watch me eat."

"You take me around food, I'll fucking vomit. I swear to Christ, Bum."

"That's fine. Their meatloaf isn't all that great anyway."

10. Signet

Bum drove them to Clifton's Cafeteria, finding a parking spot right up front on Broadway. Very few cars were parked anywhere on the block. It was a Saturday, so most of the commuters were far away from downtown. Still, the lack of weekend shopping traffic was odd.

"Check us out," Bum said with a grin. "Rock star parking. Just like the old days." As he pulled up, a dozen people wearing those same light yellow masks and black featureless outfits crossed the street without stopping for Bum's car, or any of the other moving vehicles, causing several of them to slam on their brakes. There were a number of other groups of masked people clustered up and down the block.

"Assholes," Bum grumbled, honking his horn. None of them acknowledged the car. Bum shook his head as he angled his Mercedes to the curb. "One of those nerd conventions in town?"

"No," Ganz said. "These are local. I've seen 'em all over. It's in the notes. Have you read the notes?"

Bum ignored his question. "Is this a gang thing?"

Ganz didn't respond as they both got out of the car and headed toward Clifton's.

"Maybe a bullshit modern art experiment," Bum said. "You ask me, art in this city is on the wane. It's all being painted over."

"You've seen it, too?"

"How can you miss it? Dollars to donuts this is part of the chief's secret gang injunction or something. Part of these new numbers."

"Yeah, maybe," Ganz mused. "All the street art, all the tags, all the gang leaders, all gone."

"The damnest thing."

"That's what I've been saying. Shit ain't right, Bum. Something's happening in this city. Something big and something quiet."

"But then look at that."

Bum pointed across the street to a heavily fenced parking lot, one of hundreds that utilized every square inch of unused downtown real estate. The brick wall behind it that served as a graffiti canvas for decades was now painted that same pale yellow a dozen feet up, wiping clean all those years of expression. In the center of the wall was a single black symbol that looked like a distorted triskelion, topped by a crude question mark, with a pincer jutting down on the lower left and a grasping tendril on the right. Not a drip of paint leaked from the emblem. As if it was stamped, or branded.

"That's new," Bum said.

"Yes it is."

11. Flushing Gators

Bum filled two heavy plastic trays with an assortment of gravy soaked entrées and sugary sides, anything to suck up the toxins swirling in his friend's lower GI tract. He handed a tray to Ganz and they ambled to the back corner of the nearly empty yet still claustrophobic dining hall decorated to look like a forest glade uprooted from the Sierra Madres. They passed under the gaze of a mounted moose head and sat beneath the shadow of a fake Sequoia that made up the overwrought naturalist décor that was a bizarre cross between a Ranger Rick amusement park ride and a polite 1920's dinner theatre. Bum always brought Ganz to joints like this, that mixed low economy with high camp. He was a specialist in eating cheap, even though he wasn't necessarily a stingy person, and was in fact quite well off. He was just nostalgic, and loved these old school Americana joints like Clifton's, where you could pick up a white bowl of canned corn, tapioca pudding, and grade school green jello with pears embedded inside with your Salisbury steak. In a complicated world, a man tires of caviar and hungers for the simplicity of the grade school cafeteria where everything made sense.

"So you read my notes from the Park Plaza?"

"I did, but they didn't make much sense."

"They didn't make much sense when I wrote them, but they're starting to."

"Well, I can't figure any of it out. Lots of gibberish."

"You're not concentrating. It's all in there. It's all taking shape. Order out of chaos."

"You wrote something about organized book burnings, about lizards under the city. Fucking lizards, Hank."

"The Lizard People haven't ever been disproved."

"Neither has the Loch Ness monster."

"Because you can't disprove an avatar, a metaphor that is more real than the truth. You know the Central Library was the tip of the tail, right?"

"What tail?"

"The map of the catacombs crawling under this city. It's shaped like a lizard. They're clever fuckers. Dressing up. Hiding in plain sight. Leaving maps. The head starts in Elysian Park. They're burning away the body in reverse."

"The Lizard People."

Goddamnit, Bum!" Ganz slammed his fist on the table, spilling his untouched food onto the formica. "The Lizard People are bullshit. Misdirection! A magician's trick! I'm talking about something real. Something OLDER."

"Okay, okay, calm down."

"You think I'm fucking nuts, but I'm not. There's something happening out there. All around us. A *shift*, that's been in the planning stage for years. Hundreds, thousands, maybe. I read reports on the 'net, all of them coming from writers living in neighborhoods orbiting downtown. Reporting the same thing. People disappearing. LOTS of people. They're taking down this city, remaking it. Burning the outposts of the orthodoxy."

"Who's '*they*'?"

Ganz was staring out the plate glass windows, at the trio of masked people taping a flier to a lamppost outside. Dozens of others trailed behind, all holding stacks of fliers. "Them."

Bum decided to humor Ganz, just long enough to get him home, and then call up the best psychiatrist he knew to cash in a favor. "So, Elysian Park... The Police Academy's over there. Chinatown."

"Chavez Ravine."

"You think they're targets?"

"I think all of us are..." Ganz burrowed down into his thoughts. "The play's the thing," he muttered.

A fire truck escorted by two lit up police cruisers screamed up the street outside. The triad of sound was nearly deafening, even muffled as it was amid all of the tacky woodland trappings. After a few seconds, instead of slowing fading away, the sound ended abruptly.

"The what?" Bum said.

Ganz blinked back to attention, having to remember what he just said. "The play's the thing."

Bum nodded. "To expose the consciousness of the king," he said absently, forking a greasy hillock of meatloaf into his mouth.

Ganz looked at Bum, astonished. "Did you read that on the wall?"

"Hm? ... What wall?"

"You read any Shakespeare lately?"

Bum snorted. "Yeah right... My kid said that to me two nights ago, before he left for his camping trip."

"Joseph?" Ganz asked, assuming the more bookish of Bum's two boys.

"Christian," Bum said. Christian was a wrestler in junior high, leaving behind athletics and authoritarian coaches as he worked his way through several private high schools. Had a few scrapes with the law, all of them smoothed over by daddy. Christian liked to escape Brentwood and slum it with the low rent thugs in Culver City, Echo Park. Downtown.

"He check in since then?"

"Haven't heard a peep. I figured he was just unplugging for a while, but he took his phone."

Ganz's face blanched. "Vic, I think you need to—"

It was then that the power cut, drowning Clifton's in darkness. The fake trees cut weird shadows in the fading light leaking in from the windows.

"Damn," Bum breathed. "Brown out."

Ganz peered outside. The masked figures

were gone, leaving every lamppost on the block decorated with a poster. Bold letters adorned each one, making an identical announcement.

"Let's go outside," Ganz said.

12. Playbill

Outside on the sidewalk, Ganz pulled down one of the fliers, the fading rays of sun peeking over the western horizon, giving last light to those who paid the most for it.

Bum was behind him, looking up and down the street, which was totally deserted. He looked at his watch. It was just a little past 8:00. "Where the fuck is everyone?"

Ganz held up the flyer. Hundreds of them in front of and behind him created a repeating pattern of rectangles getting smaller and smaller as they disappeared into the city. The paper was sturdy, like a manila folder. But yellow. The font was fancy, baroque.

THE PLAY
LAST L.A. PERFORMANCE - TONIGHT ONLY
DODGER STADIUM
CURTAINS UP AT SUNDOWN
FINAL BOW TBA
BRING THE FAMILY

Bum grabbed it, squinted in the dying light. "A play at Dodger Stadium? During playoffs? Is this some kind of fucking joke?"

"Dodger Stadium is in Chavez Ravine." Ganz started walking.

"Where're you going?"

"Go home, Vic. Get far away from here. Out of the city. Maybe further. I don't know…"

"*Vic*? Since when did you start calling me Vic?"

"I wanted you to know that I remember."

Bum looked around at the darkened city. "Something's happening, isn't it?"

"Something's happening," Ganz said.

"A cleansing."

Ganz nodded slowly, half turned. "Vic?"

"Yeah?"

"Christian isn't coming back."

Before Bum could respond, Ganz was already running up the street, heading north, as the last rays of sun snuffed out above, leaving skyscraper-sized shadows as the only remembrance of the day.

13. The 111 Steps

Ganz ran up Broadway, not recognizing the street. It was dark now in a way that Los Angeles had never been before. The brownout became black. Landmarks blurred, melted together. Only fires – in alleyways, on street corners, the guts of buildings – gave light to a city cloaked in quiet chaos. Yellow light, tinged on the outside with red. Screams and the pop pop of gunshots pierced the hush, but mostly it was quiet in that bloated way that fills up the space right before the perp rushes from the closet, knives out, reaching for your face.

The mask people were everywhere. They stood in groups, lined the sidewalks. They busied themselves pulling people from buildings and stringing up police officers and fire fighters from anything that jutted away from a vertical structure. Ganz gripped the play flier in his useless hands, and it seemed to grant him passage. He soon saw other people like him, faces bared to the world, clamoring up the street as fast as jellied legs would take them, all watched by a thousand sets of eyes hidden under those pallid masks. Some were yanked from the asphalt and dragged away screaming. Some went quietly, as if they knew, or maybe came to an understanding. There were kids amongst them. Little ones. Good Christ…

Still Ganz ran, stumbled, crawled on the stained asphalt like a crab. Had to keep moving, sliding through the funnel that was rapidly forming out of the melted plastic of downtown. Move, *MOVE*, you son of a bitch… Can't fight them all. Too many. Just too goddamn many, all of them armed to the fucking teeth. Clubs, long knives, SWAT issue assault rifles… What *was* this? How did this--? The Thirst was shriveling him underneath his labored breathing. Should have stopped with Bum… Baumgartner… Wait, who?

Ganz slowed, becoming dizzy. It was too much. He was less than an hour from all of his past lives, an entire world that had slipped into the howling abyss that spiraled down endlessly, sucking up the realness of memories as a black hole inhales physics. An immense blaze burned on the front steps of the justice building as well-dressed bodies were lashed to thick pillars on each side, some without heads or limbs, some with several additional protrusions stuck into their torsos like a child experimenting with Play-Do. A fire engine lay on its side, spinning red lights strobing up the side of a building like a repeating laser site. It was clear what they had done. The masks had moved on the FBI building and police stations, then the fire stations, then the consular offices and the newspaper. Then the Twin Towers Correctional and LA County Jail on the edge of downtown. Any authority figure, anyone associated with the city, state, country, or wider world was taken down, dragged out into the street and hung up on anything high. Ganz faltered, and was shoved out of the way by a woman running past him, howling like a gut-kicked canine. This was the French Revolution on peyote, Bosch painting the apocalypse in smears of human blood. He knew the history. Read about it, dreamed about it. This was the rise of the savage death cults waiting just below the boot print of civilized man. Ganz quickened his pace, determined to finish this marathon of madness. There was no other way.

He descended the hill toward Olvera Street and Avila Adobe. The entire area, boxed up years ago into a tidy historical site and touristy shopping square was teeming with the masked. They climbed on building tops like a hive of angry insects, tossing boxes and furniture and bits of dismembered humanity into their air, stuffing pieces under their masks. Each side of the street was hemmed in by either violence or the complete stoicism of those who wore the masks, with all the side streets blocked by people and things stacked on top of each other. This created a destabilizing effect on the brain, as chaos and rigid order lined up side by side, both serving the same master. Ganz reeled, sweated. He threw up as he moved, spitting slimy foam...

Chinatown now. The sidewalks were cleared of product bins, and all the trinket shops boarded up, painted over in yellow. Several had been burned down. A few still smoldered. They must have hit Chinatown early in this insane insurrection. How long had this been going on? How many knew it was coming? At every block, a few local residents shuffled from doorways and hiding spots and joined the hunched procession scuttling up Broadway like a parade route of the damned, each holding a flier for the show to come. Tonight only. Bring the family.

The pagoda architecture finally gave way to the open space of Elysian Park. The walkers moved off Broadway and down onto the parade grounds, surrounded by warehouses and the formerly smoking machinery of industrial LA. Then one by one headed down into the basin of the Los Angeles River.

14. Walk the River Dreaming

He walked down the gentle incline to the cemented riverbed, where only a trickle of water flowed, sludged with algae and the sticky sheen of industry. All the trash and discarded appliances had been cleared away and the patchwork graffiti painted over, leaving the LA River clean and uncluttered for the first time since it was paved back in '38. More people were crowded in here, of various ages and races and ease of mobility, joined by others dropping down into the river in every direction. This was the destination chute for all of the living cattle left in the city. Ganz and the rest of the citizens around him were being herded toward the bowl built on top of the hill.

On either side, before him and behind, hundreds of masked figures worked with spray paint on a continuous mural that depicted breathtakingly beautiful pastoral scenes of 19th century high society and rustic peasant frolicking in bucolic settings. Several crews teamed up on an enormous pronouncement topping the far river wall, painting the letters C-A-R-C-O, continuing on with the rounds and slopes of the next letter.

They passed under Suicide Bridge, where strange fruit hung down from the girders and exposed metalwork at the end of thick truck chains, creating a dripping curtain of barely clothed flesh, softening on the outside as the insides stiffened like drying tree branches. They would have rocked in the breeze, but there was none.

Northward the river pointed, and the walkers moved against the rumor of a current, coming to the Arroyo Seco Confluence, where the two enslaved rivers, tamed by cement, crossed paths in shame and continued on their way, dreaming of water and muddy riverbanks tousled with grass. Ganz vaguely remembered an old man with young eyes hiding behind thick glass, who told him about this place. Told him that Ganz had stolen his life, and now he'd see him again in hell. No, not in hell. On the other side. Here. CARCO…

On the right, the hills of Cypress Park and Mount Washington leered down at the quivering wretches slogging through the river. On the left, a wooden staircase led out of the cement crevasse. The masked had gathered here, and were ordering the others out of the river with blades and gun barrels, soaked feet squishing up the rough boards of the rickety stairs. Ganz looked up at the sheer hillside. At the very top, what lay on just the other side poured illumination into the dead night sky. The normally bluish white stadium lights were replaced now by a pale yellow glow that pulsed and danced. Writhed. The sky above Los Angeles used to look yellowish at night, with the smog reflecting back the city lights in on itself. A reassuring blanket of human achievement against the dark. Tonight, the sky was black, as all the lights from man were dead.

15. Dénouement

Ganz and the others climbed the hill, the interlacing cement tendrils of the 110 and the 5 Freeway growing smaller behind him. The hillside was steep, but Ganz moved steadily, grabbing hunks of stubborn brown weeds, smelling the sharp odor of the dusty soil that for generations had sucked up smog instead of rain while the city grew wild below.

Reaching the crest of the hill, where signal fires burned in six spots around the rim, Ganz stood tall and looked down into the bowl that was once Dodger Stadium. The seats had been ripped out, exposing tight stone steps like those on Mayan pyramids. Temple of Kukulcan. Chichen Itza. The terraced rings were filled to capacity with the masked figures, standing shoulder to shoulder at perfect attention. Sellout crowd. The unmasked citizens milled about on the field, in front of a stage that had been erected over home plate, six feet high and stretching from dugout to dugout on either side. Pale yellow curtains hid the preparations behind. The design of the stagework and draping was ornate to the point of decadence, channeling Louis XIV at his most sodden. The orchestra pit of two-dozen masked musicians wearing flowing robes took up a dissonant tune, heavy on brass and wheedling flute. The prelude.

The push of the crowd moved Ganz through a cut in the perimeter fence and down the stadium steps, loosing him and his companions out onto the grass. He tried to move to the back fence, to put distance between him and the repulsive symphony, but was pushed to the middle of the field, just behind second base, quickly pressed in close on all sides by breathless, moaning bodies that reeked of sweat and shit.

The orchestra swelled with a terrible spike in pitch and volume. Ganz clutched at his ears, gnashed his teeth. He wanted to fall to the ground, to die before his brain popped, but the bodies around him held him up.

A half dozen spotlights shot down from the sky, topped by the whumping sound of heavy helicopter blades. Loudspeakers mounted on the choppers buzzed out words, shouts. *Drop weapons... National Guard... By order of the President... Surrounded...* The spots raked the crowd of the masked, who hadn't moved, all focused on the stage. Two beams of light fell onto the front of the platform, perfectly illuminating the curtains as they slowly rose.

All around the stadium, those servants of the King removed their masks in one motion. The bellow from the field began at the edge and spread like a wave, wrenching wide every mouth and set of eyes as they saw what lay beneath.

The curtain was now open, exposing the players on stage. The backdrop. The costumes – what at first appeared to be costumes.

To the south, the tops of six downtown skyscrapers exploded with yellow flame, going up like ignited oilrigs. The boom and tremor arrived a second later.

Tongues fell silent. Machines fell from the sky. The play began.

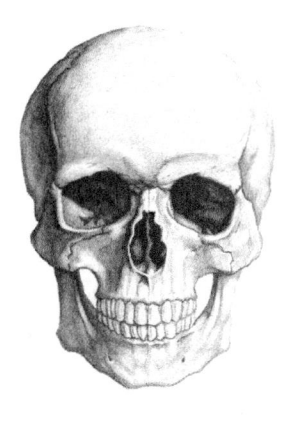

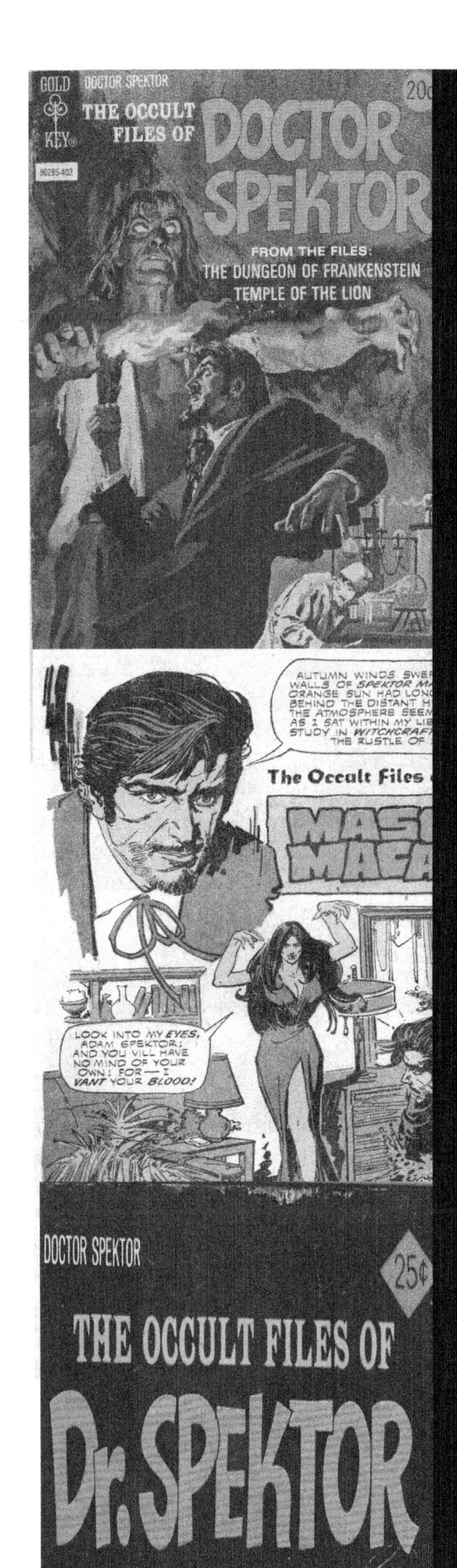

THE OCCULT FILES OF DOCTOR SPEKTOR

CHARLES R. RUTLEDGE

When people ask me who is my favorite occult detective, I'm pretty sure they expect me to mention Manly Wade Wellman's John Thunstone or Seabury Quinn's Jules de Grandin, and as worthy as those two stalwarts may be, my very favorite occult detective is actually a comic book character, Doctor Adam Spektor, created by Donald F. Glut. My introduction to Spektor was in the pages of his eponymous comic book *The Occult Files of Doctor Spektor,* issue #10, in 1974. The cover featured an Egyptian mummy crashing through a window into a costumed ball and menacing a man in a black Inverness cape, and young woman dressed as a Native American maid. Being a kid raised on the Universal Studios Mummy films, how could I resist?

The good Doctor had gotten his start a couple of years earlier in the Gold Key Comics title Mystery Comics Digest issue #5. At that point Spektor was only a narrator, introducing tales of the macabre in the grand tradition of character hosts like EC Comics' The Old Witch, and Warren Magazine's Cousin Eerie, as well as Gold Key's own witch Grimm, from *Grimm's Ghost Stories*.

The publishers at Gold Key were so pleased with the new character that they decided Doctor Spektor deserved his own comic book. They wanted him to go right on introducing creepy stories, but Spektor's creator and writer, Donald F. Glut, had other ideas. When Glut turned in his initial script for the first issue of *The Occult Files of Doctor Spektor* to his editor Del Connell, it was for a 21 page story starring Spektor as the hero of the tale. Connell agreed, somewhat reluctantly, and Spektor was off and running. As a compromise, the other early issues of Spektor's comic would be split between a story starring Spektor in the front of the comic and a shorter tale narrated by Spektor in the back.

In his introduction to The Doctor Spektor Archives Vol 1 (Darkhorse Comics 2010) Don Glut says, "I envisioned Doctor Spektor as an authority on things supernatural and the occult." He goes on to say, "He was an investigator of the unknown, a kind of combination of Sherlock Holmes and Dr. Van Helsing." (For more on the creation of Doctor Spektor, see the interview with Donald F. Glut in this issue of ODQ.)

To carry the Van Helsing connection a bit further, the menace

Spektor faced in his first issue was the vampire Baron Tibor, who would become a reoccurring character in the series. Gold Key editors weren't fond of any sort of continuity, based on their theory that no kids would read two consecutive issues of a comic or remember characters from earlier issues. But Glut paid them little heed, bringing back not only character from his own earlier stories, but using older Gold Key characters like The Owl and Dr. Solar.

Over his first dozen or so issues Adam Spektor would face supernatural menaces ranging from mummies to Mr. Hyde and from reanimated skeletons to the actual Frankenstein monster. Glut was a long time fan of horror films and there is a definite feel of the Universal Horror movies to the Spektor stories.

All of this monster mayhem was illustrated by artist Jesse Santos. Santos had a style that wasn't like that of most American comics artists. His rendering avoided the traditional brush stoke 'feathering' of standard comic book inking techniques, instead employing a use of line work to delineate form. His art was extremely detailed in the first few issues but became less so as deadlines for multiple projects piled up. Santos was also the artist on Glut's sword and sorcery title Dagar the Invincible, and drew many other features at Gold Key, such as Brothers of the Spear and Tragg and the Sky Gods. Much of the appeal of Doctor Spektor was the original and solid artwork of Jesse Santos.

Issue #11 would mark the end of the back-up stories. In that issue, Spektor was bitten by a werewolf and thus, became a werewolf. Here Don Glut broke yet another Gold Key rule, writing a story that continued over several issues, as Spektor sought a cure for his lycanthropy.

In his own quiet way, Glut broke other, less visible rules at Gold Key Comics, introducing people of color to this various series. Adam Spektor's assistant and girlfriend was the Native American Lakota Rainflower, and a continuing character, psychic Elliot Kane, was African American. Glut did this without fanfare, just making people of color a natural part of Spektor's world. A gutsy move in the early seventies.

One of the other things that Glut enjoyed was making connections between the various series he worked on. Thus characters and incidents from *Dagar the Invincible* and *Tragg and the Sky Gods* would show up in Doctor Spektor. At one point, the barbarian Durak, a comrade of Dagar's, actually traveled to the future to help Spektor fight the ancient wizard Xorkon and the Frankenstein Monster. Glut would continue this practice when he moved to working for Marvel Comics, linking his Gold Key work to the world of Robert E. Howard in Marvel's Kull and Solomon Kane comics.

One of the concepts Glut used the most was the idea of the Dark Gods, sort of his take on the Great Old Ones of H.P. Lovecraft. The Dark Gods had held power on Earth in ancient times, but had been banished from our dimension. They sought to regain control of our world, which would, of course, doom humanity. Spektor opposes the Dark Gods and they are mentioned in Dagar, Kull, and in Glut's novels and movies.

Similarly Glut's 'vampire bible', "The Ruthevenian", (named for Lord Ruthven, one of the first vampires in popular fiction, from John Polidori's short story *The Vampyre*) shows up in Doctor Spektor's adventures and also appears in Glut's 'New Adventures of Frankenstein' novels, as well as being mentioned in his movies. On a personal note, I got Don Glut's permission to use The Ruthvenian in the vampire novel I co-wrote with James A. Moore, *Congregations of the Dead*.

After Spektor was cured of being a werewolf, the next few issues would have him come up against Voodoo, zombies, and servants of the Dark Gods, and have his final encounter with the vampire, Count Tibor.

In issue #18, Spektor and Lakota traveled to Rutland, Vermont for Tom Fagan's Halloween parade. This was something of a comic book tradition. Issues of Batman, Avengers, and Justice League of America had been set at the annual event. Again, Glut made use of tropes that other Gold Key creators would never have attempted. In the story, a revived princess of the Dark Gods was able to use her evil sorcery to bring back many of Spektor's old foes, including Dracula, Ra Ka Tep the mummy, and the Frankenstein Monster. This would turn out to be the last appearances of these enemies as starting with issue #19, Don Glut would begin bringing in new opponents for the Doctor.

A swamp monster, Egyptian gods, and a big thing in a Scottish Loch would all appear in the next few issues. Spektor's world would be shaken by losing the woman he loved and other changes were in the offing.

And then, just like that, it was over.

Distribution had been an issue for Gold Key Comics for most of the seventies. The two big comics publishers, Marvel and DC were pumping out the titles, and Gold Key didn't seem to be able to compete for space on the spinner racks and newsstands. Without warning, Gold Key canceled Doctor Spektor, along with Glut's other titles Dagar and Tragg. There would be a final issue of Spektor, #25, but that was a reprint of the first issue.

Don Glut had already scripted several more issues, including an origin story for Doctor Spektor. One of these would be drawn and finally appear in the catch-all title, Gold Key Spotlight. The others would end up in limbo.

In 2015 comic book publisher IDW attempted a new Doctor Spektor comics series. More of a re-imagining than a reboot, it had little to do with the original series. It didn't last beyond a few issues.

A somewhat warped version of the original character appeared recently in the comic *Gold Key Alliance*, but Don Glut's Doctor Spektor is pretty much out of the picture. Still, Don has those scripts and he tells me he has a way to bring the character back. So who knows? We may not have seen the last Occult File of Doctor Spektor. It's hard to keep a good occult detective down.

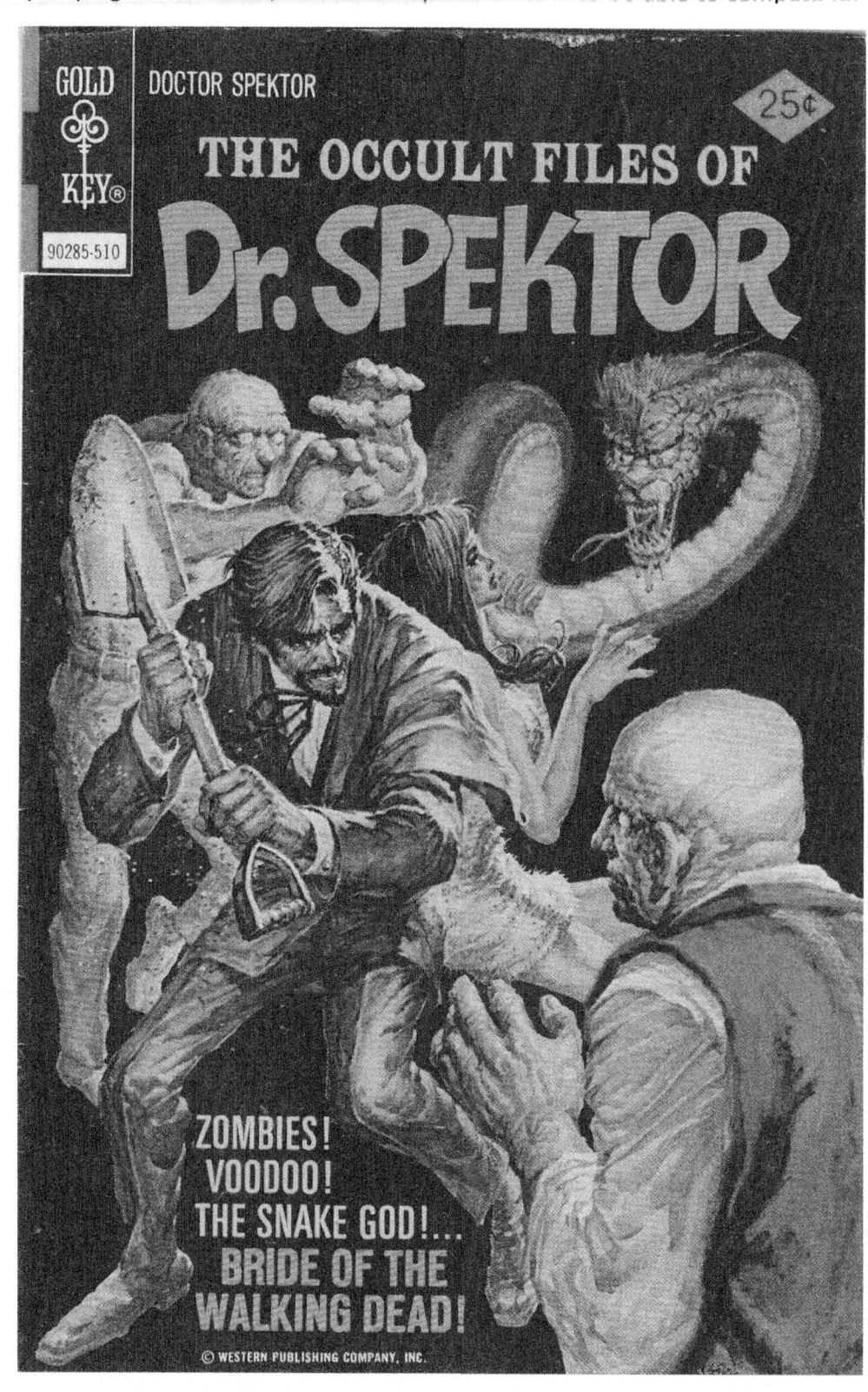

THE MAN BEHIND DOCTOR SPEKTOR!

AN INTERVIEW WITH DON F. GLUT

CHARLES R. RUTLEDGE

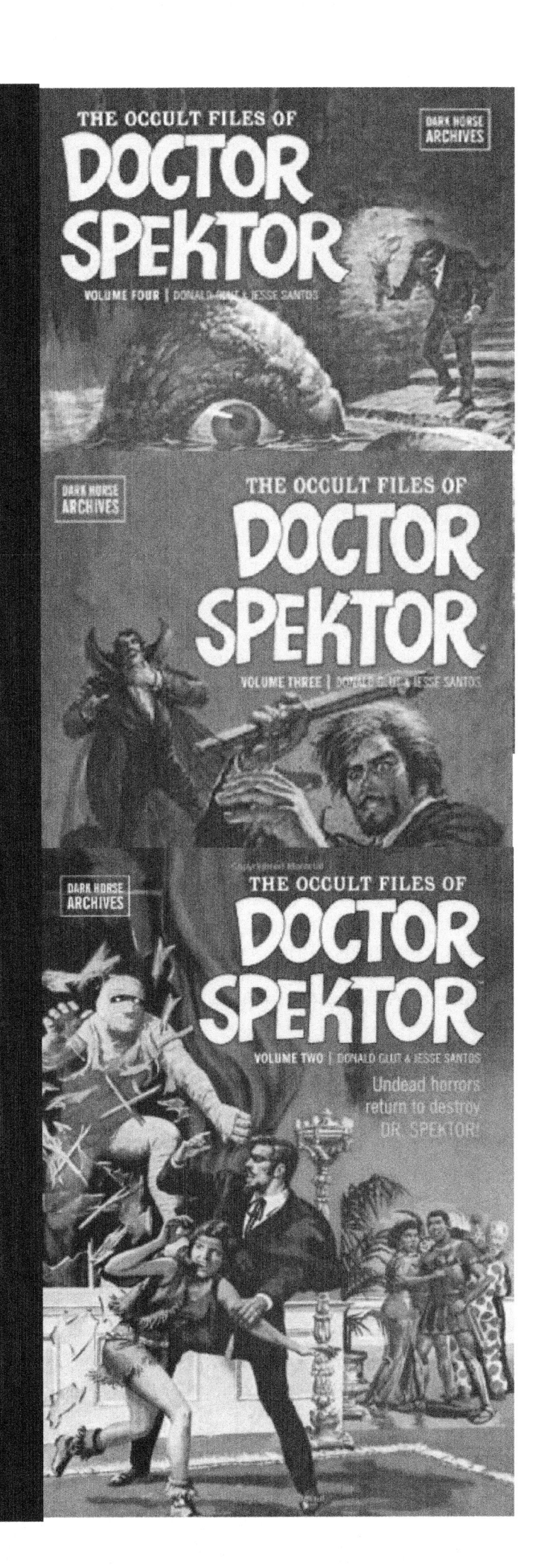

Donald F. Glut is a true Renaissance man! He is a writer, director, actor, screenwriter, musician and amateur paleontologist. Know to many as the writer of the second STAR WARS novel, THE EMPIRE STRIKES BACK, in 1980 (and still in print today), Don was a prolific writer for comic books during the 1970s during which he created the Gold Key series, THE OCCULT FILES OF DOCTOR SPEKTOR. Despite it's short run, it is a comic that is fondly remembered by many comic book and horror fans. In this exclusive interview, Don talks about his inspirations for Dr. Spektor and his plans for what would have happened if the comic had not been unexpectedly cancelled.

ODQ: Let's start with the genesis of Dr. Spektor. In the 1970s, Gold Key Comics already had several horror anthology titles like Grimm's Ghost Stories and Boris Karloff's Tales of Mystery. Dr. Spektor began as the host of a similar comic book. Where did the idea for the character come from? Did you already have plans for him to take a more active role when you created him or did that come after you had written the character for a while?

DG: Originally I pitched Dr. Spektor as just a new host character to narrate stories in MYSTERY COMICS DIGEST. I'm sure the name Spektor was influenced to some extent by DC's Spectre character and I know that the full title "The Occult Files of…" was inspired by Jerry Grandenetti's "Secret Files of Dr. Drew" from Fiction House's pre-Comics Code RANGERS COMICS. The look of the character, at least his attire, was inspired both by Sherlock Holmes and Barnabas Collins from the DARK SHADOWS television soap opera. The name "Spektor" sounded something like "Spectre" (which had more implications than just the DC superhero ghost) with Drew contributing the "Doctor." *Voila*, instant name! When I came up with the idea to make Spektor an actual continuing participant in his stories, rather than just being a talking head narrating them, I based his character on Sherlock Holmes, Dr. Van Helsing and, to a lesser extent, myself. He was envisioned as an investigator or detective of the supernatural.

ODQ: People may not realize that you're an authority on monsters and horror and that you've written non fiction books about Frankenstein and Dracula. What drew you to monsters?

DG: When I was a kid all my friends were talking about the movies INVADERS FROM MARS, THEM and, most of all, CREATURE FROM THE BLACK LAGOON. At the time I was pretty much of a scaredy cat, afraid of the dark, anything spooky and so forth. After working up as much courage as I could I went to see those movies and found them, not frightening at all, but really cool. Right after CREATURE came out, COLLIERS magazine ran a big story with color photos of the Bud Westmore make-up studio at Universal-International. The story told how the monsters were created for the screen. Being a rather creative child, who liked to draw and make clay models, I was naturally fascinated by that article and, as Ray Harryhausen often said about seeing KING KONG for the first time in 1933, I haven't been the same since.

ODQ: When you created the duel pantheons of The Dark Gods and The Warrior Gods, were you influenced by Great Old Ones or Elder Gods of the Cthulhu Mythos? I don't remember any of the Spektor stories being particularly Lovecraftian, but I wondered.

DG: You bet. I was intrigued by the continuity between Lovecraft's and also Edgar Rice Burroughs' stories and the rich backstory they'd created. It was my conscious intent to do something close to what HPL had done – and have references to that continuity spill over into my novels, short stories, eventually my movies, even into comic books published by companies other than Gold Key. I wonder how many people ever picked up on this or ever will.

ODQ: One of my favorite supporting characters in Spektor was the psychic, Elliot Kane. Do you recall where the idea for Elliot came from?

DG: I wanted to introduce a major African American character but make him different from the Doctor, hence the psychic abilities. At the time Gold Key was paranoid – even scared – about introducing a Black character of any kind, other than the ones that were already appearing in titles like TARZAN and BROTHERS OF THE SPEAR. They really believed that the slightest mistake made in a black character's portrayal would lead to the Black Community storming and maybe burning down their office building! Add to that was the problem that one of the Gold Key editors – I won't say which one – was somewhat of a racist. But fortunately I was able to work Elliott Kane and also his girlfriend Cindy Bask into the storyline and not get them rejected.

ODQ: Dr. Spektor, along with several other Gold Key titles was canceled rather abruptly. I believe that you'd already written several issues that were never drawn?

DG: Yes. In the case of SPEKTOR, I even wrote an origin issue that was bought and went through editing – that, plus the beginning of a plot involving some of the Gold Key-owned superheroes like the Owl, Purple Zombie and Man of the Atom – that would have brought back Lakota. It was terribly disappointing for me when that book was so abruptly canceled. It was very personal book for me in many ways and was a labor of love to write. I'd also written scripts that were bought and edited, but never published because of cancellation, for DAGAR THE INVINCIBLE, TRAGG AND THE SKY GODS and LOST IN SPACE.

ODQ: You made use of a lot of traditional monsters in Dr. Spektor, including, vampires, werewolves, Mr. Hyde, and so forth. The Frankenstein Monster seems to be a favorite of yours. You've written novels about the monster and he's appeared in some of your other comics work and I believe you're in the middle of a new film about Frankenstein. Could you tell us a bit about what fascinates you about Frankenstein's monster and what you're working on now?

DG: I'm a huge fan of the traditional monsters when they're done in the classic tradition, as in the old Universal and Hammer movies. I've been a Frankenstein fan ever since I was a young kid – and my Mom pointed out in a movie theater that the "Indian" we were watching in TAP ROOTS, Boris Karloff, had played "Frankenstein." At the time I'd never heard of anyone called "Frankenstein," but the name intrigued me as was the fact that the Monster had been made up from dead bodies and given life. I soon began to notice the FRANKENSTEIN comic books, the pre-Code ones drawn by Dick Briefer, which had their own allure, and my interest just kept growing. My current, in-production movie is TALES OF FRANKENSTEIN, an anthology in the mode of the old Amicus movies like DR. TERROR'S HOUSE OF HORRORS and ASYLUM, based upon five of my own short stories included in a book of that same title. We've already shot the first segment – "My Creation, My Beloved" – plus a framing story featuring the Monster. We are now completing the second story, "Crawler from the Grave." What's cool is that our second day of shooting "Crawler" happened to be Mary Shelley's 200th birthday. I want the movie to come out in 2018, the 200th anniversary of the first publication of Mary's novel. I've also written a 12th and final novel in my "New Adventures of Frankenstein" series – FRANKENSTEIN: THE FINAL HORROR – which I hope will be out before 2017 comes around. It has a slam-bang finish with a big, final one-on-one confrontation between the Monster and Burt Winslow, the scientist who revives the creature in the first book. FINAL HORROR also, if one reads between the lines and has a good memory, explains my appearances of the Monster in other media including comic books written by me…including THE OCCULT FILES OF DR. SPEKTOR.

ODQ: That's fantastic, Don. Thanks so much for talking to us for ODQ. For further information, readers can check out Don's website here: http://www.donaldfglut.com/

(Don continues to be active today! In addition to his current film project, TALES OF FRANKENSTEIN, Don has also returned to writing comics with new stories in CREEPS Magazine! Available at your local Barnes & Noble bookstore, CREEPS is a return to the classic Warren B/W horror mags of old. Highly recommended by the staff of ODQ, you can learn more about the magazine at their website: http://www.thecreepsmagazine.com/)

THE BARON OF BOURBON STREET

Aaron Vlek

The Baron strode through the river of humanity as it pulsed along Bourbon Street. Men and women, lost in nature's most primal cadence. The Baron Samedi - tall, magnificent, the color of a starless midnight, with top hat and cane and a necklace of bones, white greasepaint and the lines of the skeleton on his lean muscular body beneath the raven tails of a frock coat from a distant age.

He opened himself to all who hungrily sought his gaze, but at the touch of his soul upon their own, they quickly fled back into the crowd. He reveled in this nightly stroll and took pleasure in seeing his future children parading their finery and their flesh for his inspection. The scent of sweaty bodies caressing the darkest places of his being felt like the cold fingers of the beautiful dead. The Baron sighed, interrupted by the touch, like a child's hand knocking clumsily on the wall of his mind.

"Cartier," the Baron Samedi hissed. Freeing himself from the sea of arms and hands that brushed against his body he zigzagged through the twilight and sought the shadows of Orleans Street. Somewhere nearby, among the quiet places of New Orleans, Alfonse de Cartier was calling him.

Alfonse de Cartier's ancestress had been a matriarch of profound acumen and influence in New Orleans society. Residents of color proudly crossed Marjolaine Elise de Cartier's threshold into her elegant parlor for coffee and small French cakes, while pasty faced whites slipped around to the back door under pretense, concealed by wide brimmed hats, turned up collars and veils.

All Mimi's visitors left with what they had come for; roots and powders to fix anything from the pox to bothersome lovers, and sometimes instructions in matters both curious and arcane. Some who visited Mimi were never seen or heard from again, occasionally of their own volition. Madame de Cartier had been a poetess and painter, and the legendary beauty of her day - a mambo, a Vodou priestess of extraordinary power.

The one notable legacy that Madame was able to bestow upon her descendent emanated from her patron, the Baron Samedi himself; master of crossroads, the consumer of fine rums, expensive cigars, and the tender souls of the dead.

In an act of uncharacteristic pity, or boredom, the Baron Samedi took Alfonse into his dark tutelage. And thus, on that night of August 21st in the year 2016, when the Baron felt the call of de Cartier groping through his mind like a talentless thief picking his pockets, he turned quickly and went in search of his protégé.

***

Alfonse stood at the edge of a pool of blood. The woman was beautiful, or had been, before her throat was slit from ear to ear. Her white dress was soaked red and she was cold to the touch. Soon he'd be calling it in. Then he'd watch as Fromier and the rest swarmed over the scene like ants.

But before calling it in, the Baron would come. There was the corpse, the bloody straight razor gripped in her right hand, and a note, neatly written in a delicate hand with the single message, *Tonight is a most auspicious night, ma cherie*, and signed *Veronique*. No sign of a struggle, no defensive wounds or bruises, and not a soul in sight.

Sitting next to the corpse, upstream from the blood, de Cartier threw his arms wide to the sky. Then he opened his mind and silently called out to his patron.

***

"Yessssss," the Baron said, his fingers red with blood as he knelt beside the body. He brought his fingers to his lips and tasted. "Another suicide," he hissed.

"Are you sure?" Alfonse replied. "I thought this one looked more like a homicide."

"This is the third time this month you have called me and your corpse has been no murder!" the Baron cried with a hearty laugh. "Murder is so common in this age of bad manners and childish tempers, perhaps, but not this time. Something is happening in my territory, Alfonse. Discover what, and do not delay. You of all people know how I get when I become, *restive*."

"Yes." De Cartier winced at the implications. As he did so, sirens shattered the silence of the darkened street.

The Baron stood and turned.

"Alfonse, one more thing," he said, tapping de Cartier's chest with a long slender finger tipped menacingly by a sharpened fingernail. "There is a wrongness, an emptiness to this body, as with the first two you found. Remember that, and be wary."

Then he was gone.

Fromier was climbing out of his own vehicle as Tillman and Franklin's squad car skidded to a halt and his partner Tim Baudoin jumped out.

"Hey. I want a copy as soon as you can manage it," de Cartier said, handing Fromier the bagged note.

"Yeah, sure Al," he said. "What's this, the third time this month?" Fromier scowled and took the bag back to his car.

"Baudoin, you okay man?" De Cartier saw the tall black cop hunched over, his coat gripped around his midsection.

"Just got a chill's all," Baudoin replied, looking around the empty street.

"It's gotta be damn near 80°."

"I know. But something's off. Can't you feel it? Aw, never mind, you'd just think I'm crazy."

"Try me," said de Cartier

"Well, I got a case of the whim-whams."

De Cartier considered. Perhaps Tim was feeling the Baron, his echo. He glanced at the squad car; the rest of the crew was ready to pull out.

"Baudoin! Come on, we're getting out of here," Tillman yelled, laying on the horn.

"Go on, I got him," de Cartier yelled back.

"You sure man?" Baudoin said.

"Hell yeah, I want to hear about these whim-whams."

***

In the root place, the dark cellar of the world, the lord of the Crossroads and master of the dead drew the sweet sugary smoke into the lungs of the body he wore to walk among the living. All around him swarmed the dead; floating in the air before him, wide-eyed and unbelieving, praying they only dreamed and would soon wake up safe in their beds.

Some were intensely beautiful, drifting like wisps of cloud, delighting in freedom from the flesh and its many horrors. Others screamed for mercy where there was no mercy to be had. Some glistened uncleanly in the firelight, clinging to the Baron's body like slugs and leeches before he pulled them off and tossed them into the fire that burned forever in this place.

Here were those who had crossed the threshold that separates the living from the dead, and all who patrol the Crossroads between the two. The Baron lounged on his throne of skulls, contemplating a particularly fine bottle of rum and the three deaths that troubled de Cartier.

The Baron was not perplexed, he was amused. These three had not come running to his call when their time upon the Earth was up, and he was sure there were more. It could only mean one thing – another had interfered.

He drank deeply from the bottle of rum and sat back on his throne, pondering what to do about these ten wayward souls, and how best to convey his displeasure to the one who had crossed him.

"Ah, who ever you are in the shadows, you try my patience. You think I would not see your handiwork, that I would not smell the suicides that are your calling card on the night breeze in this, MY town?" the Baron muttered under his breath, the smile betrayed the true nature of his thoughts.

"I will have my sport, as I always do," he said out loud, his deep melodious voice echoing through his subterranean chamber as the fluttering white things thickened the air around him.

***

The Baron Samedi was just a shadow when he entered the dark places that hold the world together. A single light bulb at the end of the closed alley told seekers of the private club, le Jwèt la Mouri they called home The Baron entered the shabby club and gazed over the crowded dance floor as red spotlights pummeled sweating bodies to a cacophony of canned sound.

Le Jwèt la Mouri, the place for dark sport and blood games, the place where no rules constrained the desires of those with nothing to lose in this world. A warren of back rooms in le Jwèt were private and discrete, and they were always occupied.

Everyone in this place danced with the Baron that night, longing to be the one he took home to his bed, the one he set free with his cold hand upon their heart. But tonight was not like other nights. The Baron Samedi was distracted, bemused and pondering dark thoughts of another, a shrouded antagonist. But the one he sought was not here on the dance floor of le Jwèt la Mouri, of that he was sure.

That night, le Jwèt la Mouri burned to the ground. The Baron Samedi took everyone inside to his bed where he bestowed upon each their greatest desire.

***

At Baudoin's place the two men stared into their coffee cups like they were reading the grounds and looking for signs.

"So, what was going on back there?" de Cartier said. Tim Baudoin sighed and tossed back his coffee like it was a shot of bourbon.

Baudoin looked Alfonse square in the eyes. "You know I don't see much of my family, right?"

"Yeah, I figured, since you never talk about them. Strange for a Louisiana man born and bred," de Cartier said.

"Yeah, well, most of my family, they're church people. Good folks. I'd help them any way I could."

"But?" de Cartier prompted. "You just don't place much stock in that kind of thing?"

Baudoin chuckled. "Yeah, I guess that's about the size of it." The other man shrugged. "Anyway, my granny's side of the family? Woooo! Son, that is a whole 'nother story, I'm telling you right from the get-go," Baudoin said in a near whisper. "She, a bunch of cousins, other kin they got out there I don't know about, they're all into that weird shit, you know, spells and stuff, dancing around, singing all hours of the night, creepy drawings. You know what I'm talking about, I know you do," Baudoin growled, flashing de Cartier a glance that said they were finally getting down to business.

"Yeah, I do." De Cartier knew it, first hand and wired in the bone, as the Baron always said. "Okay, so we've established all that. What spooked you back there, made you bring all this stuff up now?"

"Just a feeling in my gut. Like worms crawling around in there trying to get out. There was something wrong about that dead girl, I tell you. Reminded me of my granny's folks, somehow."

De Cartier nodded. So maybe it wasn't only the Baron that had spooked Tim.

"Well then, let me ask you this. Your granny's folks, they good people, or are you thinking they might be mixed up in this?"

"I can't rightly say, exactly. When I was a kid I used to ride my bike out there bringing pies and such to them, and letters from Momma begging them to come to church. Whenever I did, they just laughed, and I didn't like that laughter." Baudoin took a long slug of his coffee.

"You sensitive on that stuff then, even as a kid?"

"Far back as I can remember."

"Okay, anything else you can tell me?"

"Well it sure as shit didn't feel right, if that's what you mean. I never saw them actually doing anything bad, but they'd always be whispering around me, and never looked me straight in the eye, always off to the side. And they'd pester me to come back, stay the night. But there was no damn way that was gonna happen," Baudoin took a deep breath and let it out, shaking his head.

"When I told Momma they was pestering me to stay the night, she never made me go back out there." Baudoin paused to stare at his coffee cup again.

"But one thing I never did tell Momma about," he continued, his voice not more than a hoarse whisper, "was the dreams."

"Dreams?" de Cartier said with a sharp intake of air.

"Yeah, dreams, where a woman was calling me, like 'come out and play' stuff. I could never make out her face, but she was calling me in a way that took all my power to resist. Pulling at me, always pulling at me."

"Your granny?"

Baudoin shook his head. "No, not her, but one of her people, I'm sure. As terrified as I was of those dreams, as much as I knew I didn't want to go, I wanted to! I wanted to go real bad. And I always had the whim-whams when I woke up."

"Jeez!" de Cartier exclaimed. "Sun's coming up, damn!"

They both laughed as though the arrival of daylight could somehow banish the night's conversation, and the whim-whams, to the farthest corner of unreality.

***

It was Thursday, the night sacred to Erzulie-Freda, in the basement of an elegant 19th century townhouse on Prytania Street in the Garden District. The lights burned late as they often did and the large repurposed room was an impossible contrast of images. Clean and orderly, it could have been the operating room of a small hospital. Steel instruments lay in careful array along spotless countertops while boxes, tubes, and canisters filled with dozens of medicinal solutions and topical antiseptics were stacked and ready at hand. But this is where the resemblance to the healing arts retreated and ran screaming.

In the center of the room seven corpses were laid out on surgical tables, all hooked up to hoses and dozens of IV lines that penetrated the fragile rotting flesh. The bodies were preternaturally pale, painted in a mixture of ash and egg whites and etched with a warren of delicate traceries familiar to practitioners of the arcane arts of the South, traceries which betrayed the nature of the *Doctor* who officiated at the macabre scene.

A graduate with honors from LSU Medical School, the daughter and proud heiress of one of the most notorious mambos alive, Veronique Aliette Sabatier stood tall and beautiful, her dark skin flushed with excitement beneath her flowing lavender gowns and tall headdress, her fierce intelligent eyes locked intently on the seven corpses.

She no longer had the luxury of taking her victims one by one. Other powers were becoming aware of her, closing in. Her medical training had at least allowed her to keep these seven close to her – and now each in his or her turn had given up what she needed.

Hundreds of candles lit the scene and the walls danced with spectral shapes. The air drooped with the fragrance of a thousand roses, and the sweet aroma of cakes, champagne and a dozen other beautiful offerings which adorned the altar. The gris-gris talisman of Erzulie-Freda, the one who brings success in love to her daughters and sons, covered the floor.

Papa Legba had given his permission to proceed. Veronique's offerings were the most sumptuous and costly, and she was the most beautiful and powerful of all those who called upon Erzulie, more powerful even than her own mother and all the mothers before her. Or so she believed.

The priestess raised her arms and her body shook with delight as she swayed and cried out her deepest desires. Again and again she chanted the sacred litany, her voice cresting in a hoarse throaty cry, guttural, terrifying, but enticing to any who might hear even its echo on the night breeze. It was no surprise when it was the breeze that answered, hot, sweet, and fragrant, caressing her body like the hands of a thousand lovers.

In the center of the room, a gentle creaking as of rusted locks and splintered doors rose in a symphonic crescendo as seven corpses white as ash shambled up onto dead feet and stood before their priestess.

Their sightless eyes gaped as cold limbs tore free of the tubes and groped instinctually toward Veronique like the babe for its mother's arms, grasping hungrily at her limbs and stroking her hair. Into each ear she bent with a kiss, and whispered a secret too horrible for any among the living to hear.

Veronique, priestess of Erzulie-Freda slid into each languid embrace, dancing barefoot with them in turn across a floor strewn with rose petals and painted with the stark white veve of her patron, the Lwa of true and abiding love.

***

"What do we got?" de Cartier asked while nodding his hellos. "And my God, what's that fuckin' smell?"

"See for yourself," Baudoin said.

"What the –" de Cartier bellowed as he looked over the rim of the dumpster.

"Yeah," muttered Baudoin.

"Hoo boy," Fromier groaned as he joined them.

"Where the hell's Sharkey?" de Cartier barked. "That coroner on his way already or what?"

"Here he comes," Fromier said, breaking into a sprint toward the coroner's van to escape the aroma wafting from the dumpster.

"Bodies, Sharkey. We got lots of 'em I tell ya," Fromier rattled off as Dr. Mark Sharkleton climbed out of his van and pulled his kit from the back of the vehicle. "Dumpster's full of them. Naked. Damdest shit I've ever seen. We got a real class A freakazoid on our hands, bucko," he added, as the coroner got to work.

"It's pretty bad," Sharkleton said his colleagues laid out the bodies and prepped them for the trip downtown.

"So, what do we know at this point?" de Cartier asked.

"Okay, so, seven victims, four male, three female, ages, roughly twenty-five to thirty-five, but you can see that."

"Okay Sharkey, how about you give us something we don't see?" Baudoin snapped.

"Hey, dude, I'm just doing my job. Give me a break, huh?" Sharkleton snapped back.

"Yeah, yeah, he's sorry," de Cartier said. "This is gonna to be a clusterfuck, it's got nightmare written all over it in neon lights," he continued, squaring his hands in front of their faces.

"I know that. And then there's –"

"Yeah, what's that stuff all over their skin? Paste or something?" de Cartier asked, pretending his breath wasn't stalled somewhere in his chest.

"I won't know exactly what the composition is until I run some tests. But it looks like maybe ash and something else, some binding agent. And look at these designs all over the skin, no smudging. My guess is egg whites," Sharkey said with a satisfied nod.

"Egg whites? Why's that?" Baudoin asked.

"The oldest natural binding agent there is. Used for centuries in painting. It helps create a stable surface and seals pigment. And look at the puncture marks on the skin, here, here, and here. The same on all the bodies. Looks like, you know, like IV marks. They're clean, placed with precision," Sharkleton pointed to the entry wounds on each of the bodies.

"Whoever did this, it looks like they knew what they were doing, is what you're saying?" de Cartier asked.

"Yeah, I'd say so. But I'm done here. I'll get these back to my lab and call you with whatever I have when I get it."

"Good deal Sharkey, appreciate it," de Cartier said with a thumbs up.

"Alfonse, those markings, you get a good look at all that?" Baudoin sputtered in a hushed whisper.

"How could I not?"

"Damn, it's cold all of a sudden! I'm going to grab my jacket," Baudoin said breaking into a sprint toward the car.

"Yeah, yeah," de Cartier muttered.

He turned and looked at Sharkleton. He and his team had returned to their vehicle and were just sitting there, and they'd left the bodies on the tarmac. "What the hell are they doing?" he said out loud. Then he looked at Baudoin. He was sitting on the back seat of their vehicle just staring into space.

"They're just taking a little siesta," the deep melodious voice crooned in his ear from behind. De Cartier turned and saw Baron Samedi bending over the bodies, shaking his head, a scowl on his face. "This is not right, Alfonse, oh, no-no."

"No, seven corpses is never good, and we both know what this looks like," de Cartier replied, joining his patron and looking at the corpses.

"Oh ho, young Alfonse! Of course I know, but do tell me what you see. You tell the Baron Samedi what he sees when he says something is not right among the lovely dead."

"Well, it looks like they –" de Cartier started.

"No! Look with the eyes of your inheritance! Look with the eyes that your grandmamma Marjolaine Elise gave you. See what your *colleagues* cannot see, and tell me what you feel. Feel them Alfonse, *feel* the dead."

De Cartier took a step back, filled his lungs with the putrefaction and cold emptiness that made the bodies shimmer with transparent nothingness.

"What the?" he gasped and pulled away.

"Tell me!" the Baron demanded. "Describe it! You see what is wrong, I can smell it in your sweat."

"They're empty, just rotting meat. I've never seen bodies like this before."

"Not true."

"What do you mean? I've never – Yes!" de Cartier hissed. "The woman last week! And, the two before that - you're saying that they were the same. What does it mean?"

"It means, my dear Alfonse, that you are right. They are indeed empty. That is not how it is supposed to be until I come for them. It means –"

"Somebody else took their souls! But how?"

"How indeed? Only a very great bokor could presume to trespass for even but a moment upon my sacred ground! A very great bokor, or perhaps a mambo, as it could be." The Baron was watching de Cartier closely as the implications sunk into his bowels and took root.

He turned to see Baudoin moving again, coming toward him, and when he looked back, the Baron was gone.

"Let's get out of here. I need to get some dinner, you hungry?"

"Yeah, always," Baudoin said.

"Okay, jump in the car. We'll go grab a bite. I got the copy of the note the dead girl in the alley was holding. What do you make of it?" de Cartier said, handing the note to his partner and starting the engine.

"Mon Dieu!" Baudoin groaned as he read the sheet of paper.

"What is it?"

"You think the dead girl from the other day is tied up in this thing?"

"There's a good chance. Why?" de Cartier said.

"Sharkey said whoever did these bodies knew what they was doing, the puncture marks I mean. Like they had medical training."

"That's right. What are you thinking?"

His partner sat in silence for a few seconds.

"Baudoin? What is it?"

"This note. And this, *Veronique*. My cousin's name is Veronique."

"So what? A lot of women around here are named Veronique. As for the note, we have no idea who wrote it at this point."

"Well, this cousin, she's part of the family I told you about, my cousins out there in the woods, into all that Vodou stuff."

"And?" de Cartier asked, getting a cold spot where his heart was.

"And, she's a doctor." Baudoin shivered. "She has a practice at her house on Prytania."

De Cartier didn't like this sort of coincidence.

"Well then, maybe we need to pay her a visit, find out if she's good for this, or clear her. If she's not involved, you'll sleep better tonight. We'll check it out."

"Yeah, we gotta do that," Baudoin muttered without looking at him.

***

De Cartier and Baudoin climbed the broad marble stairs to the ornate lavender painted front door of one of the most elegant addresses on Prytania Street. The place was almost overgrown with rose vines and the scent that filled the summer heat was intoxicating. After several knocks, the door opened and a beautiful tall black woman in scrubs, her hair twisted into a turban greeted them with a look of astonishment.

"I'm Dr. Sabatier, do you have an appointment?" she asked, her deep heady voice almost as captivating as the clouds of incense that wafted out of the house to compete with the roses. "I'm afraid my nurse and receptionist have gone for the day."

"No, I'm Detective de Cartier, and this is my partner —"

"Oh my god!" she cried, covering her hand with her mouth to stifle a laugh. "Cousin Timothy!"

"Veronique," Baudoin muttered.

"May we come in?" de Cartier asked.

"Of course. What's this about?" Veronique asked, her voice dropping to a seductive whisper as she caught de Cartier in her gaze. "But do come in, and make yourselves comfortable here," she said, her hand waving them into a luxuriously-appointed sitting room which opened off the large hall.

"I'll change into something more appropriate, I won't be but a moment."

She went upstairs, to return only a couple of minutes later dressed in lavender robes and head-wrap. She walked silently on small manicured bare feet over the lush Persian carpet, like a dancer, and slid onto the sofa next to de Cartier, taking his arm.

"What can I help you with, detective?" she asked, pressing her body against his and glancing briefly at Baudoin.

De Cartier coughed, the incense thick in his throat. He was having trouble concentrating. "It's an awkward matter, Dr Sabatier – may be nothing--"

A boy about thirteen in formal livery entered the room carrying a silver tray with coffee and small cakes. Baudoin looked to de Cartier, who was staring with puzzlement at their hostess.

"Who's this?" Baudoin asked as the boy bent to serve him.

"No-one who matters," Veronique purred and then laughed. "Do have one of these little cakes."

Despite themselves, they pushed the soft, sweet cakes into their mouths, chewing automatically.

"Good, good." Veronique smiled, watching as their eyes clouded.

And she whispered something into de Cartier's ear.

***

De Cartier and his partner stood outside a house on Prytania Street. The building was dark, the street quiet, and they had no recollection of why they had come to this place, or who might live inside.

"What... what are we doing here?" Baudoin shook his head as if to clear it.

"There was a woman--" de Cartier started, and then a flash of his inheritance, of Marjolaine Elise de Cartier, cut through his confusion. "Veronique, your cousin."

Baudoin groaned. "The face – the face from my dreams, those years ago. Jeez, Alfonse, it was her – I can see it now. What happened? What did she do to us?"

"She hexed us, and nearly shook us off, is what. I'd say that means she's our girl – or a big part of this mess."

"We need to get back inside." Baudoin's hand slid to his holster. "And we need to call it in."

"In more ways than one," de Cartier murmured to himself.

And once again he opened his mind, calling...

***

Veronique smiled approvingly into the mirror atop the altar in her ritual chamber. Robed and anointed, she surveyed the room that was alight with the glow of scented candles and incense. Also on the altar were the cakes and roses and champagne of her patroness Erzulie-Freda, as well as the fine cigars, the costly rum, and the other implements of power favored by the one she sought to command, compel, and take into her bed.

"Oh you, look upon me," Veronique moaned. "See me! Come and behold ME! Take *me* in your arms," she cried. Dancing before the altar with complete abandon, her passions more inflamed as the longing for the one she sought possessed her.

"See me! See how beautiful I am! You cannot resist me! I am the Woman, the woman who would command even the Guédé of the dead, the master of the grave and the lord of darkest night! Oh Samedi! Oh Baron of the graveyards of eternity, come! Come unto *ME*! How can you resist this body?

"Do you not long to do my bidding and so gain the rewards of these arms, these thighs, these breasts!" she wailed, tossing off her robes and stroking her oiled flesh with the ardor she sought to awaken in her desired one, the Baron Samedi himself.

The candles on the altar sputtered then rose up like torches several feet high, while the air in the room darkened slowly as an inky presence seeped in from unknown places and swirled around her.

"Yes! See what I have gathered before you? If you try to resist my charms, perhaps *these* will entice you!" Veronique screamed triumphantly. On the top shelf of the altar sat ten clay jars, each glowing from within and sealed with the wax crest of her name of secret power. The jars contained the souls of four men, and six women.

The inky darkness swarmed and thickened around Veronique's body, teasing her, enrapturing her, enflaming her pride with the ease of such a mighty conquest. The presence swelled within her and filled her being with its power…

There was a hammering at the door downstairs. As quickly as the moment had come, it was gone, and she screamed in heartbroken despair. How had those fools cleared their minds? Cursing, she turned to go rain her true rage on the detectives. This time, subtlety would be forgotten.

Glancing into the mirror, she clutched her throat and screamed again. Her voice was strangled and she collapsed onto the floor. From the mirror, the Baron Samedi looked down on Veronique's body, and he was laughing.

***

De Cartier and Baudoin heard the screams from above.

"We need to move," snapped de Cartier. They put their shoulders to the front door, breaking it open. The sitting room was empty. De Cartier took the winding staircase with Baudoin barreling along behind him. A smaller version of the opulent stairway coiled up to a third floor and the two detectives charged through a white door covered with veves and stormed into the ritual chamber.

"It's Veronique!" Baudoin cried, rushing to the body.

"No! Tim, you can't. Don't touch anything," de Cartier said, grabbing his partner's arm and dragging him away.

"What the hell happened here?" Baudoin roared, but de Cartier said nothing as he drew his gun and went to search the house.

"It's clear, there's no-one here," de Cartier said ten minutes later. No sign of a perpetrator – no sign either of the boy who had served them.

Baudoin looked up, his face flushed.

"There's no blood, no wounds that I can see."

"No sign of struggle, either and with all the stuff in here, there'd be signs. Come on, let's go downstairs. There's nothing more we can do right now." De Cartier pulled his partner to his feet and urged him toward the door.

Alfonse de Cartier had seen enough to give him a clear picture of what had happened here. He noted the disparate offerings on the altar, knew who had been invoked, and figured Veronique must have angered the Baron pretty badly.

Veronique would be added to the ten previous victims, and what Sharkey would make of that he had no idea. He had a feeling this was going to be a lot of paperwork, but that the bottom line would be *case closed*.

***

The walls of Baron Samedi's subterranean chamber trembled and wept. Pale mists, the pungent breath of the Earth, seeped from the floor to obscure the thousands of bottles, jars, and leather pouches that covered the massive altar he had raised to celebrate his own most glorious self. He savored every detail that was to come, drawing down from the top shelf a jar carved of blue stone that pulsed with a reddish angry glow and throbbed like a preternatural heart.

Screams and sighs, tears, moans, and wailing as from the pit of hell erupted like a symphony of despair and filled the chamber of the Lord of Death. Joy too rang out, and enough pleading to cleanse the skies of hope.

Lifting the blue decanter to his eye, the Baron Samedi chuckled as he shook its contents, causing a mournful wail to momentarily drown the cacophony.

"Where is your hubris now, my beauty? Where is your power, your charms that no man can resist, where are your magics?" He laughed and slammed the jar down on the altar.

"If I let you out, will you do all that I command of you?" he asked, his voice melodious and teasing.

"Don't toy with me!" the female voice burst from within the blue jar, then died away into tears.

"Oh, beauty, do not despair of me. Rejoice! Our time has come and I will have you, as is my right! No man, no woman, can keep from the Baron Samedi what belongs to him!"

The Baron set the jar down on the alter and opened his hand to the deepest places in his chamber, causing a huge mirror to appear before him, taller than his own great height, a glass of transparent black shimmering upon its surface. Regarding his powerful handsome visage, the Baron liked what he saw immensely and it always gave him great pleasure to gaze into the black pools of his own eyes.

Then he stripped himself of the Creole finery that was his custom, laid his hat and cane aside and stood naked before the glass. He breathed deep, filling his chest with the sacred smokes that billowed sinuously like snakes upon the altar. Grasping the jar in his right hand he pulled out the stopper and tossed it aside.

"Be with me beauty, my lovely Veronique, be with me as you desired!" he laughed again and drained the contents of the decanter down his throat. Flinging the glass into the fire pit where it shattered, the Baron closed his arms tightly around his body in a deep embrace. Then he closed his eyes and bowed his head to await the rising of his greatest magic.

***

Veronique Aliette Sabatier crawled in the utter blackness of the spirit world. Her eyes were filled with smoke and her lungs screamed for life giving breath. She sobbed pitifully and cursed in anger before surrendering to the truth. She was dead. She wandered alone in the cemetery that lies at the deep ground of all cemeteries, lost and alone, stripped of her many powers.

Her spirit-form stiffened and she shivered with dread. She was not alone. He was there, all around her, within her, his presence like the night sky, his laughing eyes like the stars. His heat filled her like the sun, and his darkness was the wellspring from which all life crawled and to which it all returned. Samedi, the Baron, the one she had sought to cheat, the one she had tried to seduce.

Veronique who delighted in sumptuous garments was naked, exposed to the mocking eyes of the dead and the cold, unloving flesh she could sense all around her. She who had always delighted in the pleasures of the bath and costly fragrances, cosmetics, oils, and tinctures, was covered with the filth of the charnel house and the moist dark earth of the tomb. She possessed nothing now but ash and sweat - and her tears, which were many.

***

The Baron stood before his spirit mirror. His chamber was quiet now, and at peace. Naked, he looked down at his body and smiled. He slowly ran his hands over the smooth delicate skin and touched his fingers to his lips. Sweet, the fragrance of rose and amber still clinging as a fine dusty oil. He felt his sumptuous breasts, heavy in his hands, full and beautiful. He threw his head back and laughed. Long slender legs supported the tall female body he now wore; thick curls and braids fell to the narrow waist. The Baron stepped closer to better examine the full sensuous lips that parted in surprise and delight and the beautiful almond eyes that looked back at him from his own face.

"You see my Veronique, all that you wanted, you have it now. You who would seduce me, have become me, you who would share my power, shall taste it every day of this, our life together, until this body wears out and drifts away like ash."

He laughed again.

"Alas, I have always been very hard on my bodies."

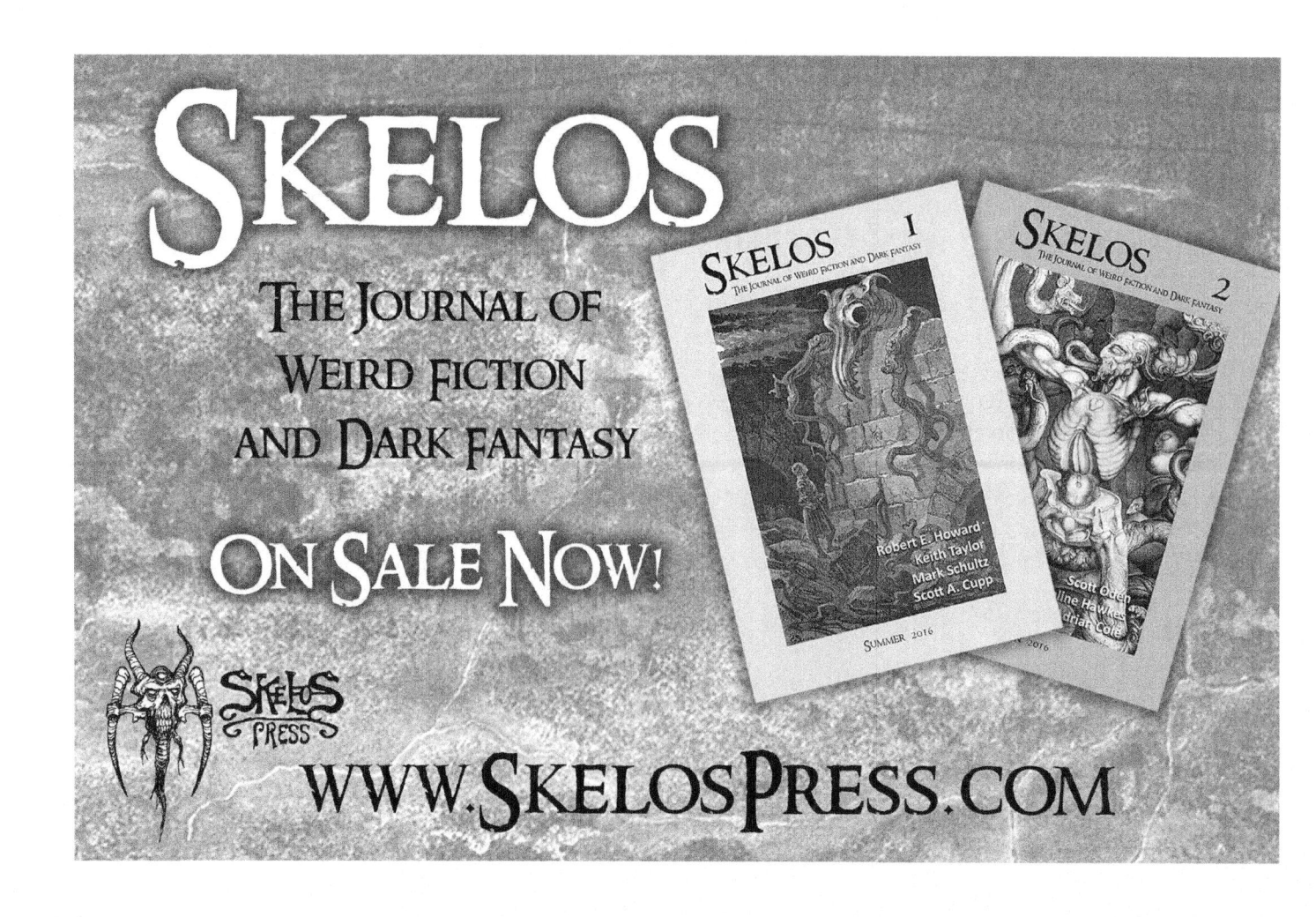

THE ADVENTURE OF THE BLACK DOG

OSCAR DOWSON

I returned from South Africa not long after the death of Queen Victoria, and London was draped in black when I arrived. I had been invalided out of the Engineers – and found my immortal place in the footnotes of arachnology – after being bitten by an unknown species of spider, following which I had been in a thrashing fever of hallucination and vomiting for a week. I wasted away drastically and was so weak when I recovered my senses that I was no use to my Regiment and not much use to myself. Having no particular ties to South Africa, I decided to return to the country of my birth, which I had not seen for some years. I was pale, purposeless, and thanks to some shrewd investments and a fortuitous legacy, dependent on no-one.

My pile was not so substantial, however, that I could expect this latter condition to last for very long. To save money, I had been staying for five weeks with my cousin Jasper and his wife, an arrangement that suited none of us. Jasper busied himself with his work at the British Museum during the day; his wife, who had never taken a liking to any member of our family except Jasper, looked on me as the worst sort of idler, a shiftless ne'er-do well who had probably feigned my spider-bite out of an unreasonable desire to avoid being shot by a Boer. Whilst Jasper liked me well enough, he did not like a fractious wife, and sombre hints began to be dropped.

I was grateful therefore to run into Dalton at my club. We had been at Trinity together and he was now something mysterious in the City. I was not interested enough to enquire very much. The shrewd investments I previously mentioned were more in the nature of gambles, as one might gamble on a horse – that is, following the advice of someone who knew the form, the turf and the thoroughbreds. In truth I had no real interest in money beyond how I might have enough of it to live well in the manner of my choosing, and the wizardry by which Dalton and his breed conjured up the stuff remained a mystery to me. It was one of many defects in my education.

'There's no magic to it, man!' said Dalton, laughing. He was a well-fed, round-faced cove, smartly dressed, with peculiarly oily skin and lively eyes. Despite the closeness in our years, he had already lost most of his hair. As he threw back his brandy I thought of him rather as an amiable egg.

'It's only a matter of knowledge rightly applied,' he went on. 'Those who make the City seem mysterious do so only because it is in their interests to do so.' He smiled in the way a parent might whilst explaining something very simple to the family dunce.

I did not mind, being filled with brandy myself. We had dined, and were now smoking our cigars in the Turkish Room of the club, a large and gloomy chamber over which Ali Pasha presided in portrait form, disapprovingly. It was not one of the best clubs, as you might surmise. Rain pattered heavily against the evening windows beside which we sat. I had been telling Dalton frankly of my irksome domestic arrangements and my worries about what I might do with myself to earn a more or less honest crust.

'Look here,' Dalton went on. 'I may be able to help you out as far as a billet goes. The business is sending me to Hong Kong at the end of this month. I'll be gone for a year at least. Why don't you park yourself in my flat?'

I declined this offer out of idiot politeness, all the while hoping he would press me to it. He did.

'No reason on earth why you shouldn't have it! I've got a ten year lease on the place and it would suit me to have it looked after in my absence.'

'That really would help me out of a jam, Dalton. But how could I possibly repay you?'

'Think nothing of it, old man!' He reached out a hand and seized another brandy from a passing servant. We continued our drinking and smoking and, rather than face Jasper's wife with the rosy cheeks of merriment, I decided to sleep at the club. As my head fell upon a cool pillow, I hoped Dalton's generosity would not evaporate with the sober dew of morning.

As things went, I needn't have worried. Dalton proved as good as his word and after seeing him off on the Hong Kong boat, I rattled his keys in my hand with a feeling of falling on my feet and made my way to his flat in Albertopolis, within sight of the Hall.

***

The apartment was on the top floor of the building, spacious and far more tastefully furnished than I would have expected from Dalton who, it seemed, was a bit of an aesthete on the sly. His bookshelves were furnished with the expected Classics, as well as a healthy dose of Swinburne and Shelley and other notorious ruffians of English letters. Even the accursed Wilde was present, which suggested to me that few of Dalton's City crowd had had the privilege of visiting him at home. There were Pre-Raphaelite prints on the walls and a French abomination over the fireplace. There was a large kitchen – I dispensed with the staff, preferring to fix for myself – and a small balcony on the main room which looked out on the Albert Hall itself. I made a note to find out if there was any music to suit my taste on the programme for the month ahead. The bedroom had a peculiar smell that I could not quite place, and while I puzzled over it, it did not prevent me sleeping like a top. I settled myself in well over that first week, eating modest meals and making the most of Dalton's wine each evening as I worked my way through Shelley before the fire, reliving my hours of idleness at Trinity.

It was during an evening of my second week in the flat that I acquired Hisser. I had gone into the kitchen to fix myself a spot of supper and found this immense black cat sitting on the counter, hissing at me. He was a savage-looking thing, one-eyed and full of obstinacy and contempt. I took an immediate liking to him. He had obviously come in the kitchen window via the fire stairs that ran down the back of the building. Perhaps he had some arrangement with Dalton that my friend had neglected to mention to me when running through the list of things-to-do in maintaining his flat. Not wanting to startle the beast, I entered the kitchen slowly, all the while talking soothingly.

'There's a good Hisser. You after some scraps, is that it?'

He regarded me as a tiger might regard Kipling's Mowgli. I fetched a few bits of cold chicken and laid them on the counter close to him then I backed away. He hissed again, a deep gassy sound. A few moments passed and then he padded slowly over to the chicken, sniffed it, and began to eat. I felt satisfied that a truce had been reached so I returned to the sitting room without closing the kitchen window, leaving Hisser to come or go as he pleased.

Twenty minutes later I was sitting on the floor – a habit I picked up through tent-living in South Africa – leaning against the couch before the fire, reading, when a silent black shadow loped slowly past me and curled up beside my feet. I petted him and felt for the first time since arriving in London that I had made a new friend.

It was through Hisser's agency that I got my first sight of the Black Dog which gives its name to the adventure I must now relate, for it was the sight of the Black Dog that led me to meet my most peculiar neighbour, who was to play such a large part in my life - Dr Henry Jerusalem Crow.

***

Some two weeks after my first encounter with Hisser, I returned to the flat on a rainy evening after a concert of Schubert's Leider. I've always thought I have rather too meaty an ear to enjoy Schubert entirely, but I refuse to give up on him. I had stopped off on my way back for a drink at the club, in hopes the rain might give way, but when after three lazy glasses it showed no sign of doing so I took a cab and found myself home and damp and in the mood for sleep. Bed was the warmest place to be, and I was out cold by midnight.

I was woken in the night by the sound of Hisser living up to his name. Rubbing my eyes, I peered around the bedroom to see if I could see him but it was impossible in the dark. I sat up and knew from the sound that he could not be in the bedroom. I resolved to give him his marching orders. I went out into the hall and saw him crouching in the most fearful condition that I have ever seen a cat: his back was arched, his ears flattened, and he was pressing himself sidelong against the rear wall of the hall and staring with horror and hatred at the front door, hissing and spitting as if his little life depended on it. My mood changed instantly and I gave the poor creature some soothing phrases, for he was in a state of real terror, but the sound of my voice seemed to do him no good at all. I looked at the front door and could see nothing amiss.

I have since learned to take better notice of what animals can sense, but on that evening, in a dozy fug, I simply walked to the front door of the flat and opened it. What a fool!

On the landing directly opposite my door, in front of my neighbour's door, there sat a huge black dog with its back to me; it was a muscular brute, panting, with steam rising from him as if he had been running in the rain. He sat just a foot or so before the door, staring at it, and he made not the slightest motion at the sound of my own door opening. From deep in his throat, however, there came a growl directed not at me but at my neighbour's door. I tried to fathom where the dog had come from. In all my time in the flat I had seen neither my neighbour nor any dog. I could not therefore be sure the dog belonged to the neighbour. If it did, why was the thing sitting on the landing in the middle of the night?

'No one home, boy?' I ventured feebly. The black dog remained motionless in his hostile vigil. After a moment, I stepped onto the landing. That seemed to break his spell. He stood up, coughed, and slowly turned his black bulk to face me. If I had hackles like Hisser, they would certainly have risen! The black dog looked at me with an expression of pure malevolence that I find difficult to describe, but it filled me with such horror, such dread that instantly I stepped back across my threshold and slammed fast the door.

I did not like the way the dog had looked at me, it is true. And that bare statement chills me even as I write it now – for the black dog had no eyes!

***

I did not sleep again that night. I sat for some time in the kitchen with a cup of tea steaming toward cold on the table in front of me. I had opened the kitchen window and Hisser had made his terrified escape. Such had been his fear I doubted whether I might see him again. For myself, I was filled with the most intense dread, and I had a covering of cold sweat such as I had only known before in the aftermath of battle. I simply could not bring myself to go into the hall again, still less to contemplate opening the front door, not while the possibility of facing that monstrous hound remained! In some deep part of my brain, I think, some atavistic warning had sounded and calculated that it would not be safe to open the door during the hours of darkness. And so I sat in perfect fear and stillness in my cold kitchen to await a creeping dawn.

The knock on my door made me start. I glanced at the window and saw light just gaining over darkness. Hours must have passed without my knowing. Who could be knocking so early? I wondered. I cannot tell you what an effort of will it took to pull myself up out of that chair and into the hall, but I managed it. Even this small action of will cleared my head somewhat. I crept toward the door soundlessly. I could hear nothing on the other side for some moments, and then again there came three determined knocks.

'Who is it?' I called.

'Your good neighbour,' was the odd reply. It was a deep, manly voice. I felt somewhat reassured. If the dog was there, its master had it under control; if the dog was gone, so much the better.

I opened the door.

'Dr Henry Jerusalem Crow,' said my neighbour.

I introduced myself. I was struck immediately by what an odd sight we must have been. I was in my dressing gown, having watched the night through for reasons I could not entirely fathom, and here was my neighbour who, despite the early hour, was dressed for dinner. He was tall, lithe, with a narrow face and gleaming green eyes. His hair was shaved very close. He stood with his hands behind his back.

'You have seen the black dog,' said Dr Crow.

'I have. He was outside your door in the night. It was the hissing of my cat that woke me.'

'O Noble feline! The dog was seeking me, so I must apologise. I would not have you disturbed.'

'Is it your dog?' I asked. The question seemed to amuse Dr Crow for he smiled thinly.

'Not in the accepted sense.' My look of confusion made his smile broader. 'You shall not be bothered again. I must make amends. Will you break your fast with me at Delmont's?'

Delmont's was a small hotel on the other side of the park. I had no idea what sort of breakfast they might whip up for a chap but trusted Dr Crow to know since he had lived here longer than I. So I accepted his invitation partly out of hunger, partly out of curiosity, but mainly out of an overwhelming desire to get out and away from the flat. The black dog was gone but still I felt oddly oppressed and heavy. I needed light and air.

Dr Crow returned to his flat while I dressed, and soon we were on the way to Delmont's. We spoke only of commonplace things. It was a bright morning and the air was fresh after the rain of the night before. I breathed hearty lungsful of the cold stuff to revive my sleepless brain. I told Dr Crow of my acquaintance with Dalton and his favour to me, while Dr Crow for his part remarked on the convenience of the location for his practice. When we arrived at Delmont's we were shown to a table without a word. A whiff of the kitchens had stiffened up my belly; any soldier will tell you that hunger can conquer fear, and all thoughts of the black dog were dissolved by a craving for food. Dr Crow had scrambled eggs and coffee, which he sweetened with honey, whilst I had coffee and rashers of bacon with buttered toast. They did me the world of good and I began to return to myself as we talked.

'Tell me, have you heard of the Tulpa?' asked Dr Crow suddenly. I owned that I had not. 'The Tulpa,' he explained, 'is what one might call a thought-form. Conjured by the great sages of Tibet, it is a willed apparition which they may send forth to carry out some task or by which they may appear many miles from their physical bodies.'

All very fascinating, to be sure, but not the sort of thing one usually discusses over scrambled eggs with a perfect stranger! You must not imagine that I had a mind closed to the mysterious elements of life. I have little patience with every species of crankery and quackery, certainly, but in South Africa I had seen many queer things among the natives and their witch-doctors, not all of which my trained mind could explain. Something in the Doctor's manner therefore, some atmosphere of quiet authority, compelled me to listen attentively. He expounded a little more on the mysterious practices of the Tibetans, of which he seemed to speak with real knowledge.

Eventually he said, 'Do you see how this relates to the black dog?'

'I think you mean to tell me that the black dog was a Tulpa of the sort you describe.'

'Quite so,' said the Doctor. 'It has proved to be quite a nuisance. This evening I mean to put an end to the unfortunate creature for good. I wonder if you might care to observe the procedure.'

A cheerful stomach had made me forget my terror of the night before, though I confess I was not eager to see that eyeless fiend again. Yet I was intrigued – who would not be? What possible procedure could be used to banish this allegedly phantasmal hound? Why did the creature appear to persecute my neighbour? What sort of man was my neighbour that he should speak so casually and confidently of such strange things?

'I'm sure I would find it very interesting,' I answered. 'But tell me, Doctor, why should you want to involve me, a stranger, in this odd business?'

At this he smiled. 'I have two reasons. First, you saw the black dog. This suggests a degree of sensitivity on your part, of which you may not have been aware until now. Second, I should like you to meet Isabella. She is a friend whom I think may interest you.'

This satisfied me and so I agreed. A time and place was fixed for the procedure – a house off Southampton Row at 8pm that same evening. I finished off my bacon and followed the Doctor's example by having coffee with honey.

'Can you tell me anything of what to expect?' I asked. 'How will you get rid of such a fearsome beast?'

Doctor Crow smiled. 'With Love,' he said.

***

As I strolled along Southampton Row that evening, I could not help but wonder what lay ahead. Was I the dupe of some confidence trickster whom the trickster Fate had provided me for a neighbour? Did the strange Doctor Crow and the woman he was eager for me to meet – a beautiful temptress, no doubt – intend to rinse me for my tin with promises of spiritual guidance? Even as I considered the possibility, it amused me to note that I had not the least inclination to turn back. Though I had wit enough to see through any sham – so I thought – there was in truth a single, simple reason why I felt compelled to keep my appointment with the occult. I was growing thoroughly bored with my life as a solitary idler in London. Since Dalton's departure, I knew no-one and did nothing - beyond read and go to concerts. There is only so much culture a fellow can take, and I longed for something that would get my blood up in the old way. It is not exactly fun to be pinned down with one's comrades by a Boer kommando who has the high ground, but by God it gets the heart pumping! I was ready for an adventure.

Following our breakfast Dr Crow had given me written directions to the house in which we were to meet again, and we had then gone our separate ways. I returned to my flat and found the oppressive atmosphere had lifted entirely, and I was pleased to catch a glimpse of Hisser from the back windows of the kitchen, prowling across the rooftops. I spent the afternoon getting in some supplies and then went to a Turkish bath that Dr Crow had recommended, where I was scalded and steamed into a pleasant stupor.

As the sun began to set, I made for the appointed place. It was not far, and I soon found myself by a narrow alleyway between two buildings. In the capstone of the arch above was engraved a scorpion, the sign for which I had been looking. I went down the alley, turned a corner, then another, and spent a few minutes wandering in a veritable labyrinth of odd, constrained turnings, my clicking heels echoing off the bricks, until eventually I emerged in the moonlit square of Beak Court. The house I sought stood before me, with a single window lit.

I rang and was admitted by a fellow I took to be a servant, a short, stocky sort with a flat nose and an iron jaw who reminded me of certain brawlers I had known. I decided that, if it should come to it, I was capable of giving him a thrashing. He spoke not a word. He took my coat and guided me to a room just off the hall.

Dr Crow rose to greet me as I entered.

'My dear fellow, welcome!' We shook hands. The doctor then introduced me to his companion, who was not at all what I had expected. 'Allow me to present Miss Isabella Woolfinder, my most trusted colleague. I have told her all about you.'

The lady was as tall as the doctor himself, wore a shimmering dress of emerald green, had a round unpainted face and a mad profusion of dark curling hair that looked as though it had never been tended by human hands. Though her face was eerily pale, I thought there was something of the gypsy about her. I took her hand – the moment I felt her clammy fingers in mine any thought of kissing that hand vanished – and presented myself. I was more than a little deflated. This was not the seductive acolyte of my imagination. Neither was the room in which we stood particularly impressive, simply an ordinary drawing room of Morris furniture with no hint of the exotic. The mantel was bare save for a ticking clock and a small bust of our late Sovereign. Indeed, the whole atmosphere of the place seemed rather Spartan. If I had walked into a trap, it was a trap whose showmanship left much to be desired.

'I am delighted that you could join us this evening for our session,' said Miss Woolfinder.

'Does he please you, Isabella?' said Doctor Crow.

'Very much,' replied the lady, with a glance at my neighbour. She smiled thinly at me and invited me to be seated. I took my place in a chair by the fire and the Doctor sat opposite me. Miss Woolfinder remained standing, motionless as a shop mannequin. For several moments there was silence.

'Shall we proceed?' asked Dr Crow suddenly. I nodded, smiling to hide my bewilderment. Miss Woolfinder moved quietly to a corner of the room and returned with a small table which she placed between Dr Crow and myself. She then took what looked like a ledger from a desk across the room and stood beside the Doctor. From the book she took a piece of paper some five inches in diameter, cut into a circle, and placed it on the table. She then returned to the spot where she had greeted me and resumed her attitude.

I observed all this in silence but as Doctor Crow reached for the circle of paper, he smiled genially at me and said, 'In order to banish the Black Dog we must first summon it with this pentacle. The procedure is quite simple, but the effect may cause you some anxiety – not unlike that which you felt last night. It is important that you keep a rein on your feelings.'

'I feel sure I can,' I replied. 'Please proceed.'

'We have already begun,' said Miss Woolfinder. 'Do you notice anything unusual?'

I neither saw nor heard anything which would be out of place in such a room as this. I shook my head. My gaze returned to the Doctor and I saw that he was drawing strange symbols upon the circle of paper before him.

'Perception of the unseen is rare and yet you saw the Black Dog,' said Doctor Crow. 'You told me of your spider-bite in South Africa and of the hallucinations which afflicted you. But not all hallucinations are the fictions of a deranged brain. Sometimes they are glimpses of the world within the world. Sometimes a drug – or a toxin – can open the doors of perception. Sometimes, the doors stay open.'

'The smell,' I said, and I looked around the room.

Miss Woolfinder smiled.

I had begun to perceive a strange odour, not unlike the odour I had sensed in Dalton's bedroom when I first moved in. A feeling of heat crept over me, passing as suddenly as it had come, but the smell remained in the air. I could not identify it exactly but it called to mind the scent of wet earth and flowers after rain. Yet there was no sense of refreshment in it. I found instead my heart had begun to beat faster and my body began to tense in expectation of danger. In accord with the Doctor's advice, I took hold of my feelings and tried to observe coolly.

Doctor Crow handed the circle of paper with its occult symbols to Miss Woolfinder. She went to the door of the room – which was closed – and placed the pentacle on the floor.

'Will the Black Dog come?' I asked as Miss Woolfinder returned to stand beside the fireplace.

'He has already,' said the lady. She began slowly to turn down the gas, and as the lamps dimmed I looked across at the pentacle. There seemed to be a misty shadow in front of the door yet no object was present which could have cast it.

And then I heard the growl.

This was no trick: as I watched, the dark shadow became a substantial thing and I would have testified under oath that I looked now upon a flesh-and-blood creature. It was indeed the same black brute that had looked on me with hellish malice the night before, now sitting upon the pentacle and growling as no earthly hound could. Once again, I felt that same dread sweep through me as the creature turned its head upwards to regard us with its sightless face.

Doctor Crow stood and I followed his example, while Miss Woolfinder moved back to join us at the fireplace so that we all three stood gazing at the thing that sat before us. Dr Crow smiled at me then stepped forward, and as I watched he went down on one knee before the panting hound.

'He is fixed by the pentacle,' he said to me, beckoning me forward. I hesitated and then moved closer, all the time not taking my eyes off the slavering jaws of the monstrosity. My heart skipped and I perspired freely, a prickly heat passing all over me. I knelt by the Doctor, my eyes wide, and he touched my arm. 'Do as I do,' he said.

He put his right hand forward and touched the chest of the dog, and the tips of his fingers vanished in the inky blackness! I wished at that moment that I might have a glass of liquid courage but I knew that moment had passed. Terror seized my belly and I had to force myself to breathe, the fear rising in me again despite my best efforts. I took a deep breath and reached slowly forward to touch the dog – but where I should have found fur and hot flesh, I found my hand passing instead into black nothingness and I hissed as my fingers were shocked by icy, stinging cold, as though I had plunged them into the water of a running stream. The freezing sensation flashed up my arm and I drew my hand back sharply.

'My God,' I exclaimed, 'It's real!' I turned to Doctor Crow with astonishment upon my face.

Doctor Crow only smiled mildly, and I felt strangely that I had passed some test, for he looked at me then as if I was the right sort. He turned his attention back to the dog.

'Now then, Dalton, we must send you on your way.'

You may easily imagine my surprise at his use of that name.

The Doctor leant forward and, reaching through the very substance of the panting creature, lifted up the paper pentacle upon which it was sitting. As he did so he said some words in a language I did not know, and the dog whined quietly. The Doctor folded the paper seven times, placed it in his mouth, and swallowed it. Then, with a kindly look upon his face, he reached forward and embraced the dog, which nuzzled into him with affection. All my fear vanished in that moment too.

As I watched, the black dog seemed somehow to resume its shadowy form and now, like smoke, began to envelop the Doctor while the serene expression on his face remained unchanging. The smoke seemed to pass into the Doctor, fading in his embrace until nothing remained.

There was silence.

This whole procedure had taken just a few minutes. Doctor Crow rose to his feet, as did I, and when I turned I saw that Miss Woolfinder held a silver tray on which there were two large brandies. I downed mine swiftly and urged my heart to slow its frantic pace. Doctor Crow nursed his for several minutes as he explained what I had just seen.

'Your friend Dalton is a tidy fellow in most things and meticulous about money – but when it comes to spiritual development he can be slovenly, a distressingly commonplace fault. People simply will not take the pains to tidy away their demons after playing with them!'

'Demons?' I was incredulous.

'I do not use the word in any Christian sense. It does not connote evil. You must abandon such ideas.'

I gladly accepted another brandy from Miss Woolfinder, who now sat down upon her couch with a drink of her own, a green thing.

'I say, do you mean to tell me Dalton – old Duffer Dalton – meddles in this sort of thing?'

'He is one of my students,' answered Doctor Crow. 'In recent months we have been trying to balance certain aspects of your friend's psyche in preparation for the next stage of his instruction. The dog – the Tulpa – was a leftover from this process. People often give personalities or characters to their own fears, and usually such avatars appear in dreams or nightmares as repeating images. In my particular branch of science the exteriorisation of such image-phenomena is possible – though not encouraged, for reasons you have observed. The poor thing was simply trying to find its way back where it came from – but Dalton has carried his carcass to the East and so the dog sought me out as the next best thing. Fortunate for you that it did: had the Tulpa resolved itself into you in error, you would have become prey to the fears that once beset Dalton.'

Doctor Crow crossed his legs and sighed heavily.

'The mind is a very strange thing,' he said (in years to come, I would reflect upon this statement often and always when I did so, in my mind I would see Doctor Crow sitting upon the couch of Miss Woolfinder's house, his eyes turned upward in dreamy consideration of his own words.)

I tried to resolve the image of jovial Dalton, the hail-fellow-well-met man of the City, the clubbable egg, with the image that the Doctor was painting of a spiritual seeker and summoner of spectres. Dalton's heretical bookshelves began now to seem less strange to me.

'Doctor Crow, this is a damned queer business!' I said. 'I can hardly believe what I've seen and felt this evening. To think that Dalton...'

'It was Dalton who recommended you for the post,' said Miss Woolfinder.

'Post?'

'I require a secretary,' said Dr Crow. 'I know that's not your usual line, but I know too that the life of an idler doesn't suit you at all. I pay well and I can assure you that the work will be interesting and varied, as you have seen. Don't you wish to get back in harness?'

He smiled as if he knew my answer already. Miss Woolfinder raised her glass. 'A toast to your new venture,' she said, regarding me with a smile of such warmth that I could only smile in return and raise my own glass. I nodded at Doctor Crow.

Thus it was that, in a state of uncanny bewilderment, I entered employment with the most peculiar man in London and, though I could not know it then, my future wife.

the OCCULT LEGION

BIGGERS FREEMAN GAFFORD MEIKLE MOORE REYNOLDS RUTLEDGE

THE OCCULT LEGION is a multi-chapter serial story written by some of the best writers of Occult Detective fiction today. ODQ is proud to serialize this landmark tale beginning with this first installment:

CHAPTER ONE: THE NEST

William Meikle

Alexander Seton wasn't much of a sailor.

But then again, this isn't much of a boat.

He pulled his deerskin cloak as tight as he could around his body, and tried to shield his legs with the leather roll-bag that contained everything he hoped he wouldn't need. It didn't help much.

"It'll only tak wan or twa hours," the old ferryman had said when Seton had been forced to take to the water for the rest of the journey south. "I'll have you there afore it gets daurk."

Now Seton was being tossed like a mouse in a box, at the whim of wind and tide, in a trip that had so far taken three hours and showed no sign of ending. And it was most definitely dark.

Cold water lapped over the bows in the rough seas and soaked into his boots, his leggings and his kilt, and all he could think about was his warm room back in Stirling. He had hoped to spend this late summer and autumn getting some heat into his bones to store up for the coming winter, but his masters were having none of it.

Seton's wellbeing was never to the forefront of His Majesty's mind, and it had been further away than usual back in the monarch's draughty chambers in Stirling Castle.

"I need you to go down to the new castle," the King said. "The master mason has stopped work, and if my queen does not have her castle by the summer after next, she will not be happy. I do not think anyone wants that."

"Do what you do best, Seton. Fix it for me, and I will fill your purse with silver."

James hadn't said it, but Seton heard the word.

Again.

A purse full of silver was all well and good, but he'd had one of those back last winter; fine while it lasted, but ale and wenches were not as cheap as they used to be, and the pursuit of oblivion was a serious business, worthy of gold at least.

But beggars cannot be choosers.

After being given his orders he'd woken the old horse from its slumber in the stable behind the inn and ridden South in the rain, until his arse was raw and his belly was empty. That only got him as far as Glasgow, where the poor beast almost took a turn under him when a hoof went down a rabbit hole. He stabled the lame steed in Gourock, at a cost that would make the King's treasurer's eyes water when time came to settle up. Now here he was, lost in the Firth in a howling gale with a mad ferryman who insisted on singing at the top of his voice the whole way.

Only two things made the trip in any way tolerable; Seton couldn't understand a single word of the old man's songs... and his dreams were quiet and had been now for several months. Any respite from his fate was always welcome.

Mayhap the bill is paid?

But he knew better than that. The price for his gift had been his soul, and Seton knew he still had that.

No one could feel this much guilt and still be soulless.

The gift was a debt that would never be repaid; a deal made with a wee man in a cavern that had cost good men their lives, and given Seton power, after a fashion. Now his soul was in hock to that same wee man, and the only way Seton knew to stave off the inevitable was to fight it with all he had in him. Sometimes the fight weighed heavy on his heart and then the ale helped. But no amount of ale was ever enough. *Service* had become his crutch—service to his King, and a cycle of sorcery, debt, ale and more sorcery. It wasn't much of a life.

But it beats the alternative.

The ferryman brought the boat to shore just as the wind finally abated and the cloud washed away under a full moon, giving him a first clear sight of his destination some half a mile inland. He could see why the Queen wanted the spot; the fells of Arran looked silver and black and gray and magical across the water. The castle itself was going to be at the foot of rolling hills and babbling brooks, sheltered in winter and standing proud at a gateway to the fertile farmlands of the interior. It wasn't just a beautiful spot—it was strategically significant, and Seton knew the Queen well enough to realize it was no accident.

But for there to be a castle in the first place, there had to be foundations, and this one was struggling to raise itself that first vital step. He paid the ferryman—another expense against the royal coffers—and had a long look at the site as he walked firstly along the rickety jetty, then up the slope to the castle mound itself.

John Douglas, master mason, was waiting for him, standing along amid a pile of worked stone and earth. If he had a team with him, there was no sign of them.

"You will be the King's man, then?" the man said, then, as he put out a hand to be shook, looked straight into Seton's eyes. "Have we met?"

They had indeed, but Seton couldn't admit to it—it had been nearly forty years past, at the rebuilding of Arbroath Abbey—and while the master mason had gained a long beard and a stoop, Seton himself had not aged a day.

"I do not think so," he replied cagily. "Although I have been told I take after my grandfather in the face."

The old man's gaze never left Seton's eyes.

"Aye. That will be it. He was a queer cove too, if I have the right man. Well, you had better come and see what has caused the stooshie. If I ken the King's mind, he'll want this sorted fast."

The old mason led Seton to the main diggings—a large square hole in the ground some fifteen feet deep that they had already started to shore up with a perimeter underpinning.

"We needed to go almost half as deep as we want to go high," the old man said. "The ground is damp and heavy and it was hard going. Then, just as I was thinking that we had broken the back of the task and could get some height built up before winter, we found it."

"Found what?"

"The thing your king has sent you to see," Douglas replied. "It is doon here."

They went down a sturdy wooden ladder to the bottom of the workings. Seton immediately felt even colder, all too aware of his recent soaking that had not yet had a chance to dry. The moonlight scarcely penetrated down here, and dark shadows flitted and capered, demons among the black. Seton's roll bag swung alarmingly, threatening to topple him backward off the ladder, but he could not leave it up top—every one of his senses was telling him that the King had been right—whatever was here, Seton was the only one who might stop it.

But I have to understand it first.

The old mason led them through a mire of sucking mud to where the diggings slumped alarmingly into a deeper hole, pitch black in the dark depths of the foundations.

"It is down there," Douglas said, and spat into the hole. "I dinnae right ken what it is, but there is not a man will work here. So if you are the King's man, here is what you have been sent for. Good luck."

With a look that spoke of relief to be away from the spot, the mason left Seton there in the dark.

Seton heard him climb the ladder, setting the old wood creaking, then all went silent.

He was left alone, with the dark, the hole, and whatever it was that sat in the bottom of it.

***

Seton felt cold, wet and tired—but there was a new thing to see here, he could feel it. And that simple fact was more than enough to ensure his attention. There was indeed a power in this spot—it spoke to the part of Seton that came from the same place, the dark speaking to the dark, a conversation he barely understood, but was all too aware of its happening.

He unrolled the long leather bag on the ground at his feet and fetched out a candle lantern and tinderbox. It took him three tries to get a spark but finally he had the lantern lit and could survey the scene properly.

At first it looked like no more than a deep muddy hole, but as he approached the edge he saw that the very bottom had collapsed inward, a darker hole, opening out into some kind of cavern below. He rolled up his bag and took it with him as he went down the muddy sides, more sliding than climbing, finishing up somewhat precariously above a three-foot wide entry that went down into complete blackness. The darkness in his mind came from there, whispering and entreating his to come closer.

"There is no need for that," Seton whispered back. "I am coming."

He lowered himself down gingerly until he sat on the edge of the hole. The light of the lantern showed him a floor some four feet below so, trusting to luck, he let himself drop down, and had a bad moment when his left foot slipped under him on landing, nearly sending him tumbling. The sound he made on trying to recover his footing caused an echo to ring around him, one that immediately rose in tenor and timbre.

It began with a reverberating vibration that shook the ground beneath him, as if a giant might be attempting an awakening from a buried sleep. Seton again tried to stand but the shaking was so violent that he immediately fell back to lie on the ground. The vibrations soon shook him to his very core, threatening to loosen flesh from bones. Darkness seeped in at the edge of his sight.

In less time than it took to draw a breath he was completely blinded, groping in the darkness. The ground rose and fell around him as if something huge attempted to rise up from below.

But that was not the worst of it. He was in blackness. But he was not alone.

A drumbeat had started and he felt it just as much in the pit of his stomach as he heard it in his ears—a giant drum, distantly far, but getting closer every second, beating as fast as his terrorized heart. Something moved in the dark, something huge. He was lost in a world of fear, like a child in a dark room when he senses movement under his bed. The blackness surged, washing over him in waves. Seton wished he were dead so that he might be free of this. He was utterly lost, utterly alone.

And just as he thought he could take no more, something in the blackness reached for him.

His own darkness, the thing inside, answered back, and it was only then that the great drum faltered, and finally failed, the interloper drawing away as it met something it recognized.

Seton's eyesight returned. Slowly, the dim glow of his lantern leading him back to what passed for normality. The chamber fell deadly quiet once again. He sensed that he was being watched—tested—but put that away, trusting to his strength as he stood and managed for the first time to have a look around. Any inconvenience was immediately forgotten when he saw where he had ended up.

***

He had dropped down into a longbarrow, the mason having had the great misfortune to be building atop an earlier—much earlier—structure. The walls were built of large blocks of sandstone, beautifully engineered and dovetailed together so tight that you could scarce slip a layer of silk between them. Seton had visited several of these old tombs, in Carnac in France, on Orkney and on the great moors in the South of England. This one gave the same sense of age, of a time long past.

What was completely different here was the overwhelming feeling that this place was in use.

The initial chamber where he had landed was some ten feet long, and half as wide. Small passages led off on either side leading to sub-chambers, all of which were dry, but empty. The ground descended at the far end of the chamber, leading Seton down an incline and into a larger room beyond.

It was a rough-hewn chamber of some antiquity, and unlike the smaller chambers near the entrance, this one was far from empty, The walls were covered in small carvings. At first Seton thought it might be a language, but it was none that he recognized from his studies, indeed, it seemed to bear no resemblance to anything he had ever seen before. Whoever had drawn the figures had packed them tightly, a miniature army ranked side by side in tightly regimented formation. Some had all four limbs, some were missing an arm or a leg, and some were just a single streak with a dot for the head. It did not take Seton long to realize that he was not actually looking at crude representations of men at all—it was a code—perhaps even a language, albeit one with which he was completely unfamiliar.

All the time he had been in the mound he was aware that the vibrations underfoot continued apace. As yet there was no sign of any drumming or anything that might suggest a return to the full shaking terrors. But thinking of drumming brought an idea.
What if it is not language or code at all—what if it is simply instructions?

If a single line of the figure was a single beat, then Seton surmised that the other figures might also signify beats, or multiple drum strikes. He took his dirk out of his boot and, using the hilt, started tapping on the walls.

Left arm gone, right leg gone, all limbs intact, no head, legs gone, no arms, limbs intact, left leg and left arm gone.

After the first group of eight, Seton felt a responding vibration on the floor. And as he followed the tracks on the wall and associated beats, he started to spot something else—there was a repeating pattern amid the scrawls, and by a process of trial and elimination he was able to determine the associated beats.

No limbs, no limbs, no head, no head, left arm gone, left leg gone, no legs, no head.

He rapped the beats on the rock.

"Two beats, two, four, four, five, seven, three, four."

Something beneath pounded back in time. Then came the first indication that there was more to this than mere spectral drumming. A tear in space appeared in the center of the chamber, blacker still than any shadow. It floated at Seton' eye level and span slowly in a clockwise direction. As he watched it changed shape, settling into a new configuration, a black, somewhat oily in appearance droplet little more than an inch across at the thickest point. It seemed to be held in mid-air by some strange force.

And it looked most like an egg.

As Seton stepped forward a rainbow aura thickened around it, casting the whole chamber in dancing washes of soft colors as it continued to spin.

The dirk hummed, hot in Seton's hand as he moved closer. The egg quivered and pulsed. And now it seemed larger than before. The chamber started to throb, like a heartbeat. The egg pulsed in time. And now it was more than obvious—it was most definitely growing. The dirk sent a new flash of heat, like a searing burn in his palm as he lifted the weapon, but before he could strike the egg the throb became a rapid thumping; the chamber shook and trembled. The vibration rattled his teeth and set his guts roiling. A blinding flare of blue blasted all coherent thought from his head.

When he recovered enough to look back there was nothing to be seen hanging there but empty space. The black egg was gone as quickly as it had come and the chamber was once again dark and quiet.

***

Seton realized that to proceed any further at that juncture would be most injudicious—he had learned enough to know that he would be in peril if he did not take care. He made his way out of the main chamber, and, not without some difficulty, climbed up and out into the muddy foundations. The old mason was up above at the tip of the ladder, and seemed surprised to see him.

"I thought it had swallowed you up," he said. "And after all that drumming, I was sure we had seen the last of you."

"You heard it?" Seton asked as he hauled himself up the ladder to stand beside the man.

"Aye. It is all I have been hearing for a week now. Come on down to the bothy and we'll get you warm—I'll tell you the tale over a wee *uisque* or twa."

"I cannot guarantee I will stay awake," Seton replied, realizing that he was suddenly dog tired.

"And I cannot guarantee that your sleep will

be dreamless," the old man replied. "But the *uisque* will help. Trust me on that much, at least."

As it turned out, the old man did not have much to tell that Seton could not have surmised for himself—they had started in on the foundations, the ground had caved in to reveal the chamber, and the drumming had started up at nights. Douglas' men—five of them—had fled to the nearest tavern and were refusing to come out until something was done—which brought them back to the reason that Seton was here.

"Can you banish this bogle?" the old man asked.

By that stage the *uisque* was having the desired effect and Seton was starting to drift.

"It is not a bogle," he started to say, but then the exertions of the day finally caught up with him and he fell down into a black sleep.

***

If Seton dreamed, he did not remember it in the morning, although he did not feel as rested as he might have hoped. He broke his fast with a bowl of thin gruel and some stale bread, then turned his attentions back to the chamber under the foundations.

His encounter of the night before had merely confirmed an idea that had been forming. His foe here was not a bogle or a haunt—this was something older and more fey than either, an ancient thing, lying in this ground long before men came—perhaps even from before the formation of the rock itself. The chamber, like others he had visited, was both a shrine, and a cage, of sorts. No doubt the chamber had seen many grim mummeries—initiations, sacrifices, and hermits, a small army of seekers after truth—and now Seton himself, who had already found one kind of truth and was in no hurry to find any more.

The carvings denoting the rhythm—and the fact that they had actually worked and summoned something—also told him that he was not the first to delve into these secrets. And he might not be the last if he did not carry out his appointed task with every ounce of his strength and intellect.

He went back down into the chamber armed only with dirk, lantern, and what he carried inside him.

I can only hope it will be enough.

***

Weak sunlight filtered a little way down into the chambers below, but the larger, deepest cavern containing the carvings was almost in total darkness, and the lantern did little to dispel the feeling that something yet lurked in the shadows watching, waiting.

Seton rapped on the rock with the dirk.

No limbs, no limbs, no head, no head, left arm gone, left leg gone, no legs, no head.

As if it had been waiting for just this circumstance, the dark tear in space formed immediately in the center of the cavern.

Two shimmering black eggs now hung in the air side by side, just touching, each as black as the other, twin bubbles held in check by dancing rainbow colors. The whole chamber throbbed like a heartbeat. The eggs pulsed in synchronized agreement and calved.

Four eggs hung in a tight group, all now pulsing in time with the throb. Colors danced and flowed across the sheer black surface; blues and greens and shimmering silvers that filled the chamber with washes of color. The heartbeat got louder. Soon there were eight, then sixteen.

Seton started to back away, back toward the chamber above and escape.

Thirty-two now, and the chamber filled with dancing aurora of shimmering light that pulsed in time with the heartbeat as the eggs calved again, and again, everything careening along in a big happy dance.

Seton stepped forward. The dirk screamed as he aimed a blow at the growing mass of eggs. He felt the strike all the way through his upper body, as if he'd just hit a wall. The rainbow aura seemed to breathe in, breathe out, twice. There was a sudden burst of color; red, blue and shimmering silver filled his head with a glare brighter than the brightest sun.

Then, suddenly, he was elsewhere, elsewhen, a century and more before—in a chamber under Stirling Castle—in a room full of bubbling pots and burning coals, a room of chants and incantations and the end of an old life—the beginning of a new. He felt the darkness flow in and through him once again, felt it take root in every fiber of his being, felt the insidious whispering in his head that he had heard every day since. He heard again his Magister call out the old words, attempting to retract something that would not be retracted, something that was already taking root.

And this time there was something else with him—something new—something that beat in a peculiar rhythm.

No limbs, no limbs, no head, no head, left arm gone, left leg gone, no legs, no head.

The drum went still, Seton blinked—and was back in the chamber under the foundations of Law Castle.

He looked around. The eggs were gone again, as quickly as they had come—there was only the empty chamber. But he knew more now.

We are made of the same stuff.

He had finally recognized the cluster of black eggs—had a name for the phenomenon, one as old as mankind itself. People have long searched for a way through to the other side—whatever their idea of that other side might be. It seemed only logical that over the course of those long millennia, from primitive tribesmen, through great civilizations and all the way up to Seton's day, that some had succeeded, in some small part. The gates are there for any that want to look hard enough. And just as he recognized the gate, he also recognized the configuration of hanging eggs from a tome he'd read back in Stirling; an etching of something the Persians had discovered nearly three thousand years before. They had called it *Darbān* but it has had many names in many places—Seton knew it as *The Opener of the Way*.

His family had already spent several lifetimes looking for something like this. And now, in this remote corner of a Scottish field, Seton had found it, and opened it, just a fraction.

Now it had to be closed; otherwise The Outer Darkness would quickly surge through and engulf this site, these fields—the whole country, given the chance.

***

He felt as old as the surrounding hills as he dragged himself out of the chamber again and up into the light, although on this occasion he was quickly revived by more of the old mason's *uisque*.

"Did you see the bogle?" the old man asked.

"Yon black hair and red eyes—if nearly had me running, I can tell you that."

It took some coaxing, and more *uisque* but Seton got the rest of the man's tale—what little there was of it—a story of a night time encounter with a large hairy thing, more bear than man. He also found that the rest of the workmen had all seen something—indeed, they had all seen something different—one had seen an old crone, another his own dead sister, back to claim a kiss. They had each encountered that which they most feared—which gave Seton cause to remember his own vision, of that long ago day in the alchemist's chambers, and the fear in his Magister's voice as he called out the old words.

Fear is the key—and mayhap also the lock.

Given this latest insight there was nothing else for it. He put a fresh candle in his lantern, gripped his dirk hard, and went back down into the chamber.

Third time's a charm.

***

Now that he had an inkling of what he was dealing with, he moved more purposefully, heading straight for the lowermost chamber.

This time he did not even have to rap out the beat with his dirk—whatever was there had been waiting for his return. A black tear opened in the air above the center of the chamber, accompanied by what sounded like the ripping of paper. A singe black egg, no bigger than a thumb, hung there.

The egg quivered, a rainbow aura danced over it, and ever so slowly it became two, oily sheen running over their sleek black surfaces. They hummed to themselves, a high singing that was taken up and amplified by an answering whine from the surrounding rock itself.

As two eggs became four, the whole chamber rocked from side to side in rhythm.

The dance had begun again.

***

Seton heard a rustle to his left, and turned, expecting an attack. The old mason, Douglas, stood there, wide eyes, his knuckles showing white where he gripped a dirk of his own.

"I cannae let you stand alone, laddie," he said.

"This is my castle now, and it is best that this thing kens it."

Eight black eggs hung impossibly in the air between the two men, oily and glistening, thrumming in time with the vibration from the walls that was getting ever louder, ever more insistent. Seton had to resist a sudden urge to start clapping in time to the beat.

Thick fog glowed in an aurora of rainbow color and swirled angrily in the darkened chamber.

Eight eggs became sixteen, and thirty-two seconds later, clustered in a tight ball that spun lazily in the air. The walls of rock were changing too—the stone had become noticeably thinner, almost translucent and swirling rainbow fog clearly moved through them. The walls thinned further, almost ghostly now, then vanished completely until there was only the dark and the darker eggs hanging in it—sixty-four now, and singing louder.

The dirt on the ground underfoot started to tremble and shake, then, as if taken by a wind, rose in a tight funnel spiraling up toward the hanging eggs, faster and faster still. The eggs sucked up the material and sang louder, as if requesting more.

Seton felt them suck at him too, and had the old mason not been there he might have been taken—and gone almost willingly—to whatever was on the other side.

There were too many eggs to count now—into the hundreds. They almost filled the space in the chamber, their song rising higher, the beat and thrum of the rhythm filling Seton's head, and the dancing rainbow colors filling his eyes with blue and green and gold and wonderment.

His whole body shook, vibrating with the rhythm. His head swam, and it seemed as if everything melted and ran. The scene receded into a great distance until it was little more than a pinpoint in a blanket of darkness, and he was alone, in a cathedral of emptiness where nothing existed save the dark and the pounding.

And then there was light.

He saw stars—vast swathes of gold and blue and silver, all dancing in great purple and red clouds that spun webs of grandeur across unending vistas. Shapes moved in and among the nebulae; dark, wispy shadows casting a pallor over everything they covered—shadows that capered and whirled as the dance grew ever more frenetic. Seton felt buffeted, as if by a strong, surging tide, but as the beat grew ever stronger he cared little. He gave himself to it, lost in the dance, lost in the stars.

He did not know how long he wandered in the space between. He forgot myself, forgot the King's business, forgot the old mason, dancing in the vastness where only rhythm mattered.

He may never have returned had the old man not brought him back.

Douglas had Seton gripped by the shoulders and was screaming into his face.

"Fight it, laddie. Help me. I will no' let a bloody bogle have my castle."

It was that simple request to his humanity that brought Seton back—back from a place where humankind was as insignificant as one of those motes of dancing dust. But when Seton managed to focus on the old man, he could see that the mason was now as far gone from humanity as the stars among which he had been dancing. The mason's head looked misshapen and deformed, as if his brain had grown too large for his skull and was threatening to expunge itself. His hands had taken on a peculiar rough aspect, as had his feet. The left one in particular bothered Seton—it had thickened and hardened into black cuticle. It looked like it wanted to become a claw. What is more, thick wiry hair ran, not just over the old man's face but up and down both his arms.

"It is taking me. I dinna have much time, laddie," Douglas said—even his voice was going, barely more than a throaty gurgle. 'We can finish this—I think. It calls to me, and I must go to it. But when I do, when the way is opened—then you shall have your chance. Watch closely—and take it. Do not falter or flinch—it might be the only chance we have."

He pointed at Seton's dirk.

"And dinna be slow to use that if you need to. Ye ken fine what I'm talking about?"

Seton nodded as the old man went to stand at the edge of the hanging batch of eggs then, without a pause, stepped inside and quickly moved to the center where he raised his hands until they seemed to be engulfed in the mass. Seton could hardly see him inside the swirling aurora of dancing color.

The eggs danced faster—thousands of them filling the chamber with song and dance that Seton had to fight to resist. The mason sank his hands completely into them.

"Now. Dae it now, while I am still me," he shouted.

Seton's darkness shifted inside, and suddenly he knew what was wanted—the memory of the time when he too had faced his own fate in a similar manner. On that occasion Seton's Magister had faltered—ultimately failed—leaving Seton as the man he had become. But he at least could prevent a similar fate from befalling the mason.

Just as ways could be opened, there were ways and means by which they could be closed—he only hoped that this time, it would be done completely. Seton raised his voice in the chant of completion that he had last heard on that day he had been filled with his dark.

Ri linn dioladh na beatha, Ri linn bruchdadh na falluis, Ri linn iobar na creadha, Ri linn dortadh na fala.

The drumbeat in the chamber got louder. Dust disturbed by the vibration drifted down from the roof to fall around them. Voices seemed to rise from below to join in as Seton continued, a repeat of the previous phrase sung now by a choir, a throng, a myriad of singers in a chorus that rang and bellowed like a huge raging beast.

Ri linn dioladh na beatha, Ri linn bruchdadh na falluis, Ri linn iobar na creadha, Ri linn dortadh na fala.

Seton staggered, almost fell, buffeted by a cold wind that blew through the chamber like a gale.

The chorus rose to one final cry, Seton's throat tearing with the strain of the shout.

Dhumna Ort!

The floor bucked and swayed, and once again Seton almost fell.

The myriad of eggs popped, burst and disappeared as if they had never been there at all. Dancing fog swirled, a dark funnel that brought more howling, screaming wind.

The old mason screamed.

"The castle is mine."

Everything went black as a pit of hell, and a thunderous blast came down like a hammer from above, driving Seton down into a place where he dreamed of empty spaces filled with oily, glistening bubbles. They popped and spawned yet more bubbles, then even more, until he swam in a swirling sea of colors.

Lost.

***

Seton woke in the dark, lying on cold rock. He had to feel his way to the exit by touch, and on finally making his way out of the lowermost chamber found that the rest of the way up was lit by dim moonlight—he had dreamed the whole day away.

There was no sign of the mason, nor of any of the eggs. He had succeeded—the old man had gone through—and the Keeper of the Gate had closed the way behind him. When Seton turned and looked back into the darkness of the chamber he saw only rubble and dust—and just as he was about to turn away a dim rainbow aura, already fading, sinking slowly into the ground.

Over the coming weeks he did his job—hiring a new mason, a new team, and getting a fresh start on the foundations. They filled in the underground chambers with packed earth, laid a stone floor on top, and pronounced it done. Seton went back to Stirling, reported to the King and was paid enough silver to keep him in ale and *uisque* for the winter.

The liquor did not stop the dreams, although they came with decreasing frequency as the sky span round to Spring—dreams of stars and blackness, swirling clouds and peace.

One day he would go back to Law Castle and see if the way could be opened again—see if he could even be tempted to follow the old mason through.

One day.

Just not yet.

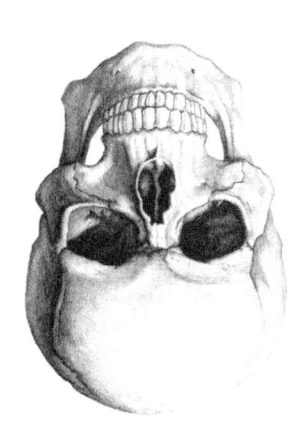

How to Be a Fictional Victorian Ghost Hunter (in Five Easy Lessons)
By Tim Prasil

Over the summer of 2016, I very carefully read 28 works of ghost hunter fiction. What I call ghost hunter fiction is a sub-genre of ghost stories and, I think, a curious branch of the occult detective cross-genre. According to my definition, it's is made up of imaginative writing that features characters who investigate cases of ghosts specifically (rather than, say, vampires, werewolves, etc.)—but only when such characters *haven't* been haunted by the ghost beforehand. This last point might be better understood by looking at typical ghost stories, in which characters find themselves haunted and, consequently, either run away or investigate the situation in order to rid themselves of the ghost. These characters do not qualify because, as I see true *ghost hunters*, the ghost has to be someone else's problem.

My reading those 28 works stemmed from editing an anthology titled *Those Who Haunt Ghosts: A Century of Ghost Hunter Fiction*, published by Coachwhip Publications. Included in the collection are works by such luminous authors as Edward Bulwer-Lytton, Henry James, Ambrose Bierce, H.G. Wells, Arthur Conan Doyle, Algernon Blackwood, Rudyard Kipling, Sax Rohmer, and H.P. Lovecraft. Though the original publication dates of these 28 stories span from 1823 to 1928, reaching beyond the Victorian period with both hands, my reading gave me a good sense of the fictional ghost hunter of that very significant and very charming era of ghost stories.

I began to notice certain patterns in the tales. Clearly, ghost hunter fiction quickly became a tradition, one that constantly evolved as authors flipped and twisted and, yes, "paid tribute to" the authors who had preceded them. I present some of these key patterns here in the form of five lessons. These should prove most valuable to any and all readers who aspire to become a fictional ghost hunter of the Victorian period.

Lesson 1: Partly Safari—Partly Slumber Party

According to this body of fiction, a ghost hunt might seem to be concocted of *one part safari* and *two parts slumber party*. The fundamental procedure is this: 1) learn of a haunted site—usually, a house—not too far away, 2) make arrangements to spend the night there, 3) spend the night there, and 4) dispel or validate alleged paranormal activity. Let me add here that *validation* of supernatural goings-on can lead to uncertain and often dangerous consequences, including a failure to survive the evening.

Though it's common to include an initial examination of the entire premises, a right and proper investigation is usually centered in one room. If I'm correct in thinking that Victorian ghost hunters are a species of occult detective, they tend to be particularly leisurely sleuths. They patiently wait for the ghostly "suspect" to appear.

As with most slumber parties, one should not expect to get much slumber. In the anonymous "The Haunted Chamber" (1823), the first selection in *Those Who Haunt Ghosts*, the ghost hunter character scoffs at reports of a haunted room at an inn and insists upon sleeping there. Thusly accommodated, he suffers a touch of insomnia: "It was in vain that he endeavored to compose himself to sleep, for his thoughts were too busy with the novelty of his situation." The phantom follower in William Howlett's "The Haunted House in Charnwood Forest" (1850) fairs about the same during his probe of a farmhouse bedroom: "Midnight came and found John Basford wide awake and watchfully expectant. Nothing stirred, but he lay still on the watch."

THOSE WHO HAUNT GHOSTS

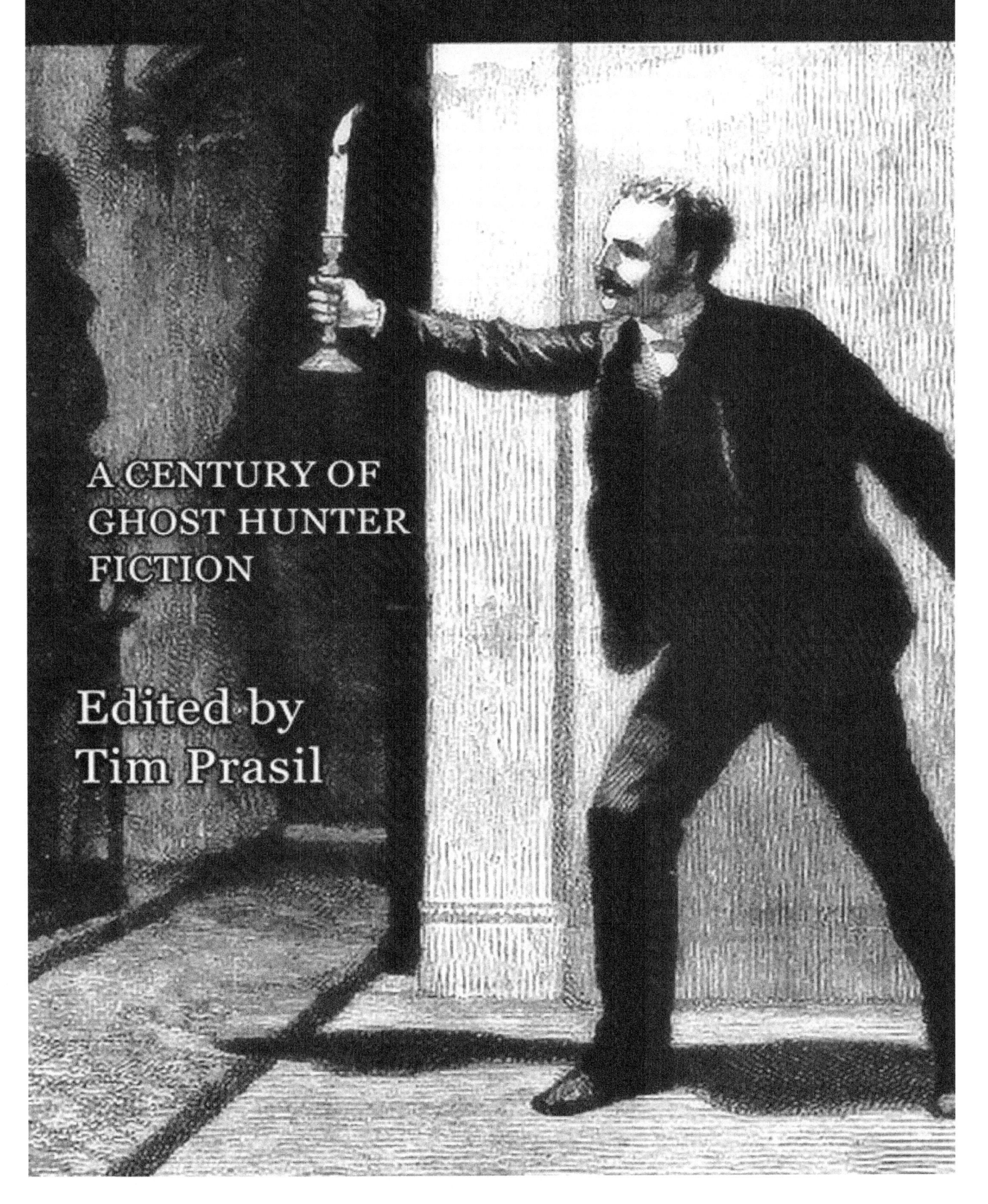

A CENTURY OF GHOST HUNTER FICTION

Edited by Tim Prasil

And in Doyle's "The Brown Hand" (1889), the wraith wrangler declares: "So interested was I in the result of my experiment that sleep was out of the question."

To the side of these sleepless soldiers are some characters who find staying awake downright exhausting. In Ralph Adams Cram's "No. 252 Rue M. le Prince" (1895), the narrator describes his nightly vigil in a house reputed to be infested with spooks: "It was certainly gratifying to know that I could sleep, that my courage was by me to that extent, but in the interests of science, I must keep awake. . . . Half a hundred times nearly, I would doze for an instant, only to awake with a start and find my pipe gone out." Some do eventually succumb to Morpheus—and awaken to terrible peril! The anonymous tale "The Ghost of Stanton Hall" (1868) features a narrator who is awakened by a ghostly woman weeping, whom he follows down a series of hidden stairwells in which he risks becoming helplessly trapped. In Lettice Galbraith's "The Blue Room" (1897), one of the rare female ghost hunters awakens to find in her bedroom a man who *isn't* a man—and who isn't exactly a *ghost,* either—but who *is* a treacherous supernatural entity. A fictional Victorian ghost hunter, you see, must be prepared to *rise* to an unexpected and inhospitable threat.

Lesson 2: Bullets Pass Through Ghosts—but Through Flesh, Too

Regarding such threats, the ghost hunter in "The Haunted Chamber" suggests why one in his position should holster a pistol or two: "'Against human visitors, here is my protection;' said he, drawing forth a small case of pistols and placing them in the chair; 'and from superhuman ones, I have not much to fear.'" Some of these characters are motivated by the urge to *debunk* supernatural explanations of a haunting, and in seeking a material cause—or even simply knowing that there might be one—the smart hunter knows that the "ghost" might be some unsavory criminal in disguise. Therefore, firearms could prove useful.

This logic persisted throughout the Victorian era. In another anonymous tale, "A Night in a Haunted House: Being a Passage in the Life Mr. Midas Oldwyche" (1848), the titular character also packs a couple of pistols among his ghost-hunting supplies. In Bulwer-Lytton's *The Haunters and the Haunted* (1859), that classic horror novella, the manly narrator tells his manly assistant: "Take with you my revolver and my dagger for my weapons. Arm yourself equally well, and if we are not a match for a dozen ghosts, we shall be but a sorry couple of Englishmen." Theophilus Edlyd, a ghost hunter hoping to *prove* his manliness in J.H. Riddell's "The Open Door" (1882), brings his own rifle and borrows a revolver.

Even in the comical "My Only Ghost" (1884), by Angelo J. Lewis, the main character packs a piece. When asked if he would "pot a ghost," that narrator replies, "I don't suppose I shall pot the ghost, but if anybody attempts to play any tricks I shan't have the smallest hesitation in potting him, so if you know of anybody who would be likely to attempt a practical joke, just give him a caution." In the far-from-comical "A Fruitless Assignment" (1888), by Ambrose Bierce, and "The Red Room" (1896), by H.G. Wells, both ghost hunters carry revolvers. While ghost hunters in the twenty-first century might aim their EVP recorders and full-spectrum cameras at their quarry, their Victorian forebears did so with firearms.

Lesson 3: Bring Along a Dog—Preferably One You Don't Love

Much like a pistol, a pooch can be handy if what's haunting the house is short on the ethereal as well as the ethical. This is nicely illustrated in Maurice Davies' "A Night in a Ghost-Chamber" (1873), when one of a team of ghost hunters says this regarding his dog, Brush: "If anybody in the flesh attempts to play us a trick and Brush pins him, I pity that practical joker. He will devoutly wish himself a ghost." And, in cases of actual ghosts, the keen eyes and noses of our canine companions often prove invaluable. Some say their senses penetrate into the supernatural realm more deeply than those of humble humanity.

Nonetheless, ghost hunting might become a bone of contention for some pups. In *The Haunters and the Haunted,* Bulwer-Lytton's ghost hunter recounts his investigation: "I took with me a favourite dog,—an exceedingly sharp, bold, and vigilant bull-terrier,—a dog fond of prowling about strange ghostly corners and passages at night in search of rats—a dog of dogs for a ghost." I regret to report that this bull terrier "meets his matador," so to speak, during his first night of investigation. In B.M. Crocker's "Number Ninety" (1895), the ghost hunter's doggy, Crib, meets a sadly similar fate.

Even when the results aren't quite so dire, ghost hunters are repeatedly revealed to *not* be a dog's best friend. When the usually ruff-and-ready Brush, mentioned above, notices the presence of a Presence in a nearby room, "instead of rushing at the door, he bolted hastily from it into the extreme opposite corner of the room where we were sitting. There he sat with his face to the wall howling with terror." There's an unnamed dog that belongs to a character named only "the ghost hunter" in Francis Tracy Moreland's "Grimbyville's Last Boom" (1902). After it is unleashed upon its phantasmal fox, this "dog followed, barking, but in a moment its bark changed to a howl of pain, and it came back whining piteously." The lesson seems to have been learned by Riddell's Theophilus Edlyd, despite his readiness for a rifle and a revolver. After being offered the company of a dog by the haunted house's owner, this ghost hunter kindly replies, "I think a dog might hamper me." I suspect the dog was grateful.

Lesson 4: Bring Something to Read—But Not Something Too Diverting

Since ghost hunting Victorian-style involves a good deal of waiting for something to happen, it's best to bring reading material. There's an honorable history that accompanies this, one traceable as far back as Pliny the Younger (c. AD 61-115). In a letter, the ancient Greek reports on Athenodorus, a philosopher who rented a house in order to verify claims about it being haunted. To avoid dwelling upon supernatural subjects—thoughts that might fool him into seeing things that aren't there—Athenodorus focused on getting some writing done. One presumes reading could serve as well.

That being the case, in two of the earliest works, Joseph Clinton Robertson and Thomas Byerley's "Seizing a Ghost" (1823) and Charles May's "The Haunted House" (1831), the respective ghost hunters, Madame Deshoulieres and Cuthbert Foster, begin their spectral stake-outs with a good book. Bulwer-Lytton's fellow brings a copy of Macaulay's *Essays* specifically. Do take some care when choosing the book, however, or one might become distracted—as Croker's narrator does: "My novel proved absorbing. I read on greedily, chapter after chapter, and I was so interested and amused—for it was a lively book—that I positively lost sight of my whereabouts and fancied myself reading in my own chamber!" This is a hazardous state of mind for a ghost hunter!

Lesson 5: Spirits and Spirits—an Obvious yet Noteworthy Pun

You might think that imbibing "on the job" clashes with the Victorian penchant for prudence and propriety. Not so among the fictional ghost hunters—in fact, quite the opposite. The works in *Those Who Haunt Ghosts* include a long shelf of liquor. In "A Night in a Haunted House: Being a Passage in the Life of Mr. Midas Oldwich," the narrator describes how he settled into his spooky night: "Still more comforted did I feel after I had drawn a chair to the fire, thrown on a fresh shovelful of coals, unpacked my basket, drawn the cork of a bottle of Madeira, poured myself out a glass, tossed it off, poured out another, and left that standing at my elbow." And Mr. Oldwich is hardly alone in strengthening his spirit for spirits with spirits.

His name perfectly suited to a ghost hunter's life, A. Wynter Knight brings several bottles of Bass's ale on his investigation in the anonymous "Midnight at Marshland Grange" (1863). Similarly, Lewis's ghost hunter pours himself a couple of toddies. Before his nocturnal search of the Red Room, the investigator in Wells' story is allowed a glass of beer. In "The Toll-House," by W.W. Jacobs—a name you might recognize as the author of "The Monkey's Paw"—a team of ghost hunters bring the whisky but forget the water. I suppose one must find ways to keep cozy on those chilly nights that so often seem to surround haunted houses, and if warmth comes in a bottle . . .

Of course, many of the key characters in these stories do *abstain* from alcohol (or, at least, such indulging was stricken from the literary record). These five lessons should be seen as general guidelines, not stringent rules. The short stories and novellas I edited illustrate a wide range of ghost hunting techniques as well as a multiplicity of conditions and outcomes that accompany such an avocation. After all, each author brings his or her own unique imagination to the challenge of netting a specter.

Indeed, while following the trail of *what happens next?* these 28 stories split and wander and split again in labyrinthine directions. Some of the characters manage to reveal perfectly natural explanations for what had been mistaken as otherworldly. But some skeptical ghost hunters are forced to become believers. While many others encounter the spooks they had been anticipating, only some are then able to vanquish those entities. And other characters, expecting to meet a ghost, come to face supernatural beings *even more terrifying!*

If Coachwhip Publication's *Those Who Haunt Ghosts: A Century of Ghost Hunter Fiction*, edited by Tim Prasil, is not already available at online bookstores as you finish reading this, it will be very soon. Think of it as your guidebook to Victorian ghost hunting.

Remember Lesson 4, though. It's probably best to finish the book *before* spending the night in any haunted house, inn, or castle.

greydogtales.com

the home of weird fiction & art

features, interviews, news, illustrations
and all manner of good things

greydogtales.com - still not banned in Finland!

REVIEWS

Help For the Haunted: A Decade of Vera Van Slyke Ghostly Mysteries (1899-1909)
Author: Tim Prasil / Publisher: Emby Press /Format: Paperback/Kindle /Reviewer: Dave Brzeski

As the title suggests, the eponymous character of this collection is a Victorian/Edwardian female occult investigator. It soon becomes apparent that the tone is, for the most part, light-hearted. Vera van Slyke is a debunker of fake mediums, who actually believes in ghosts. I loved her reasoning for this seeming incongruity: "It's not really a contradiction. I know that Spiritualists are frauds because, well, ghosts are like *cats.* They're real, but they hardly come when called. They act of their own accord."

Her assistant/partner is one of the fake mediums that she exposed, then took pity on. Ludmila Prášilová, Anglicized to Lucille Parsell, more often referred to by her pet name, Lida, is the Watson to van Slyke's Holmes. She is, the author claims, his great grand-aunt, and the (unpublished) stories passed through the family, finally ending up in his hands. Like Watson, she is not only Vera van Slyke's chronicler and assistant, she also acts as a buffer between her employer's eccentricities and the people she has to deal with. Vera van Slyke might well have been described as "an odd bird." She's appallingly bad at remembering names, and she has a tendency to speak in downright peculiar metaphors.

There are thirteen tales in the book—one, or two per year from 1899-1909—between which the two often lead totally separate lives, sometimes not even in the same city. Indeed, Lida even gets married during one of these extended separations. We find out more details about van Slyke's family background and early life at the same pace Lida does, which is sometimes a cause of some little tension between them. Van Slyke doesn't like to talk about her family origins. We discover the reason behind this when revelations about her origins cause a man with whom van Slyke has become close, to back off suddenly.

Like most right-thinking people, I loathe racism. More often than not, when the spectre of racism is broached in fiction, the author will make the racist characters totally evil. While such types obviously do exist, people are rarely that uncomplicated. Kudos to Tim Prasil for doing what few authors do by giving us a character who actually appears to be a good person in all respects until his ingrained bigotry is revealed. I suspect many of us have had the experience of being bitterly disappointed by someone we liked and respected when we discover their views on certain subjects.

The general light-hearted feel of these stories is underpinned by the, some may consider, absurd method they discover for uncovering evidence of supernatural incursions. I found this contrasted very well with the interplay between the characters as they got to know each other better. It's in these scenes, when discussing delicate, or embarrassing subjects, that Prasil uses van Slyke's habit of talking in odd metaphors to illustrate her discomfort with the subject being discussed to great and often very moving effect. But more than that, it's one of the strengths of Tim Prasil's writing that he absolutely shows, rather than tells. He has a facility for allowing the reader to understand what his characters are thinking and feeling without actually stating it outright, which lends a great deal of veracity to his storytelling.

As for the stories, we have ghosts who just need reassurance that their life's work mattered, ghosts pretending to be poltergeists, ghosts of beached whales... there's no shortage of originality here. The one common factor in the cases van Slyke investigates is guilt. Apart from the aforementioned odd method of ascertaining whether, or not there is actually an incursion from the other side, they have no gimmicks: no ancient manuscripts with banishing spells, no electric pentacles. More often than not, van Slyke has to simply convince the ghosts that they should move on.

In his postscript, the author reveals that he is working on editing the story of van Slyke and Lida's first meeting, which was too long to include in this volume, plus another couple of their investigations. I, for one, will be waiting for the publication of that collection with bated breath.

The Complete Weird Epistles of Penelope Pettiweather, Ghost Hunter
Author: Jessica Amanda Salmonson / Publisher: The Alchemy Press / Format: Paperback/Kindle/ Reviewer: Dave Brzeski

It became quickly apparent that Penelope Pettiweather wasn't your typical sort of fictional occult detective. What Jessica Amanda Salmonson has done here, for the most part, is to use reports of "real" ghost stories as a basis for her fictional protagonist's adventures. Also, Penelope Pettiweather isn't generally all that concerned with banishing restless spirits—to some extent, she's mainly interested in researching material for the various books she writes on the subject.

She's also something of an anachronism. It took me some while to narrow down the period setting for the stories, which was not nearly as early as I'd initially assumed. Being a middle-aged, scholarly lady, Penelope Pettiweather is somewhat old-fashioned in her habits. That combined with the stories being written and set in the eighties, through the early nineties—just prior to the mobile phone, home computer and email communication taking over our lives, with the protagonist communicating regularly via actual written letters—had me thinking for a while that I might be reading something set sometime between the 20s and the 50s.

The book opens with *"The Hounds of the Hearth"*, an account of a supernatural event which Miss Pettiweather decides to investigate in the hope of adding a new chapter to her work in progress. Salmonson admits she found the central idea—that of an entire library of rare books being reduced to ash—far more horrifying than any mere ghost. I tend to concur. It quite unsettled me.

Following another story which did involve some personal investigation by Miss Pettiweather, we get several letters to her correspondents which are little more than the passing on of local legends, with some speculation as to the truth of the matter. This is not to say that they are not interesting, containing as they do some of Miss Pettiweather's personal observations on the effects of the white man on the environment. The subject matter even moves in the direction of Cryptozoology with discussion of sea-beasts in general & giant cephalopods in particular.

Not all the stories are presented in the form of letters to her fellow occult investigators, but it would have been easy enough to adjust *"The Woman Who Turned to Soap"* to fit that format. I wonder if, perhaps, the original publisher simply preferred to have it presented as a non-epistolatry story. In either case, it's one of my favourites in the book. Penelope Pettiweather once again experiences a personal paranormal encounter as part of her information gathering, rather than just passing on local legend.

Even better is, *"Sarah, the Ghost of Georgetown Castle"* in which Miss Pettiweather finally hints that she has some real experience in banishing unwanted spirits.

By this point, I'd come to like Penelope Pettiweather quite a bit, but it was in *"Fritz, the Gentle Ghost of Shaw Island"* that I really grew to love her as a character. The concept of a ghost-breaker who has sympathy for the incumbent spirits and recognises that some are harmless and might even be friendly is a refreshing variant. I particularly liked the comparison between Miss Pettiweather and her colleague, Mrs Byrne-Hurliphant, who took a much more uncompromising attitude to the restless dead.

Miss Pettiweather finally has her own encounter with a lake monster in *"Ogopogo"*. Again, it's based on actual legends. An ancient Native American woman takes Miss Pettiweather to witness the legendary Ogopogo, aka: N'ha'a'itk. Salmonson portrays the awe Miss Pettiweather feels so well that I actually felt it along with her.

It's in *"The Burnley School Ghost"* that Miss Pettiweather really starts to get personally involved and, inevitably, puts herself in grave personal danger. Based on real reports as usual, Salmonson had herself intended to spend the night in the haunted basement in Burnley Art Academy, but permission was withdrawn for fear of bad publicity. The latter part of the story is a fictional account of Miss Pettiweather's terrifying experiences in that basement. Salmonson admits to not actually believing in ghosts, so I find myself wondering how an overnight stay in that basement might have influenced the story, had it been allowed.

Most of the stories are in the form of Miss Pettiweather's letters to her contemporaries in the occult investigation business. Quite a few are not, but *"The Queen Mum"* is unusual in that it takes the form of a letter to Miss Pettiweather, from an old friend who has retired from 'the ghostie habit' due to her husband's disapproval. It's a lighter tale than most, based on a report of a Portland woman who died a few months short of her 121st year. Miss Pettiweather's old friend suspects that she may have been much older than that.

Salmonson regards the final story in the collection—*"Jeremiah"*—as the scariest. She's quite right. It's also the most moving and, in my opinion, the best story in the book. Had it not been a reprint, I would certainly have suggested it for a best short story nominee in the British Fantasy awards. I will say no more about it, other than to say it's easily worth the price of the book on its own.

It's interesting to note that one of Penelope Pettiweather's regular correspondents is not a character Salmonson created herself. I was suspicious when I noted her address was in Oundle, just a few miles down the road from where I live—all the other places (apart from major cities) are made up. It turns out that Jane Bradshaw is a character created by Rosemary Pardoe, whose tales are collected in a small press chapbook, *The Angry Dead*, written as by Mary Ann Allen & published by Crimson Altar Press in 1986. I found that I actually owned a copy of this chapbook, shamefully unread, so I endeavoured to put that oversight right as soon as I'd finished Salmonson's collection. A couple of the Bradshaw stories are available in the Tor Books anthologies, *Tales by Moonlight* and *Tales by Moonlight 2*, both edited by Salmonson. If you can track down a copy of *The Angry Dead* chapbook, which contains all the Jane Bradshaw stories, I urge you to do so, albeit with a warning that the print is uncomfortably small.

Title: Carnacki The Ghost-Finder
Author(s): William Hope Hodgson (author), Scott Handcock (director) /Starring: Dan Starkey (Thomas Carnacki), Joseph Kloska (Dodgson) / **Big Finish Productions / Reviewer:** James Bojaciuk

Thomas Carnacki may be as much the forefather of his own genre as Sherlock Holmes is of his, but, altogether, Carnacki is a rather thin character. We know nothing of his attitudes, feelings, thoughts—he ends up nothing but a slightly distant host, apparently warm and friendly, but with no characterization beyond that. Even the sudden appearance of his mother (in "The Searcher of the End House") does nothing to advance his character, or tell the reader more than the bland and obvious fact that he was, obviously, born.

This is not a criticism of William Hope Hodgson, per se. He knew his talents, and he clung to them. Characterization was not his suit.

This is reflected in the stories' scattered, brief adaptions.

Donald Pleasence ("The Horse of the Invisible," *The Rivals of Sherlock Holmes*), who saved so many thin roles, seems finally put out of his depth. Alan Napier's Carnacki ("The Whistling Room," *The Pepsi-Cola Playhouse*) is not only a madman, but a crank, and "The Whistling Room" can only offer a lame, mundane explanation. "The Casebook of Carnacki – Curse of the Mummy's Tomb," the only other Carnacki "adaption" of note, sidesteps the issue of characterization entirely. For a man usually so talkative, the Carnacki puppet is silent.

Thence, Big Finish Productions.

Big Finish is in the business of expanding thin characterization. They built the sixth Doctor (Who), once the series' shame, into one of the most beloved Doctors. His companion, Mel, was given much more to work with than television allowed. Characters who had been treated well by the whims of television—the seventh Doctor, Ace, Ian Chesterton, to pull three names at random—were suddenly blessed with new depth, and, in time, literary characters were treated to the same process. Alexander Vlahos' Dorian Gray found depths Wilde never would have imagined, and even a series as faithful as Big Finish's Sherlock Holmes deepens and widens Holmes and his Boswell.

For everything else Big Finish got right, and for everything else Big Finish excels at, this is the best way to understand their production of *Carnacki the*

Ghost-Finder: it's about his character.

In an interview with *greydogtales*, Dan Starkey admits as much. "Reading the stories a bit closer, in preparation for performing them, gave me a deeper appreciation for the character and he's quite fun in that he's a balance of the bluff and vulnerable. He affects his listeners in that he lets them into his thought processes, the shame and terror, as well as his rational, methodical attitude to the supernatural."

Through this, Starkey is able to take Hodgson's thin characterization and—with nothing more than acting and emphasis—make Carnacki a compelling, full character. He has presence, and life. This, too, is something Starkey found in the period diction. "I think the feeling of the period is evoked very clearly in the writing, and that is very helpful in locating the voices for me. Carnacki's obviously an Edwardian agent judging by his diction, and I think that rather than being an impediment, the rather florid language in some passages gives you more to chew on and play with, than a bit of bland neutral prose would."

Perhaps what helps these stories the most is the sheer enjoyment radiating off Starkey's performance. There is nothing of the weary actor biding his time. Instead, this infectious merriment works on two levels. First, the audience is immediately captured by any actor having so much fun. Second, it proves Carnacki's quality as a host. He is not self-serious. He is a born storyteller, who lives for the joy of the story—something that even extends to his quotes from the Sigsand Manuscript. Something that could have been dull and dry is delivered in such a voice to make Hodgson's attempt at fifteen or sixteenth century English engaging—an unexpected feat, especially to those who have struggled with *The Night land*—and, even better, these excerpts have a spot of humor.

The stories stride the line between audiobook and audio drama. As with audiobooks, the cast is limited, and all focus is laid on a main actor reading his part. But as with audio drama, there is mood set through quiet music, there are sound effects, and, despite only Starkey performing the bulk of the story, he performs conversations among himself with the elan of two actors. This is an audiobook performed as audio drama, and the stories come off all the better for it. Neil Gardner and Tanja Glittenberg, the collection's sound designers, are to be congratulated. They've outdone themselves with this release. As did the musicians, Ioan Morris and Rhys Downin. Everyone worked together as a perfect unit, presenting each story without an aural misstep.

There is one minor downside. *Carnacki the Ghost-Finder* only adapts the stories from the book of the same name. Skipping "The Find" and "The Haunted *Jarvee*" is no great loss. But in skipping "The Hog," Big Finish missed out on adapting the greatest Carnacki story. But, then, this is understandable. These are full-length recordings, already weighing in at a hefty 300 minutes. "The Hog" would add another hour and a half to two hours onto an already full package.

Thus, I can only hope for a second collection. And, considering Big Finish's great skill at telling new stories in established worlds, I can only hope for a further collection full of new stories. I would not argue if these stories were written by such men as William Meikle or Josh Reynolds, or the editors of this magazine ...nor would I argue if Big Finish nomads The Scorchies one day wandered into Carnacki's corner of the worlds of Big Finish.

As for *Carnacki the Ghost-Finder* itself...

Most generations have their definitive Sherlock Holmes. Gillette, Rathbone, Brett—Dan Starkey is not only among these, to Carnacki, but surpasses them all in one way. He has no competition. There is no other Carnacki who matters. Starkey is not only Carnacki, but the first Carnacki; Starkey is not only the first Carnacki, but the only Carnacki.

Dan Starkey *is* Thomas Carnacki.

Big Finish Productions' *Carnacki the Ghost-Finder*, then, is not only highly recommended, but indispensable to even the most casual fan of occult detectives.

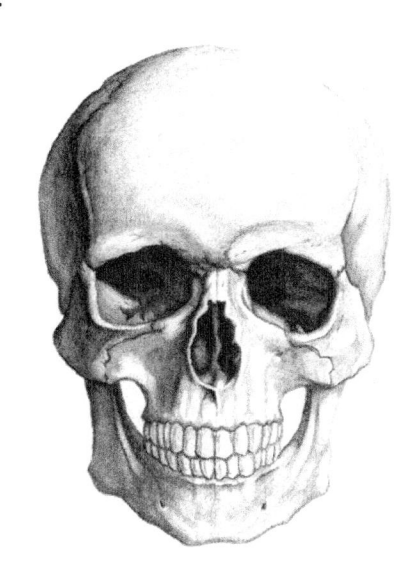

DESCRIBIN' THE SCRIBES

ADRIAN COLE is an inhabitant of Southwest England. He has had over twenty novels published, and is known to science fiction/fantasy readers for his "Dreamlords" trilogy and other books. His latest gritty collection "Tough Guys" was released this year. A prolific short story writer, his Nick Nightmare series already has many occult detective fans in its grip, and a collection of Nick Nightmare stories, *Nick Nightmare Investigates*, won a British Fantasy Award for "Best Collection".

AMANDA DEWEES is an American author who received her PhD in English literature from the University of Georgia and likes to startle people by announcing that her dissertation topic was vampire literature. She is already known for her stylish dark romances and thrillers, such as "With This Curse" which won the 2015 Daphne du Maurier Award in historical mystery/suspense. Her most recent novel "The Last Serenade" features the same Sybil Ingram as her story in this issue.

OSCAR DOWSON lives in Scotland, and has had comic-strips and SF published under various names. He is currently working on his own comic-book series, BRITISH POWER:1957. He advises you not to call up that which ye cannot put down.

TED E GRAU lives in Los Angeles with his wife and daughter, and last year released his striking debut collection "The Nameless Dark", which was nominated for a Shirley Jackson Award for Single-Author Collection. He has been widely praised for his dark, thought-provoking fiction, and in November 2016 released his novella "They Don't Come Home Anymore" through UK Press This is Horror.

WILLIE MEIKLE is a Scotsman now living in Newfoundland, Canada. A prolific writer with a back-catalogue of hundreds of short stories and many novels, his works range from new tales of Carnacki the Ghost Finder and Sherlock Holmes to Lovecraftian horror and dark SF. He is involved in numerous projects, and has recently contributed to the new "Veil Knights" series, a blend of urban and post-Arthurian fantasy from Harbinger.

JOSHUA M REYNOLDS is another transplanted man, originally from Carolina but now based in Yorkshire, England. He's a dual-purpose favourite, widely followed for both his gripping Warhammer fantasy novels and his occult detective series The Royal Occultist, of which the novel "The Infernal Express", published this year, is the latest major work. He has just had a new Age of Sigmar novel published, "Fabius Bile: Progenitor", from the Black Library.

DAVID T WILBANKS is a Minnesotan writer and enthusiast of both heavy metal and classic sword & sorcery. He makes a welcome return to writing here, having previously been known particularly for his "Dead Earth" series, written with the late Mark Justice.

AARON VLEK is an American writer who works with the trickster mythos in its role as bringer of delight and proponent of disquieting humours. Some of her stories centre around the goings on of the jinn, and of the Native American character, Coyote. Featured in the "Miskatonic Dreams" anthology, she's also been heavily involved in the Wicked Library and other podcasts.

THE OCCULT LEGION is a collective of writers producing linked stories, and currently comprises (in alphabetical order) Cliff Biggers, Bob Freeman, Sam Gafford, Willie Meikle, James A Moore, Joshua M Reynolds, and Charles R. Rutledge.

THANK YOU!!!!

ODQ Kickstarter Backers

A huge thanks to all the following, who helped us achieve and exceed our targets, and to those who helped spread the word and bring Occult Detective Quarterly to life.

- A Orde
- Aaron Cummins
- Alexandra Dimou
- Allan Beiderman
- Allison Eleazer
- Alvin Helms
- Amanda DeWees
- Andrew Evans
- Andrew Hatchell
- Andrew Ivey
- Angelo Benuzzi
- Autumn Barlow
- Barry Gregory
- Bill Thom
- Bobby D.
- Bret Burks
- Bryce Beattie
- Buck Weiss
- Charles Prepolec
- Chris Kalley
- Chris Wegner
- Dale Glaser
- Dan Hunt
- Darrell Grizzle
- Dave Brzeski
- David
- David Annandale
- David Chamberlain
- Davide Mana
- Debra Bourdeau
- Dominic Voyce
- Don Lee
- Eddie Coulter
- Eileen Kelly
- Elaine Corvidae
- Flannigan
- Floyd Brigdon
- Frank Coffman
- Frederick Siem
- FredH
- Gavin
- Gene Moyers
- Jake Maraia
- James Barron
- James Bojaciuk
- James Lowder
- Jane Keller
- Jeffrey Shanks
- Joe Kontor
- John Bullard
- John Smith
- Johnnie Nemec
- Jonathan Ly Davis
- Jørn Kristian Johansen
- Josephine Mori
- Jowell Hearn
- Justin Gustainis
- Keith West
- Kevin
- Lemuel M. Nash
- Loren Rhoads
- Matt Cowan
- Matt Nixon
- Matthew Masucci
- Matthew Willis
- Michael Adams
- Michael Brown
- Michael Kellar
- Mike Chinn
- Mike Hunter
- Mike Meltzer
- Natascha McGilvray
- Nathan Meyer
- Niall Gordon
- Nicholas
- Nick Williams
- Nina Zumel
- Paul Brian McCoy
- Paul Leone
- Paul M. Feeney
- Paul McNamee
- Peyton Smith-Hopman
- Phil Breach
- Randy Haldeman
- Richard Zwicker
- Rick Oberuc
- Robert Caple
- Robert Pohle
- Russell Smeaton
- Sarah Mooring
- Scott David Aniolowski
- Scott McClung
- Shawn Michael Vogt
- Simone Peruzzi
- Stephen Willcott
- Steve Eckart
- Steve Loucks
- Steven Rowe
- T. Everett
- Tarl Hutchens
- Trevor Prinn
- Tricia Owens
- William Lohman
- William R Rieder

Printed in Great Britain
by Amazon